Tom didn't wait for an answer

"Have you thought of what it'd do to Matt if you got yourself killed?"

The words hurt, but Ann refused to let him see it. "I'm aware of my responsibility to Matt." She stuck her hands deep into her skirt pockets so he couldn't see them tremble. "But I can't afford to sit back and wait for you guys."

Tom said nothing for several long moments. "You've always had the courage to reach out for what makes you happy. That's what makes you such a good fighter." He grinned, a sensual smile that left her heart pounding.

Ann couldn't tear her gaze away. There was a powerful virility about Tom. She had to be careful. Otherwise, she and Tom could end up creating a bigger mess than the one they were attempting to resolve....

ABOUT THE AUTHOR

Aimée Thurlo says she's thrilled that in building the background for *Suitable for Framing* she's finally found a use for her longtime interest in comic books and cartoons. But she must admit that the real inspiration came out of watching the wonderful blossoming she saw in the life of an unmarried friend with a small son, when the woman found the right man to love. When not writing, Aimée enjoys riding her horses, playing with her pack of dogs and practicing her marksmanship. She and her husband David live in New Mexico.

Books by Aimée Thurlo

HARLEQUIN INTRIGUE
109—EXPIRATION DATE
131—BLACK MESA

HARLEQUIN SUPERROMANCE
312—THE RIGHT COMBINATION

Suitable
for Framing
Aimée Thurlo

Harlequin Books

TORONTO • NEW YORK • LONDON
AMSTERDAM • PARIS • SYDNEY • HAMBURG
STOCKHOLM • ATHENS • TOKYO • MILAN

To my two favorite collectors,
Sergio and Lourdes Rodriguez,
for sharing the joys of "Booping."
And to Sue Stone
because she knows what it's like
to camp out with wild animals.

Acknowledgment

With special thanks to Doris Andrus for
sharing her real estate expertise.

Harlequin Intrigue edition published July 1990

ISBN 0-373-22141-X

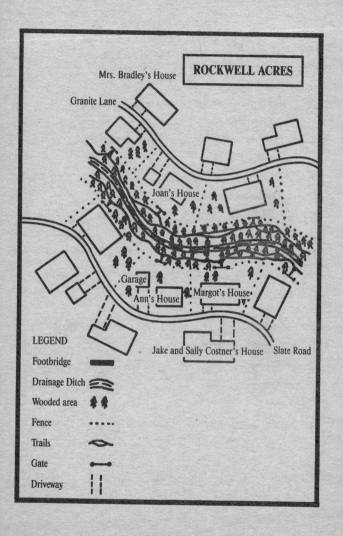

ROCKWELL ACRES

Mrs. Bradley's House

Granite Lane

Joan's House

Garage
Ann's House   Margot's House

LEGEND

Footbridge

Drainage Ditch

Wooded area

Fence

Trails

Gate

Driveway

Jake and Sally Costner's House   Slate Road

CAST OF CHARACTERS

Ann Dixon—Whoever had framed her was a real artist.

Tom Keller—Was he right to bet everything on Ann's innocence?

Matt Dixon—Ann would risk anything to protect him.

Joan Richardson—Was Ann's friend in need a friend in deed?

Chuck Adams—Was he Sean Jackson's partner in crime?

Captain Lambert—Had his ambition led him astray?

Lenora—Would she lead them to the killer—or in circles?

Bob Glenn—His sharp questions could be an investigation—or a cover-up.

Sean Jackson—Whoever said dead men tell no tales, lied.

Chapter One

The controlled mayhem of Saturday-morning cartoons filtered through Ann Dixon's closed door, nudging her awake. Placing a pillow over her head, she grumbled in the half-darkened room. The whine of a battery-powered "alien invader" marching across the tiled kitchen floor finally defeated her. With a groan, she rolled onto her back and stared at the ceiling. Sometimes it was better just to give up.

Ann heard the knob of her door being turned, and a small face peered in. "Mom?" the voice whispered. "Are you awake?"

"No," she teased, putting her hands over her eyes.

"Aw, Mom," Matt laughed, jumping onto her bed and crawling under the covers, slippers and all.

A familiar game ensued. Ann tickled her son in the ribs as he attempted to escape by tunneling farther under the covers.

"Hey, partner, you ready for breakfast?" she asked after a moment.

Matt poked his head out of the covers by her feet. "Pancakes, Mommy. Can we have pancakes?"

There was an expectant look in his eyes. Matt's blond hair and fair skin had come from his father, but his deep violet eyes were the mirror image of Ann's own. "Let's have a race. If you get dressed first, then we'll go get pancakes, but if I win, then it's cereal and toast. Go!"

Matt bolted off her bed and across the bedroom. Ann watched the four-year-old leave, a smile on her face. Her son, she thought with a sigh, was a morning person. It was one trait he most certainly had not inherited from her.

Like his father...

With a sigh, she glanced at the empty far side of the bed. Her thoughts drifted back to that terrible day two years ago when Warren had been killed in an air-force training accident. Without her son, she really wasn't sure how she'd have found the courage to go on.

Nowadays, things were good, however. Together, Matt and she had found happiness again.

Slipping on jeans and a T-shirt, Ann stood before the mirror. She brushed her black, shoulder-length hair into a ponytail and fastened it with a silver barrette.

"Mom!" Matt rushed back into her bedroom. "I'm ready!" He opened his arms to illustrate his point. "I won! You don't have shoes on yet."

Ann smiled. Her son's Broncos T-shirt was inside out and his orange sweatpants had been grabbed from the clothes hamper in the hall, but he was completely dressed. "You beat me fair and square. So pancakes it is this morning."

"Okay, hurry!" With a yell, Matt bounded down the hall.

As she turned to look for her shoes, she could hear the squeak of his rubber soles on the kitchen floor, then the slam of the back door that indicated he was going to their detached garage. "Mommy, I'm going to get Commando out of the garage so we can take him with us."

She noted with a rueful smile that he really hadn't expected no for an answer.

Ann had stopped halfway down the hall to tie her shoes when Matt came rushing back inside, his eyes wide with alarm.

"There's a man in the car and he's hurt!" Matt clutched Commando, a brown-and-white guinea pig, to his chest protectively.

"In *our* car?" Instinctively, Ann stepped between Matt and the back door.

"He's lying down. And there's a trash bag on his head. Mom, you've got to go help him! He's bleeding!"

She glanced anxiously through the hallway entrance to the kitchen. "Bleeding, with a trash bag over his head? Honey, that can't be right." She searched her mind for an explanation that made more sense. Maybe a transient had spent the night in the car. It had been left in the driveway instead of the garage. "You mean he's asleep using a trash bag for a pillow?" It was possible that what Matt had assumed to be blood was just mud.

Matt shook his head. "No, not like a pillow." He stopped, his eyebrows furrowed tightly, as he considered the matter. "Like a trick-or-treat mask."

Ann gave her son a skeptical look. She'd have to go and check for herself. If someone was hurt, it was possible she could help. She'd taken an extensive first-aid course a few years ago when she'd worked at Matt's day school.

First, however, she had to take care of Matt. Ann urged him farther into the house. "Matt, go to your room and close the door. Don't come out until I get you, do you understand?"

He nodded.

As he ran back to his room with Commando, Ann went into the kitchen and pulled out a rolling pin. If this was a trick of some sort to get her outside, whoever it was had one big surprise coming. Ann called the police, quickly informing them of what was going on. Then, taking a deep breath and grabbing her keys from the counter, she went outside and locked the door behind herself.

She walked to within a few feet of her car, parked on the driveway. The rear door was open, obstructing her view. The only thing she could see was a pair of legs dangling out of the car.

"Whoever you are, I suggest you leave immediately," Ann said. "The police are on their way."

There was no response. A chill swept over her. "Can you hear me?"

She stretched her foot out and lightly tapped one of the outstretched legs. "Go on, get out of here!"

With a soft *whssht*, the body slid from the back seat to the ground, where it sprawled like a rag doll. Ann squelched her initial urge to scream by covering her mouth with one hand. Matt was in his room, probably scared stiff. This was no time to lose control.

Forcing herself to breathe deeply, she went to the man's side. His blue sports shirt was speckled with blood. And Matt had been right. His head was obscured by a white garbage bag held in place by a rubber band fastened around his neck. Through the vinyl, she got a vague impression of grossly contorted features. Ann shuddered and fought the urge to run back inside. But she couldn't leave. It was possible there was still a spark of life left in the man. Her hands trembled wildly as she tried to slip off the tight rubber band. "Oh, please don't be dead, please don't be dead," she murmured to herself.

She worked the elastic band over the man's head and pulled open the bottom of the bag. As she drew her hands away, she realized her fingers were covered with blood. Her heart pounded. Forcing herself to continue, she pulled at the bag, slowly uncovering the man's head. She was halfway done when what she saw stopped her cold. He was definitely past any help she could give him. Bile rose in her throat and she rushed back to the house, fumbling with her keys to get inside.

Ann dropped the rolling pin on the kitchen floor, then ran to the bathroom. She washed her hands vigorously as if trying to remove the memory and the shock of what she'd seen along with the traces of blood. She felt weak all over, and splashing cold water on her face did little to help. Where were the cops? As she leaned over the sink trying to steady herself, Ann heard Matt moving around down the hall. Concern for her son quickly overshadowed everything else. What was Matt doing out of his room? Was he okay?

She dried off her face and hands and stepped out of the bathroom. As she turned to go down the hall, she saw her son a few feet ahead of her. He was sitting over the furnace grating playing with the toy fishing pole she'd given him last Christmas. "Matt, honey, not now! You can go fishing later, okay?'' Loud, insistent knocking at the door interrupted her.

''Police,'' a loud voice echoed from the front porch.

''Matt, go to your room while Mommy takes care of this, all right? I'll be right in there.''

''But you said I could go fishing whenever I wanted,'' he protested. ''And, Mommy, what about my pancakes? You promised.''

''In a while, sweetie, okay?'' she replied, leading him to his bedroom, toy fishing pole in hand.

''Police, open up!''

''Coming,'' she yelled back down the hall.

She gave Matt her most reassuring smile. ''Help Mommy out by being a good boy right now, please?''

He nodded dolefully.

Leaving him in his room, she walked quickly to the front door and opened it. A very young patrolman was standing there anxiously, shotgun pointed upward, but ready for use.

''He's dead,'' Ann said immediately. ''I tried to help him, but it was already too late. There was this bag on his head, and the blood...'' She could hear herself talking and knew that she wasn't making much sense. Angry with herself, she tried again. ''He's in such bad shape. I've never...'' She shook her head, her voice wavering.

''Just show us where the body is, ma'am,'' the officer said, never taking his eyes off her. ''We'll handle it from there.''

As she started to answer, another patrolman came onto the porch. ''He's in my car, in the driveway.'' She stopped and shook her head. ''No, he *was* in my car, but then he fell out.''

''I thought you said he was already dead.'' The young policeman's eyes narrowed.

''He was...is,'' she corrected then explained. ''You'll have to see for yourself.'' She led them to the back door. ''And, please, just go down the driveway from now on, okay? My son's only four and I don't want him frightened,'' she said, forcing her voice to remain steady. She stopped by the back door. "I'm not going. I've seen enough to last a lifetime."

The officers walked out to the driveway, then returned a minute later. The younger of the two had paled considerably.

"Ma'am, we're going to have to ask you some questions," the senior officer began, taking out a pad and pencil.

"Fine. We can do that in the living room." At that instant Matt came rushing around the corner. "Why are the police here, Mommy? Is that man still in our car?"

She cut him off before he could get any farther into the kitchen. "Matt, I asked you to wait for me in your room."

"I want to stay out here with you."

"Matt," Ann's voice grew sharp, and immediately she regretted it. "Sweetie, I need you to be good right now, please. Mommy has to take care of a few things. Play with Commando and the toys in your room, and I'll be with you just as soon as I can."

"Okay," he answered glumly.

She waited until she heard Matt's door close before turning back to the policeman. "I'm sorry, but I just don't want him exposed to any more of this. He found the man, but I don't think he realizes what's really happening."

"It's probably best that way," the officer conceded. "Did you know the victim?"

"I don't think so. I'm not sure," she admitted miserably. "His face was distorted and there was so much blood...." Ann paused as she heard someone come through the back door.

Ann stared at the tall, dark-haired man who strode into the room. Recognition triggered dozens of memories from the past and her heart began to hammer. "Tom, what are you doing here?"

"Hello, Ann." He nodded, then spoke to the officer. "I'm Lieutenant Keller, Homicide. Can you give me a rundown?"

"I've just started questioning Mrs. Dixon, Lieutenant," the officer answered. "The men outside might be able to tell you more about the victim."

"I've already spoken to them," he answered. "I'll take over here now. Your assistance is needed outside, to help preserve the crime scene." As the officer left, Tom turned to Ann. "Are you all right?" His voice had softened somewhat.

She nodded, recovering from the shock of seeing him under these circumstances. "Why don't you come into the living room and sit down? I'll tell you what happened." Suddenly she heard rapid footsteps coming toward them from the back of the house. She glanced up and saw her neighbor coming from the kitchen. The tall, stocky young woman was wearing a loose-fitting jogging suit and her hair was damp, as if she'd just stepped out of the shower.

"Joan! What are you doing here?"

"Ann, I've been worried sick! I looked out my bedroom window and saw all the patrol cars through the trees. I thought you or Matt had been hurt. The cops wouldn't let me through at first, until I told them I was Matt's baby-sitter. What's happened?"

"I'm not sure what's going on. Matt and I woke up, and there was this dead man in the car.... Oh, everything's just crazy around here!" Ann clamped down on the words, upset at her inability to keep her voice from wavering. She'd always prided herself on being good in a crisis. This was no time to start a new trend.

"Dead man?" Joan's eyes widened. "How—"

"I think she'd better tell *me* that first, if you don't mind," Tom stated brusquely. "I'm Lieutenant Keller of the Crystal Police Department, Ms...."

"Joan Richardson," Joan replied. Giving Keller an annoyed glance, she placed a hand on Ann's arm. "I don't think I'm going to be much help here. Would you like me to take Matt home with me until this is cleared up?"

"Joan, would you? He's hungry and I haven't had time to get him any breakfast at all. He's in his room."

"Consider it done." Joan started down the hall. "Matt?"

Ann saw her son peer out of his bedroom and smile at Joan. Within seconds, they were gone. With a sigh, Ann walked back to her living room couch. "It's been a long time."

Tom sat in the chair facing her. "Almost three years, right?"

She nodded. "Tom, is there any way you can hurry up the men outside and get these questions over with quickly? I don't want Matt upset."

"You and Warren were my neighbors for years. You know I'll treat you fairly. But I need to do a thorough job of gathering the physical evidence and conducting interviews. Remember, I'm a cop, first, last and always."

"Yes, that's always been so," she muttered, almost to herself. She also knew that the tension of his profession had led to the breakup of Tom's marriage. She and Warren had known Tom and his former wife, Jessica. They'd lived right next to each other. They'd been friends then. But they'd lost touch over the years. Now in the midst of chaos, Tom had suddenly reappeared in her life, bringing with him conflicting emotions she was ill-prepared to face. She shied away from the memories and related to him, as calmly as she could, the events of that morning preceding the arrival of the police.

He thought her words over for a moment then spoke. "You said you have no idea who the victim was. Are you sure you want to stick to that story?"

"Get real!" Ann shot back, upset at his implication. "I wasn't about to sit there and study his face. It was all I could do to keep from getting sick."

Impassive eyes stared at her. "The man in your driveway is Sean Jackson." He stood and paced around the living room, his eyes darting everywhere, alert and curious. "Sean is—was—a very successful con man and thief. He enjoyed the easy life and bilked quite a few women out of their savings. We've also had him down at the station several times for assault and battery. He was a dangerous felon, and no one's going to blame you for defending yourself. A widow with a young child would get the support of the court. If you're keeping anything back, now's the time to level with me. But first I have to advise you of your rights. You don't have to say anything without an attorney present."

Ann jumped to her feet and stood in front of him, hands on her hips. Her slender frame seemed delicate contrasted against his six-foot-three, athletic build. "You're not seriously accusing me of having something to do with all this!"

For a moment a flicker of something crossed Tom's eyes. The change was undefinable, like a ripple over still water. He exhaled slowly and moved away to the window. "Ann, sit down." His voice softened. "I'm going to be honest with you. From what I've seen and heard so far, things look bad right now. The district attorney could easily argue that you invited Jackson into your home, then killed him, perhaps in self-defense. He'd say you put the body in your car, intending to take it elsewhere and dispose of it, but your little boy woke up. Once he saw the body, you were forced to call the police."

"That's nonsense, Tom, and I think you know it," she replied firmly.

"Maybe, but my personal opinion won't help you." He loosened his tie, then sat back down in the chair. "I was called here because I was available and on duty. But before long, word will get around the department that I'm investigating a friend and former neighbor. Unless I'm hard-nosed about this, they'll say that friendship is interfering with my judgment. Then even if I tell them you're innocent, it won't carry much weight. I need to build a case based on the facts and then see what kind of picture comes together." He paused. "And Ann, I hate surprises. You might as well tell me everything you know, because sooner or later I'll find out anyway."

It took all her will power to do nothing more than glare at him. "If you remember anything about me at all, Tom, then you must know how I feel about Matt," she said in an arctic tone. "I'd never expose him to danger. As a Realtor, I deal with a great number of people and I've learned to be a good judge of character. I wouldn't have invited a man like the one you've described into my home to visit," she argued logically. "And believe me, those types I can recognize. Some people think widows are easy marks. I've learned to be hard in order to survive."

"Good point." He started to say more but one of the uniformed officers strode into the room and signaled to him. "Excuse me for a second," Tom said and walked off.

Ann watched the two men speak in urgent whispers. Eventually the police would realize that she was innocent. There was no way they could tie her to a man she'd never met. Yet the interim worried her. She'd worked hard to give Matt a home filled with stability and love. She didn't want him exposed to the uncertainty and pressures of a long criminal investigation.

Tom returned a moment later. "The medical examiner has just finished his preliminary examination. It shouldn't be too long before he can take the body away for a complete autopsy." He showed her a driver's license photo. "This is the man in your garage. Have you ever seen him before?"

She looked at the photo, then handed it back to Tom. "No, I don't think so."

He glanced out the window, watching the growing circle of neighbors and passersby. "The coroner's office better send their wagon here soon," he observed. "Otherwise, this'll turn into a sideshow."

She walked to where he stood and groaned as she saw the gathering. "This is going to generate gossip that could ruin me, Tom. Isn't there something you can do?"

"I can ask the crowd to disperse, but that won't stop people from talking."

Her throat constricted, but she masked her emotions well. She'd spent the last few years proving herself, both personally and in business. She'd found the best rule of survival lay in learning to hide her weaknesses. "Then find your answers fast," she said crisply. "I'm my family's sole support."

"I'm very aware of that." He met her eyes.

It didn't used to be that way. She'd felt so safe and secure before Warren died. Nowadays, everything depended on her. With effort, she focused on the present. "What did the medical examiner find?"

Tom studied her speculatively. "There were wood splinters imbedded in the victim's fractured skull. That tends to indicate he was bludgeoned to death with a heavy wooden object."

Outwardly Tom appeared emotionless, but the spark that flickered behind the veiled eyes suggested there was much beneath the surface. "Look around all you want," Ann said. "I can't imagine any large wooden object around here except some garden tools in the garage."

"Let's go check," he answered, following her to the garage. Once they were back in the house, Tom asked to inspect her broom, then glanced around. "Do you have a plumber's helper?"

She led him to the main bathroom. "Beneath the sink."

"Well, that's that," he said, looking it over carefully. "Anything else you can think of?"

"Oh, of course," she said sarcastically. "I forgot the deadliest weapon of all. My son's little toy fishing rod. It's wood and plastic."

He didn't even blink. "Where is it?"

Seething, she crossed the hall and led the way into a small bedroom filled with posters of movie heroes and cartoon characters. She glanced around and out of the corner of her eye caught a glimpse of Commando scurrying underneath the bed. She'd have to try and catch him later. Concentrating on the problem at hand, she searched the room and found the pole on top of her's son's storage chest. Removing a piece of gum from the plastic fish hook, she handed Tom the toy. "Satisfied?" she added cynically. "All the table legs throughout the house, as I'm sure you've noticed, are still attached. I think this should set your mind at ease. Off hand, I can't think of anything else I have that's wooden and that could be used as a weapon except my rolling pin. You're welcome to study that, too."

"Why don't you let me take a look around? You're not obligated in any way to do that, but it would help your case."

She fumed silently. He should have been chasing the real criminal, not harassing her! "Fine," she said in a clipped tone. "Anything to get this over with. I have to pick up my son and quite frankly, I want to spend the rest of my Saturday with him."

Tom's gaze met hers and held it. For long moments the impasse continued. Finally, Tom looked away.

Ann swallowed. Her throat was as parched as sand. The years hadn't diminished the effect he had on her. They'd never done anything, but back when they'd both been married, the attraction had been dangerously inappropriate. Even more inappropriate than it was now.

Closing the door to Matt's room, Ann followed Tom around the house. As they traversed the kitchen, he stopped and carefully picked up her rolling pin from the floor. Traces of blood stained one of the handles. "Why is this out here and where did the blood come from?"

"I took it with me when I went outside to check Matt's story. When I came back inside, I just tossed it on the counter and I guess it rolled to the floor." She saw the interest flicker in his eyes. "I had blood on my hands at the time, so it's little wonder I got it on the rolling pin."

"Why did you take it with you in the first place?"

"I had no idea what was waiting for me out there," she snapped.

"So why did you go out?" he challenged. "Most people would have waited for the cops."

"I have first-aid training. Matt said the man was bleeding. If he had needed immediate help, I was the only one in a position to provide it."

Tom's look was filled with grudging admiration. "You've always had courage, Ann."

As they returned to the living room, one of the officers approached them. "Lieutenant, we'll be taking the body away to the morgue now."

"Wait here," Tom said, glancing at Ann, then walked off with the officer.

Ann could hear the voices outside. It seemed that everyone in the neighborhood had congregated behind the yellow-tape police line around her house. When news of this reached the general public, her real-estate business could be deeply affected. She thought of Matt and her responsibility to him, and began to worry once again.

"The lab boys took the rolling pin so they can verify your story, and they'll be working in your driveway and examining the car for a while longer," Tom said, returning to where she waited. "You won't be able to go back there until they're finished. If you're going to need anything from the garage, let me get it for you now."

"There's nothing," she said, then stopped. "No, there is. The cage for Matt's guinea pig. It's just inside the garage door, on a bench. I don't want Commando loose in Matt's room all morning."

"I'll talk to the officers." A moment later Tom reappeared, cage in hand. "Here you go."

As Ann started down the hall, the morning's events came rushing back to her. "Poor Matt! He won't really understand any of this. He just wants his special day. I try to set aside Saturdays to do whatever he wants since I have to work so hard the rest of the time." She set the cage down on Matt's dresser.

As she turned to leave the room, Ann collided with Tom. "Oops, I'm sorry. I thought you were waiting by the door." She glanced up, his eyes capturing her attention. The greenish-gray pools told fascinating, and maybe even dangerous stories. It was hard not to be affected by him. Averting her eyes, she moved around him.

Tom followed her back to the living room. When he finally spoke, his tone of voice suggested he hadn't been totally unaffected by their encounter. "I'm having the driver's license photo shown to the neighbors gathered outside. I want to see if anyone recognizes Jackson. One of the things we need to find out is what he was doing here."

She lapsed into a thoughtful silence. "The back of my house faces a small wooded area," she said at last. "There's a large ditch, part of a system that extends for miles, that cuts right through the middle of it. Maybe Jackson was meeting someone back there on one of the foot bridges.

Suitable for Framing

That person could have killed him, and dumped him in my car to hide the body. Maybe he was planning to switch the body to his own car and drive away with it, only Matt showed up before he could complete his plan."

"It's a convenient explanation, but it doesn't work. If someone met Jackson near the ditch and killed him, why not just hide the body in the trees out there? It might have taken days before Jackson's body was discovered. The thing that bothers me most is the bag that was placed over his head. I think it was there to avoid leaving a trail of blood that would reveal where the murder actually happened." He pursed his lips and shook his head slowly. "Can you think of any other explanation?"

Something about his tone warned her. "You still haven't ruled me out as a suspect, have you?" she observed grimly. "Is it really the evidence, Tom, or is it because of the past?" she challenged in a quiet voice. "Once I got pregnant, Jessica put a great deal of pressure on you to start a family."

His gaze hardened slightly, and his jaw clenched. He remained silent for a moment then spoke. "I'm just investigating the facts of this case," he said, his words too measured to pass as calm and natural. "That's my job. As far as my resenting you, you're wrong. I've always believed that men in professions like Warren's or mine shouldn't have dependents. What happened to you supports that. You've had to take on a great deal of responsibility as Matt's only parent. And he's a constant reminder of Warren and the life you might have had."

"Yes, that's true," she admitted, "but Matt's also the best thing that's ever happened to me. I learn so much from him. He's taught me about a different kind of love." She smiled. "And he's shown me all about hope. No matter what the circumstances, I wouldn't trade—"

A uniformed officer came to the door and drew Tom aside. They spoke in low tones for about thirty seconds.

By the time Tom came back to her his features held a rigid cast. His eyes were steely. Only one emotion, anger, flickered across his face, and it showed in the clipped tone of his voice. "One of your neighbors recognized Sean Jackson. She says she saw him come visit you late yesterday afternoon."

Chapter Two

She stared at Tom uncomprehendingly. "That's impossible. I was here alone with Matt all day. He wasn't feeling well, so I stayed home."

"Your neighbor claims that Sean Jackson's car was parked in front of your house for quite a while," Tom maintained in a flat tone.

"But I didn't have any visitors all day except... Wait a minute. Let me see that driver's license again." She took it from Tom's hand and studied the photo more carefully this time. "This *might* be the man who came in to use my phone. He called the auto club, then sat out in the shade of my porch to wait. His car was parked out front. I was busy with Matt at the time, so I scarcely paid attention to him. Then later when I looked out again, he was gone."

"Check on a tow truck. See if anyone saw one," he ordered the officer, then turned back to her. "I'll check the auto clubs myself as soon as I get back to the office. Maybe we can track down someone who can support your story."

"Tom, I know how this looks, but believe me, I've told you the truth." She stared directly at him, trying to convince him of her honesty through sheer force of will.

He seemed unmoved. "Ann, if you're withholding anything at all, tell me now. I give you my word that I'll do my best to help you." The uniformed officer returned and approached Tom, whispering something in his ear. Tom's jaw clenched. "There was no tow truck, Ann," he said without inflection. "Your neighbor saw Jackson drive off in his own car, a white sedan."

She felt as if the walls were converging upon her and there was nothing she could do to stop them. "Maybe he managed to fix the car himself." It sounded lame, but the truth was all she had, even if at the moment it wasn't much of a shield.

A clamor near the back door added to the confusion that gripped her. As she glanced inside the kitchen, bright lights from video cameras glared into her face. "What on earth..." She looked at Tom for help as a half dozen people scrambled into her house.

"Davis, get those reporters out of here," Tom ordered. As they were hustled out, he focused his attention back on her. "How do you explain the fact that there was no tow truck?"

"I don't know, I'm not a mechanic!" she shot back. "You explain it!" She stood angrily near the window and watched the news people gathered around her front porch. "Can't you at least get the reporters out of my yard?"

"I could, but they'd either go stand on the sidewalk or come back later when we're not here. I'm going to have to ask you to go downtown with me to make a statement, and that will make them even worse. It's your choice if you want to talk to them before we go."

Ann swallowed hard. "I might as well face it. This isn't going to fade away like a bad dream. I'll answer their questions, let them take their pictures, then maybe they'll be satisfied and leave." She took a deep breath, opened the door and stepped outside.

It was the look of suspicion on her neighbors' faces that hurt the most. The whir of cameras sounded as reporters jockeyed for position around her.

"Did you kill Sean Jackson, Mrs. Dixon?" one queried.

"Was it self-defense?" another added before she could answer.

"What about your son? Will the police question him, too?" a third interjected.

"Lieutenant Keller, have you arrested Mrs. Dixon yet?" a woman at the back shouted.

"There've been no charges made against Mrs. Dixon," Tom stated flatly. "In a few minutes, she's going to go with me down to the station to make a formal statement. Then she's free to go. Now give her a break, will you? A police spokesperson will be briefing the press this afternoon."

"I came out here to tell you I had nothing to do with this man's death," Ann said firmly. "What happened here is as much a mystery to me as it is to the police—"

Ann heard quick, light running footsteps. Then suddenly Matt came rushing at her. He leaped into her arms and clutched her tightly. "You're not going away like Daddy did, are you, Mommy? You stay here with Commando and me, okay?"

She hugged her son tightly, then stared defiantly at the people around her. "I'm not going anywhere, sweetheart," she said loud enough for everyone to hear. "I haven't done anything wrong."

A second later Joan pushed her way through the crowd. "I'm so sorry, Ann! We came back down to check on Commando, and when Matt saw you out here, he rushed right past me. I couldn't catch him in time."

"Matt, go with Joan for now. Commando's just fine, he's in your room. I'll come for you in a little while." The fear in his eyes made her heart ache. "I will be back, sweetie, I promise."

As Joan led Matt away, Ann faced the reporters again. The impromptu press conference took only about fifteen minutes, but she handled it with the aplomb of a general facing the troops. By the time she got into the car with Tom to go downtown, she felt invigorated. She was determined not to let anyone, police or reporters, upset her little boy's world.

"How long before we're through?" she asked briskly.

"It won't be much longer." Tom took a deep breath, then let it out slowly. "You're scared, Ann. I can feel it. Only you deal with fear the same way I do. You don't retreat. You come out fighting." His gaze traveled over her gently.

"You're going to have to learn to relax. At this rate, you won't make it if this turns out to be a long haul."

"Then help me out. Find the person who's really responsible for this before it ruins the life I've made here with my son."

ANN RETURNED FROM the police station an hour later. As the officers dropped her off, two men stepped out of a white van and hurried toward her.

"Mrs. Dixon, we're from the *Rocky Mountain Confidential*. We'd like to talk to you for a minute," a tall redhead informed her. An overweight man carrying a camera followed a short distance behind.

"I've already given a statement," she replied wearily, recognizing the name of the regional scandal sheet. "You'd better check with the others."

"Ma'am, what we'd like is an exclusive. We thought this would make a great human-interest story. We did some research. Your husband was the air-force hero who ordered his navigator to eject when one of the engines caught fire, and wouldn't bail out himself because the aircraft was over a residential area. He was killed when he tried to ditch in Cherry Creek Lake."

Hearing the story again made Ann want to start shaking, just like she had the evening she'd been notified. "It was a long time ago," she responded in a thin voice. "What exactly do you want?"

"We'd like to do an in-depth story about your relationship with Sean Jackson," the man answered. "We can make you look really sympathetic to the public, being a widow with a son. I guarantee it'll help your defense." His companion began to take pictures.

It took a few seconds for the words to sink in. Even after making a statement to the press, people still believed that she'd played a part in Jackson's death. "Get out of my driveway," she snapped. "I didn't know Sean Jackson, and I don't want to know you." Ann started to close the door, but the man reached in to push his business card in her face.

"Here, take it. You might change your mind after you spend a few more hours downtown with the cops."

Ann let the man drop the card and move away from the door. Then, with a curse, she pushed the door shut. Exhaustion made every muscle in her body ache. She fought the tears stinging her eyes. How could she protect her son or herself from what was happening? She stood at the door for several minutes, trying to regain control.

Slowly her thoughts drifted to Tom, and an emotion she couldn't quite define swirled through her. As a police officer, his duty was clear. He wasn't an old friend who'd believe in her, but a detective out to do a job. Only, as it had been in the past, her heart still beat a little faster whenever she was around him. Tom wasn't a pretty boy by any means. His appeal was a more rugged kind. There was a toughness about him that pushed some people away. But through the years, she'd also caught glimpses of the gentle side of him. They'd come unexpectedly, shattering his steel-hard shell with their warm intensity. She found that conflicting blend compelling somehow, drawing her to him.

The last thing Ann felt like doing was tending to business. But she couldn't afford to neglect it now. Her survival and that of her son depended on it. Forcing herself to find comfort in her daily routines, she checked for messages. Once she'd done that she could go get Matt.

Her first two messages were nasty crank calls meant to provoke and frighten her. The third was from her boss, Jonathan Randall. Two prospective clients she'd scheduled to meet tomorrow had cancelled. He wanted to speak to her as soon as possible.

Dialing the office quickly, she tried to prepare herself for what was to come. Randall and Associates was a very conservative real-estate brokerage firm. Scandal did not go hand in hand with the image they wanted to project.

The conversation matched her expectations, upsetting her even further. None of what had happened was her fault and she refused to be held accountable for it. When they had finished talking she slammed the receiver down. It was then that her eyes fell on a photo of Matt and her taken last year. His smiling face filled her with a rush of love.

Feeling better, she grabbed her house keys. It was time to pick up her son. Cutting through the wooded area behind her house, Ann crossed the foot bridge over the ditch and went through Joan's back gate. As she approached the patio door, she could hear Matt's loud voice inside.

Joan responded to Ann's knock almost immediately. "Hi! Matt and I have been watching television. I started getting the children's channel on cable for the times he comes over."

"Can I stay and watch the rest of the show, Mommy?" Matt's face was covered with chocolate and caramel.

"You're a mess, kiddo," she observed.

"I'll wash up, I promise, but can I stay, huh, please? It's almost over."

She nodded, unable to suppress a smile as he ran back quickly into the other room. That kid of hers would melt hearts someday.

Joan led her to the kitchen. It was cozy and cluttered, with shelves full of old salt-and-pepper sets and antique cookware. "Come on. I'll split a soda with you, and you can tell me what's happened. I still can't believe you found a dead man in your car! By the way, your boss called here a while ago, hoping to catch you. He figured I'd have Matt today, after all that's been happening."

"I just spoke with him, Joan, thanks. He left a message with my service." She exhaled loudly. "Jonathan's worried about how this is going to affect his company. You see, the news is starting to get around. Two clients have already cancelled with me."

"That's really rotten, not only of Jonathan, but of the public."

"Jonathan's not really trying to be a skunk, though," Ann conceded. "In his own way, he's tried to help. He spoke to his attorney and got the man to agree to represent me, if necessary. Jonathan doesn't think I should speak to the cops or the press anymore unless the lawyer's there with me. He's got a point, too. I probably shouldn't have said anything without an attorney." She paused and sipped her cola.

"There's one way Jonathan could really help you out, if he wanted to. Do you think you can persuade him to give you an office job for a while? That way you wouldn't have to deal with the public until your name's cleared."

She shook her head. "I can't afford the cut in pay. Besides, I refuse to hide out."

Joan shrugged. "If I was in a predicament like yours, I'd keep to myself for a while. To me, it wouldn't be a matter of hiding out, but rather of saving my sanity."

Matt came bounding into the room. "Can we have hot dogs for lunch, Mommy? I want hot dogs. Lots of hot dogs."

"Well, I don't know about lots, but we can go get *a* hot dog for you now, if you'd like."

He ran to the door, then stopped and looked back. "Right now, Mommy?" he asked. "I'm hungry!"

Joan stared in surprise. "Ann, I give you my word, the kid hasn't stopped eating since breakfast."

Ann laughed. "I believe it." Saying goodbye to Joan, she took her son's hand and led him back down the path to her home. Inside, Ann retrieved her wallet from the table and started back toward the driveway. She stopped in midstep, a vivid image of the corpse flashing into her mind. "Maybe we ought to see what's in the refrigerator first," she suggested tentatively.

Matt's face fell. "No hot dogs?"

She took a deep breath. She couldn't afford to buy a new car, so sooner or later she'd have to use the one she had. She glanced at Matt, who was looking up at her.

"Mommy, you want me to go see if there's any more grown-ups there?"

"Good grief!" She gathered her composure quickly. "No, dear. There's no need. Let's go get the hot dogs."

Her cherry-red sedan was even cleaner than usual. The police had only checked the door for fingerprints and Tom had asked them to clean that up. Since they'd also carefully vacuumed the car in a search for cloth fibers and microscopic evidence, the interior was neat and tidy. Without hesitation, her son jumped onto the front seat. Blocking the morning's incident from her mind, Ann started the car and pulled out of the driveway.

"See Mommy? You didn't have to be scared. There's no more guys in here."

With a smile, Ann switched on the radio. It took less than five minutes for them to arrive at Deputy Long Dog's, her son's favorite fast-food restaurant. When she came to a stop by the drive-through window, the news came on. Hearing her name over the radio caught her attention immediately. As she turned up the sound, she saw the puzzled expression on her young son's face.

"Mommy, are they talking about you?" he asked in a very serious voice.

"Yes, sweetheart, but you shouldn't let it upset you. It'll be okay once the police find the person who's responsible for all that's happened." She gave him a reassuring smile.

Matt's eyes lit up as the young woman handed Ann the bag filled with hot dogs and French fries. "Lunch!"

So for now the subject was forgotten. She breathed a silent sigh of relief, but her mind remained on the news report. If her prospective clients had heard this bulletin, it was little wonder they'd cancelled. The story had made it sound as if she'd played an integral part in the murder, though few actual details had been given out.

She saw Matt's happy face as he pulled out the small sack of fries. She'd have traded her soul to give her son a childhood filled with only smiles and laughter. Yet, no matter how hard she'd tried to protect him, her efforts hadn't been enough. His reaction with the press today had been proof of that. Matt still carried the scars left by his father's death.

To be fair, she doubted that Matt actually remembered his father. What he did understand, however, was that other kids had daddies and he didn't. Perhaps that's why he needed so desperately to know he could always count on her to be there. The situation with the press and the police threatened Matt with his greatest fear. She could not let this go on.

"Can I ask Jeremy over to play this afternoon?" Matt asked, interrupting her thoughts.

Two rambunctious four-year-olds would certainly take her mind off things. But Jeremy was one of the neighborhood children. She recalled seeing the boy's mother outside with the others this morning when the police had come. They hadn't spoken, but under the circumstances Ann doubted that she would allow Jeremy over until everything was cleared up. How could she explain that to Matt? "Let it be just the two of us today, okay, Matt?"

He nodded with a seriousness rarely seen from a four-year-old. "You tired of company, huh, Mommy?"

"Yes, I am. Thanks for understanding, Matt." She reached over and gave his hand a squeeze.

"I'll play with Commando, then." He glanced at her. "And, Mommy, don't worry. I'll catch him and put him back in his cage."

"Please do!" She couldn't hide a smile.

She played with her son at home that afternoon, but her mind remained miles away. Had the police done anything to clear her? Would Tom even trust her enough to keep her informed?

She stared at the telephone as calls came in and were answered by her service. She'd pick up her messages later, once Matt was asleep. Her son could sense her moods too easily and she didn't want him to guess how precarious their situation really was.

"Mommy, let's play outside in the backyard." Matt held up his plastic ball and bat.

"Sure." She took the ball and followed him out to the lawn. Spotting Jeremy in the yard next door, Matt dashed over to the fence. Suddenly Jeremy's mother appeared and whisked her boy inside the house.

Without saying a word, the point had been made. Matt's downcast face tore her heart. "I guess his mommy doesn't want him to play," he said softly.

"Come on, Matt. I'll throw the ball," Ann replied, and was gratified to see his face brighten.

As she pitched the ball to him, her thoughts raced in a different direction. The first chance she got, she'd start questioning the others in the neighborhood. If she was persistent enough, she might be able to discover something more about the dead man.

Like most little boys Matt had an unbelievable amount of energy, but a short attention span. Before too long he wanted to go back inside. Ann was helping Matt put away some of his toys when the doorbell rang.

"You finish here while I go answer it," she told her son, and went to the door. Peering through the peephole, she saw Joan. "Well, hi," she greeted, inviting her neighbor inside.

"I'm here because I need an excuse to play hooky from work and I'm hoping that you'll let me take Matt to see a movie." Joan was a freelance word-processor operator in her late twenties. She was single, but she rarely dated. Going out to a matinee was one of her regular breaks from work.

"I don't mind at all, but are you sure? You take care of Matt so often for me as it is!"

"I like doing it. Matt's a neat little guy. I have as much fun with him as he does with me." Seeing his head appear in the doorway, she smiled. "Yo, Matt! How about catching the matinee with me this afternoon? *The Revenge of the Ninja Rangers* is playing."

"Oh Mommy, can I, please?" Matt's voice rose as he ran up to them.

"Sure, but change your pants. Those have a tear at the knee and grass stains." As he ducked out of sight, Ann glanced at Joan. In a whisper-soft voice, she said, "I don't see how you do it. Watching a movie like that must be as appealing as a visit to the dentist."

Joan laughed. "My father taught me to really enjoy cartoons. And I'm having a great time going through my second childhood with Matt."

Ann waited until her son and Joan drove away, then checked the answering service again. The realty office had called. A buyer had asked to see one of her listings. If she was unable to make the appointment that afternoon, Ann was to call the office and make arrangements to have someone else meet the client.

She thought seriously about having another agent show the house. It was her day off, after all. And she realized that it could be a crackpot, or worse, those reporters. But if she took this attitude about every new contact, she'd soon be unemployed. Changing into her agency blazer and a matching skirt, Ann picked up her briefcase and went to the car.

The house was near the old downtown district of Crystal, a small college town not far from Denver, Colorado. It was a recently remodeled brick home much like her own, but two story instead of one. She'd shown the house before and knew it would be difficult to find a buyer. It was, frankly, a good house in a bad neighborhood.

Locking her car carefully, she stepped out onto the sidewalk and looked at the nearby parked cars. All were unoccupied. Ann decided to give the house the once over, quickly, before her client arrived. Going to the back door, she reached up and opened the lock box with her key. Inside was the key to the front door.

Ann walked back around the side, noting once again that for the neighborhood, the yard was in surprisingly good shape. Seeing no new cars had pulled up, Ann opened the massive wooden door and walked inside. Ahead, in the empty living room, she could hear a curtain flapping in the breeze. She stepped forward cautiously. The house should have been completely closed up.

Glancing through the open doorway, Ann noticed a window had been opened. A broken pane and shards of glass on the hardwood floor told her how the intruder had gained entry. She started to back out of the room when she saw something that stopped her in her tracks. Spray-painted crudely in red over the lilac wallpaper on the opposite wall, was a message meant for her. *Murderer. If the police don't get you, I will.*

THIRTY MINUTES LATER, Ann was on her way home. Her hands were still trembling, so she kept them gripped to the wheel. Two policemen had arrived shortly after she'd called from a phone booth. They'd checked the place out, but found no clues that would enable them to identify the culprit. Although they'd filled out a vandalism report, the officers had dismissed the threat to her as the work of a crank.

She cursed softly, her temper rising to the surface. So far, her boss, Jonathan, had been more help than the police. He'd told her to refuse any more meetings with new prospects unless they agreed to meet at her office first. With the transient problem in Crystal, women Realtors had to be careful, anyway.

Ann glanced into her rearview mirror for the third time in the past minute. She was getting jumpy. If the message was to be believed, her only hope lay in having the real killer apprehended. Just being exonerated by the police would not satisfy the person who'd left that warning. She definitely had to do something on her own behalf.

Now that Matt was at the movies, she'd begin by canvassing the neighborhood. After leaving her car at home, Ann got underway on foot. She went to her neighbor's house and rang the door bell. The woman peered past the window curtain, then opened the door a crack. From the sounds behind her, it was obvious she was keeping her son, Jeremy, back. Her smile seemed pasted on her face.

"Hi, Margot. I'd like to talk to you, if you have a minute." Refusing to take the woman's blank stare as an answer, Ann continued. "Have you seen any strangers hanging around the neighborhood lately?"

"You mean like the one who turned up in your driveway?"

Ann imposed an icy calm over herself. "Look, I need some help." She forced her tone to remain cool and logical. "Someone dumped that man's body in my car and I've got to figure out who put him there. One way to do that is to learn what he was doing in this neighborhood. I won't take too much of your time, I promise."

"I'm sorry, Ann." Margot gave her an apologetic half smile. "I shouldn't have been so sarcastic. I guess you have enough problems already. But why are you asking these questions? That's the police's job.''

Ann shrugged, suppressing her annoyance at not being invited in. ''I have a vested interest in this. Come on, Margot. What have you got to lose by helping me out a bit?''

''I saw what the press did to you this morning, Ann. Now I'm afraid to answer the door. Reporters have been trying to get me to talk all day.'' She shook her head. ''I'm sorry, but I just don't want to get involved. I have a son to think about, too. I hope everything works out for you, but please keep Jeremy and me out of it.'' With that, she closed the door slowly in Ann's face.

Ann hurried down the street to catch up with another neighbor, Jake Costner, coming back from his weekly foursome of golf. He seemed willing to cooperate. She'd just started to question him when his wife came rushing outside. She insisted he'd received an important telephone call and led him quickly into the house.

A few seconds later, Sally Costner emerged again. ''We're both sure you didn't kill that man. But please don't get us involved with your problems, Jake's got a bad heart. The police will clear you soon. Just give them a chance.''

''I was only going to ask Jake a couple of questions. He might have seen something important earlier this morning, Sally. He might not even be aware of it.''

''Jake works for a government contractor, you know that. We can't afford to have this kind of trouble touch us. It wouldn't take much to jeopardize his security clearance, believe me.'' Mumbling another apology, she returned to her house.

For the next ninety minutes Ann went from door to door. The people who were sympathetic were no more help than the ones who weren't. The question foremost in her mind still remained. How had the corpse turned up in her driveway? Obviously he hadn't walked there.

If only she could find out why Jackson had been in the neighborhood to begin with! That would undoubtedly lead to the rest of the answers she needed. Either the murderer or the murdered man must have left some kind of trail. For instance, if Jackson had driven to the area, where was his car? If he hadn't, who'd brought him here?

Ann tried to recall everything she'd overheard about Sean Jackson that morning, but she couldn't remember anyone mentioning car keys. Their absence or presence could be a very important clue. Quickening her steps, she returned home and called Tom Keller. He'd have a list of every item that had been found inside Sean Jackson's pockets.

The telephone rang four times before the desk sergeant picked it up. Informing her that Lieutenant Keller was not in his office, he offered to take a message.

Ann left her name, then replaced the receiver in its cradle. She couldn't bear to sit around and do nothing when she had so much at stake. With renewed determination, she picked up her wallet and keys and went back out. She'd drive around and ask people if they'd noticed an unfamiliar vehicle parked near their homes.

She circled the block slowly, speaking to people as she went. As she turned the corner, she spotted a faded blue sedan about half a block behind her. The car looked familiar, but she couldn't remember who it belonged to. When it disappeared down a side street, she focused her attention back on her task.

Her gaze fell over the weathered brick houses on the twisting residential streets. Some of the dwellings dated back to the mid 1920s. She watched her neighbors, marveling at the uniform life-styles of those in her neighborhood. It seemed that everyone either washed their cars or mowed their lawns on Saturday. There was comfort in the familiar patterns and routines. No wonder they had found this incident so threatening.

She spoke briefly to three more people. Then, when she started toward the next corner, she spotted the blue sedan again. An uneasy feeling crept through her. Could the neighborhood watch have increased their patrols? Or was the person in the car the same one who'd threatened her? Occasionally, she checked her rearview mirror. The car stayed in sight, though it kept a discreet distance behind.

She went back to Mrs. Bradley's house. The elderly woman was one of the few who had answered her questions and even offered to help.

As she walked to the door, Ann noted that the blue sedan had pulled over against the curb farther down the block. Explaining quickly what she needed to do, Ann entered Mrs. Bradley's home and sneaked out the back. She stayed low, using the shrubs for cover while she made her way through the dense thicket to the drainage ditch. She moved swiftly but quietly along the edge of the canal, cut across the far end of the block and came up from behind the sedan. Sheltered beside two large pine trees, the car was almost obscured from view.

She rushed forward, eager to put an end to the game, when suddenly a man stepped out of the shadows and blocked her path.

Chapter Three

Ann gasped and jumped back. As recognition hit, her temper came bubbling to the surface. "I don't believe this! Someone dumps a body in my car, another person threatens revenge, and you're out following *me*?" She stared at Tom as if he were a gross and previously undiscovered form of insect life. "You think I've been lying to you and I'm guilty of murder, is that it?"

He shook his head. "At this point, I'm only searching for evidence. I must admit, though, your actions this afternoon got me curious."

What had she expected? Warren had told her once that Tom lacked the ability to trust anyone outside himself.

"I was on my way to talk to you, but when I saw you leave the house, I decided to stay back and watch. What on earth have you been up to?" He paused then added, "And what's this about a threat?"

"You would know if you'd been at your office."

"I've been out in the field most of today. Did you try to call?"

"Yes, I wanted to talk to you. I was wondering if the police had found any keys in Sean Jackson's pockets."

"Why? Are you missing some?"

"No." She exhaled softly. Tom's response didn't surprise her. It wouldn't be like him to give out information, no matter how trivial. "I was wondering about Sean Jackson's car. If he brought one, where is it? And if he didn't, how did he get here?''

"Sean Jackson's white Chevy was found a few blocks north of here near the mouth of the drainage ditch.''

"That means he walked into the neighborhood. For whatever the reason, he didn't want his car to be seen." Her shoulders slumped. "That still doesn't tell us much, does it?''

"No, but it's a start. Now tell me, what did you mean about getting threatened? Did the crank calls start already?''

"Yes, but that's not the worst of it. I halfway expected those," she explained slowly. "It's the way I was set up at my job that frightens me." She explained about the phony client and the spray-painted message she'd found in the empty house.

"It seems that someone went out of their way, even risking criminal charges, to threaten you. You shouldn't take that lightly.''

The shadow of fear in her eyes was clear. "I'm not taking anything lightly—not after this morning. But the officers who responded seemed unconcerned. Maybe it's just because they knew there wasn't much they could do. That doesn't help me much, does it?'' she observed wryly.

"The officers realize that many threats are never carried out. But complacency is a dangerous fault. Don't dwell on what happened, Ann, but stay alert. That's the best advice I can give you." Tom cocked his head, gesturing toward his car. "Now come on. Let me give you a lift back to your car.''

She slipped into the passenger's seat. "No wonder this car looked familiar,'' she said. "It's the one you took me downtown in.''

He looked at her and nodded. "Ann, no matter how it seems to you, I'm really not your enemy. Maybe I am being hard-nosed about this, but I do want to clear you. That means proving *conclusively* that you didn't commit the murder, whether or not we ever find the real killer.''

She smiled ruefully. "It's not just you. It's this entire situation. It's frustrating not to be able to convince people I had nothing to do with that man." She exhaled softly. "I'll tell you what. Why don't you come over and have something to drink? It's a hot afternoon, and I've got some lemonade in the refrigerator."

He hesitated for an instant then nodded. "All right. Sounds like a good idea."

Ten minutes later they were at her kitchen table, sipping lemonade. Tom looked pensive. "How did you end up in real estate?"

"It was a matter of survival," she answered candidly. "I couldn't afford to spend years training for a career. After Warren died, things were really rough for us and I spent quite a bit of time being angry with life. For a while I blamed Warren for having chosen such a dangerous career and for having been taken from us." She shook her head. "But then I realized that Warren had loved flying. I'd known that and had accepted the risks when I married him."

Tom nodded in acknowledgement but remained silent.

Ann grew quiet. Looking back on those days still filled her with longing. Her life had been so different then. She'd been so much in love and her future had seemed filled with wonderful possibilities. "Have you kept in touch with Jessica?"

"She remarried. She has a little girl now, and another child on the way. I guess she's happy."

"And you?"

He stood and paced around the kitchen. "I've got my work, and my life's the way I wanted it."

But Tom hadn't answered her question. She'd asked if he was happy, not if his life was well organized. She was about to say more when the front doorbell began to ring.

Ann smiled. "Matt's here." She opened the door and her son came bounding inside. Joan, following right behind him, laughed. "Well, he ate a little too much popcorn, but otherwise he's safe and sound."

"Thanks, Joan."

Joan caught a glimpse of Tom and looked at Ann, eyebrows raised. "Are you okay?" she mouthed.

Ann smiled. "It's a friendly visit. You're welcome to join us for something to drink."

She shook her head. "I'll be back later," she said in a conspiratorial whisper.

"It was a great movie, Mommy!" Matt said as Joan left. "You should have come with us." He ran into the kitchen and stopped as he saw Tom. He seemed to study the man briefly. Then, as if making up his mind, he smiled. "Hi, I'm Matt."

"Pleased to meet you."

Matt accepted Tom's offer to shake hands then ran to the cookie jar on the counter. "Can you reach the cookies?" he asked Tom. "We can share."

Ann watched her son, surprised. Matt didn't usually warm up to strangers so quickly.

"I think you better ask your mother about that." Tom smiled politely.

Ann handed Matt a chocolate chip cookie, then watched as her son offered it to Tom. "They're good. You want one? Mommy will give me another."

"No, thanks, Matt." Tom looked uncomfortable as he stood and glanced at Ann. "Well, it's time for me to go." He walked to the door with her. "I'll let you know if anything new comes up. Be sure to lock everything tonight."

Ann watched him leave. Had her questions made him nervous? Perhaps she should have known better than to ask. As she walked back to the kitchen, she smiled at her son. "It was very nice of you to offer Lieutenant Keller your cookie, Matt. Do you like him?"

The little boy considered the question and then shrugged. "He looked like he needed a cookie."

She'd heard many things from her four-year-old, but this attempt at psychology baffled her. "What do you mean?"

"He looks sad, Mommy. A cookie would help."

With that bit of wisdom Matt ran to his room. Ann stared after her son for several moments. What had Matt sensed in Tom?

It was a little past eight that evening when she switched off the television. Matt had fallen asleep on the couch beside her. She roused him gently. "Time for you to go to bed, Matt."

The little boy looked at her through sleepy eyes. "Mommy, I don't want to sleep by myself."

"Matt, why? You like your room, and Commando will be with you. Besides, I'll be right here."

"Can't I sleep in your room? Just for tonight?"

Ann knew she shouldn't allow that. Warren would have told her that she was spoiling Matt, and she probably was, but she couldn't turn him down. Not after what had happened today.

"All right, son, just this once. But remember, you have nothing to worry about. I'll always be right here for you."

Matt placed his hand in hers as they walked down the hall. "I'm not worried," he said, but he still didn't sound sure.

Ann helped him get ready for bed, then tucked him in. She decided to stay with him until he fell asleep. She propped herself up on several pillows and allowed Matt to snuggle close against her.

As Matt's breathing evened, she remained beside him, awake yet unwilling to move away yet. Guilt assailed her. If she'd been a better mother, she would have stopped Matt from going out to the driveway alone. Or perhaps she should have been more alert to intruders. She replayed the events in her mind, second-guessing herself in scenario after scenario. Finally, exhaustion overcame her and she drifted into a fitful and restless sleep.

It was morning before she knew it. Sunlight poked through a gap in her curtains, and she shifted, trying to avoid the little ray. Outside her door, she could hear Matt already watching his favorite Sunday-morning cartoons in the den.

Though her eyes remained closed, her mind refused to relax. She wondered about the day ahead and speculated on how she could protect Matt from the publicity that was sure to come.

Finally she opened her eyes, remembering the spray-painted message on the wall. It was hopeless. This wasn't her morning for sleeping late. Tossing the covers aside, she slipped out of the wrinkled clothes she'd slept in, wrapped a housecoat around herself and went to find Matt.

"Mommy, are we ready for breakfast?"

Ann managed a smile. She didn't know what she'd do without him. Thoughts of waking up in a silent, empty home seemed painfully lonely by comparison. "I'll start the waffles while you go outside and get the funny papers for me."

"Okay!" he ran to the front door, slippered feet padding upon the carpeting.

She was at the kitchen counter when she heard voices outside. Curious, she stepped into the living room and glanced out the window. Matt was surrounded by adults and he was crying. She rushed outside.

Seeing his mother, Matt dashed between two people and into her arms. Several cameras clicked and whirred as the reporters began shooting questions at her. "Would you get off my property?" she demanded angrily. "How dare you come here and frighten my son!"

"We were only talking to him, Mrs. Dixon. How about answering some of our questions right now? The readers want to hear your side of the story." She recognized the man as the same reporter she'd run off the day before.

Ann took Matt's hand and hustled him back inside the house. "Get off my property," she ordered, glancing back, "or I'm calling the police." She slammed the door hard and locked it.

"Sweetie, you're okay, aren't you?" she said as she crouched down in front of Matt.

Nodding, he handed her the newspaper, which he'd held tucked tightly under his arm. Then he wiped a tear off his cheek with a sleeve and hugged her tightly. "Here's the funnies," he said. He eased his hold and looked up at her. "Now can we have waffles?"

"You bet," she answered, relieved that he was already willing to go on to another concern.

Thirty minutes later, with Matt back in the den playing with his robots, she was finally able to read the newspaper. Two photos were centered at the bottom of the first page. One was Sean Jackson's and the other was of her, taken yesterday.

She stared at it aghast, unable to turn the page. The ringing of the telephone jolted her out of her trance.

Matt ran over and handed her the cordless telephone. "It's Mr. Randall," he said in the respectful tone he used for people he felt were very important.

"Hello, Jonathan, how are you?"

"Have you seen the Sunday paper yet, Ann?" Jonathan's voice echoed from the speaker.

"Unfortunately, I have." She exhaled softly. "Is that why you're calling?"

"I thought you might like to take tomorrow off," he hedged. "I wouldn't like you to have to deal with cranks calling here at the office."

"I need to work, Jonathan. I can't hide out. I have an appointment with a client."

"Well, if you're sure..."

"I'm sure." Saying goodbye, she switched the handset to Off and stared pensively across the room. Jonathan would not be immune to the pressure of public opinion for long. From his tone she suspected he was already hoping she'd stay away from the office until matters were cleared up. But, he hadn't asked her not to come in.

She walked to the den where Matt was playing. Today, she'd stay at home with her son. But tomorrow she'd have to find a way to keep him safe until the police got to the bottom of things.

AS SHE GOT READY FOR WORK the following morning, she tried to prepare herself for whatever lay ahead. She thought if she could anticipate problems, then she'd be better equipped to deal with them. Her son was the first priority. Ann telephoned the day-care center to speak to the owner. Allison MacKenzie had known Matt since the day of his birth, and Ann trusted her completely. Assured that Matt would be protected from the people hounding her, Ann was able to relax a bit more.

She dropped Matt off, then went to her office. As she stepped through the doorway of Randall and Associates Realty, the receptionist gave her a worried glance.

"Any messages for me?" Ann asked.

The thin brunette hesitated. "Just a few from jerks who want to ruin your day."

"So you've had crank calls here, too," she muttered. Now Jonathan's attitude was making more sense. "I'm sorry you've had to deal with that, Cindy, but it should blow over soon."

"I hope so," she answered a bit uncertainly.

As Ann walked to the back where her small office was, she could feel the stares of those around her. She couldn't blame them, really. Anything that brought negative publicity to the firm affected all their livelihoods.

Ann tried to keep busy. The clients coming to see her today were from out of town. With a bit of luck, they wouldn't have read the local papers or heard the news. Perhaps if she made a sale, she'd boost her co-workers' sagging spirits.

Her clients arrived a short time later and seemed eager to get started. She drove them around Crystal and kept the radio turned on to an all-music station. Things looked promising. "Did you like this last three-bedroom, Mrs. Fontaine? It had all the features you said you wanted."

"Greg and I need a chance to discuss it more, but it was just what I had in mind," she answered in an excited tone.

As a Realtor, Ann had learned to spot an imminent sale, and right now her instincts told her she was close. "Let's go back to my office. You two can talk it over there in private. Then, if you'd like, we can work up an offer."

Thankful that things finally seemed to be going her way, she led them inside the building of Randall and Associates. It was close to five-thirty by the time they finished writing up a purchase offer. In a great mood, Ann walked her clients outside and saw them off.

"How'd you do?" Jonathan asked, as she came back inside.

"I've got their purchase offer and earnest money check in my office now. I'll talk to the sellers tomorrow."

"That's fantastic! Even with all this hanging over you, you've still managed to come through. No wonder you're our top agent."

"They were from Colorado Springs," Pat Miller, Ann's fiercest competitor countered. She regarded Ann with a venomous gaze. "Ann shouldn't be coming into the office, Jonathan, until this murder thing is settled. We can't all count on out of town clients."

Jonathan was quiet for a moment, then spoke. "You'll see to it that it's cleared up soon, won't you, Ann?"

"Count on it." Five minutes later, purse in hand, she stepped out to the parking lot. It was time to pick up Matt and go home. Afterward, she'd call Tom to find out what progress had been made. If his answers didn't satisfy her, she'd have to take things into her own hands. She didn't plan on doing anything that would endanger herself or Matt. But perhaps she could find some leads for the police to pursue.

Ann walked out to her parking space, then stopped abruptly, wondering if she was going crazy. She glanced around the parking lot, then headed back to the office at a run.

Chapter Four

"Cindy, call the police. Someone's stolen my car!"

"Your car's been taken from our parking lot?" Jonathan stepped out the door to check for his Mercedes. Finding it still in its place, he came back inside.

"It looks like trouble is following her here, too," Pat said acerbically. "Think it over, Jonathan." With a glacial stare directed at Ann, Pat strode past her and went outside.

Ann walked to her office, feeling dejected again. She needed to talk to someone who'd understand. She dialed Tom's office and felt an irrational wave of relief when she heard his voice.

He listened to her story in silence and responded in a crisp tone. "Give the officers who respond a full report, then wait for me inside. I'll be there in twenty minutes or so."

She'd called him needing a friend. But now, faced with the cop in him, she suddenly felt awkward and a little foolish. "I'm going to have to leave as soon as the officers are finished, Tom. The day-care center closes at six and I've got to call a cab so I can pick up Matt."

"Hang on for a minute." He exchanged a few words with someone then returned to the telephone. "Don't worry about Matt." Tom's voice sounded softer now. "I'll give you a ride to the day school. I'm off duty as of right now."

She smiled. So his concern *was* more than official. The gesture of friendship warmed her. "That would be great. Getting a cab always takes so long!"

Ann walked to the reception area to wait for the police. A short time later a patrol car arrived. She explained briefly what had happened. "Do you have an idea why your car was stolen?" the ranking officer asked.

"No, not at all. It's fairly new, but there were others parked outside that are worth a lot more."

It took about ten minutes to complete the questioning. Ann knew her answers reflected her confusion, however, and she realized she hadn't been much help.

"We'll turn in a report, ma'am, then pass it along to Homicide. I think they might be interested."

"I wish you guys could find out who's doing this to me. Yesterday it was vandalism and threats, now, today, my car is stolen."

"All we can do is our best, ma'am. We'll let you know if your car turns up. Most of the time we find them abandoned, sometimes stripped, but your insurance should cover that loss."

"Look, it's not a matter of insurance..." she started to say, then she clamped her mouth shut. "All right officer, thank you. Is that all?"

"For now." The man closed his notebook and went to join his partner in the patrol car.

Ann watched them drive away. Fighting her anger, she walked back inside. Most of the others had left. As she sat in the reception area, she fought the loneliness that swept over her. It was frightening to think there was no one, beside Matt, who would stand in her corner and believe in her no matter what the evidence said.

She took a deep breath, stood and started to pace. Since Warren's death, she'd had to rely only on her own strength. She'd do so again now. Still, she couldn't quiet the restlessness that nagged at her, hinting at a longing for more. It wasn't a new feeling.

She saw Tom pull up outside. Eager to leave, she rushed to join him and gave him directions to the day-care center. "Thanks for offering to pick me up."

"I wasn't about to leave you stranded." He gave her an embarrassed half smile. "It may not look like it at times,

Ann, but I really care...." He cleared his throat. "I care about the people involved in my cases."

His statement took her by surprise. She didn't think that had been what he was about to say.

"We weren't speaking about the case," she said with a gentle smile. Then she took a deep breath and let it out slowly. "But now that we are, I think I should give you fair warning. Reporters are making my life miserable and frightening my son. I can't let this go on much longer."

"Ann, let us handle this. You can't go off half cocked. We'll get to the truth soon."

"But will it be soon enough?" she answered. "What if the theft of my car is connected to the murder? It could be. That's where Jackson's body was dumped. Maybe some valuable item or piece of evidence remained in the car. The killer might believe the cops hadn't found it. That's where I can help you. I can ask around. People are much more likely to let their guard down around a Realtor than a cop."

"Wait a second," he protested. "You're jumping to conclusions. We don't even know for sure that the incidents are related."

"We have to start somewhere." She looked at him and thrust her chin out stubbornly. "Your problem is that you go too much by the book. I suppose that as a cop you have to. Fortunately, I'm not encumbered that way. That's why you need me to help."

"I need *you*?" He shook his head. "No, Ann. It's not worth the risk. You could find yourself in way over your head," he warned her roughly. "Sean Jackson was a low-life. His known associates included burglars, smugglers and fences. He was smart, too. He always managed to slither out from under whatever charges we brought against him. His murder proves that he had some particularly nasty enemies. So if you're trying to protect your son and yourself, stay out of this."

"For heaven's sake, Tom. I'm already involved! Even *you* aren't really sure to what extent. And I've noticed that you haven't come right out and said that you believe I had nothing to do with Jackson."

Tom pulled to a stop in the day-care center's parking lot. "Finding the body in your car makes impressive circumstantial evidence."

"See? That's precisely what I mean."

"Let me finish," he admonished. "I do think it's possible you might be keeping something from me. But that doesn't necessarily mean I believe you're guilty."

"Oh, gee, thanks!" Ann answered, sarcasm dripping from every syllable. She opened the car door, then glanced back at him. "We'll talk more about this later, but not in front of Matt."

She returned a moment later. Matt was in high spirits, but seeing Tom made his eyes light up even more. He rushed to the car. "Hi! Guess what! I drew this today." He pulled out a sheet of paper filled with crayon markings.

"That's nice," Tom said noncommittally.

"It's our house," Matt insisted. "This," he pointed a stubby little finger at a glob of crayon on the side, "is the doggie I want."

"Nice hint, son, but forget it," Ann said, laughing. "Ever since he saw an old rerun of *Lassie*, he's been pressing me to get a dog for him. I've tried to explain that we're not home enough to take care of one properly, but I'm not getting through. Once he makes up his mind, logic and facts seldom deter him."

Tom laughed. "Gosh, I wonder who he gets that from."

"Hey! What's that supposed to mean?" Ann protested.

Tom was about to answer when Matt leaned forward, sticking his face between the two bucket seats. "Do you like to play ball, 'Tenant? We could play when we get home."

"I'm not much on games, Matt, thanks." Tom started the car engine. "Fasten your seat belt, okay?"

Ann glanced at Tom, then at her son. Tom seemed really uncomfortable around Matt. He was avoiding talking to him directly, always shifting the conversation back to her. This kind of tactic would normally have dampened her son's enthusiasm. In this case, however, Matt appeared determined to win the man over.

"We could watch TV," Matt suggested, as if reading her mind.

"I can't stay tonight, Matt. Maybe another time," Tom answered.

He was being polite, but his indifference to Matt hurt. Then again, perhaps Ann wasn't being fair. Tom was thirty-eight years old. He'd chosen to remain childless and wasn't used to being around kids.

When they reached home a short time later, Tom walked inside with them. Matt rushed to his room to visit with Commando. "Are you sure you won't stay for a bit?" Ann asked. "It'd be no trouble to stretch dinner for all of us."

"No, I can't tonight. There're a few things I have to do. Thanks for the offer, though."

"Still the same cop I used to know," she teased. "You'd rather be working than doing anything else."

Tom stopped by the door and faced her. For a moment their gazes met and she couldn't seem to breathe. "You're wrong. Things have changed since then and so have we." His voice had grown smoky, hinting at the depth of emotion behind his words. "Years ago you and I worked hard to avoid each other, Annie," he said softly. "Though we seldom agreed on anything, the attraction between us was always there."

The warmth radiating from his body seemed to envelop her, setting her nerves afire. "What we felt was wrong."

"Yes, back then it was. That's why we both worked hard to suppress it. But now we're both alone." He reached out to embrace her gently.

His hands cupped her neck. The kiss was soft at first, its pleasant warmth drifting through her veins. He traced the line between her lips with his tongue and the warmth grew until she was engulfed by it.

Ann's knees felt wobbly. She clung to him, enjoying his strength, loving the way he held her. A rush of emotions she hadn't experienced in years made her body tremble.

"Mommy," Matt's voice echoed from down the hall, "Commando's hiding under the bed and he won't come out."

Tom released her slowly, his breathing uneven. "I'm sorry Ann. We're not alone and I had no right to forget that, even for a moment."

"Help me with Matt, then we can talk," she urged.

He shook his head. "You go on, Matt needs you. I'll let myself out."

Hearing the front door close made an aching emptiness sweep through her. Why had he left? Mommies were still women. Didn't he realize that?

Then again, perhaps that was part of the problem. Tom had never been interested in children. To get involved with her would mean opening his heart to Matt, too.

As she stepped into Matt's room, she forced herself to shake off the sadness she was feeling. She would not put this on Matt's little shoulders, too. "Okay, let's see what we can do to get Commando back," she said with a smile.

It took half an hour on hands and knees before they got the guinea pig back in the cage. When it was over, Matt stared at her with large, soulful eyes. "Are you mad at me, Mommy?"

"No, Matt." She gave him a long hug. "You're my best pal. Sometimes you do things that you shouldn't, but believe me, we all make mistakes."

"Is 'Tenant Keller staying for dinner?" he asked. "I could ask him, if you want."

She watched her son pensively for a few moments. "You like him, don't you? Why?"

He shrugged. "I wish he could be your friend, Mommy. I have friends I play with, but you don't. You need a grown-up to play with, so you can do grown-up things."

She sat on the edge of Matt's bed and watched her son bring out a toy airplane from the storage box. "Matt, I get lots of time with other adults at my job. I like to spend my free time with you."

His eyebrows furrowed as he concentrated. "Mommy, I want a daddy like Joey and Danny and Jimmy at school," he said at last. "They do neat things together. They go to ball games and fishing, you know, guy stuff."

Ann stared at her budding male chauvinist. "Girls can do that stuff, too. If you want to go fishing or to a ball game, I'll be glad to take you."

He shook his head. "Jimmy's dad says that it's better with just guys."

She pursed her lips. She'd have liked to give Jimmy's dad a good swift kick in the shins. "He's wrong, sweetie, believe me. The important thing is to like the person you're with."

"Will I ever get another daddy?"

Ann recognized the tone. Matt wouldn't be deterred from this subject without a real answer. "I don't know. I'd have to fall in love before I could ever think of marrying anyone. So far that hasn't happened."

"If it does, will you tell me?"

She chuckled softly. "You can count on it."

"What's for dinner?"

Matt's abrupt change of subject indicated that, for now at least, he was satisfied with her answers. She smiled with relief. "Spaghetti," she said, knowing it was his favorite.

"Saguetti!" He giggled and deliberately mispronounced the word. "I'm hungry!"

The evening passed slowly. It was a bit after seven-thirty when the doorbell rang. Ann's body tensed. More reporters? The thought made her go cold all over.

"I'll answer it, Mommy," Matt said, rushing out of the den.

Ann followed him quickly. "No, let me get it."

Matt stopped and gave her an odd look. "But Mommy..."

"Go back into the den." She waited until he'd left the entryway, then peered through the security peephole. Smiling, she opened the door. "Joan, you gave me a scare. I had the worst feeling it might be reporters. They've been driving me crazy lately."

"I'm sorry," she said, immediately contrite. "I should have called you first, I guess."

"No, don't be silly. I'm just getting jumpy." Ann invited Joan inside.

"I wanted to tell you that a cop from Homicide came over—a Detective Glenn—and he asked all sorts of questions about your love life."

"*What* love life?" Ann replied with a wry smile.

"Exactly. I told him the only love in your life was your son."

"Thanks, Joan." She shook her head sadly. "I'm really sorry they dragged you into this."

"Don't worry about it. I can handle them." She walked to the den with Ann. "You know, I've been sitting in front of that darned word processor all day long. I'm about to lapse into a coma from boredom. You're so lucky you have Matt to keep you company. I really envy you. He's such a neat kid."

Matt sat on the carpet, a half dozen small robots scattered around him. "Hi, Joan."

"Hiya, sport!" She smiled and sat beside Ann on the sofa. "You've done a great job, Ann. Your son doesn't lack for anything." Her gaze drifted over the toy robots scattered all around the little boy. "Speaking as a collector, you might give serious thought to hanging on to his toys even after he loses interest in them. Some of the old Barbie dolls go for thousands of dollars nowadays. You never know what's going to increase in value over time. And even if you're not particularly interested in collectible toys, you can always use them to trade for something else."

Matt glanced up. "Joan, wanna play?"

"I'd love to!" She shifted onto the floor next to him. "Do you mind, Ann?"

"Not at all. It'll give me a chance to work up some ads that have to go in next weekend's paper. I've got a handyman's special that's going to be really hard to sell."

Ann watched them for a while as she paused to gather her thoughts. Joan seemed to enjoy Matt's company as much as he enjoyed hers. It was easy to visualize Joan with a husband and half a dozen kids. Yet in the past two years, Ann had never known Joan to have anyone special in her life. She should go out more. It would be a shame if she never had the family she obviously wanted. How could Tom doubt that a child was the best thing a man in a dangerous profession could give his wife?

"Can I put Matt to bed for you? It's eight," Joan asked, interrupting Ann's reverie.

"Sure, go ahead."

"Come on, kiddo. I'll read your favorite story and then tuck you in. What do you say?"

"I don't want to go to bed."

"Maybe the regular way, you wouldn't. But how about if I carry you piggyback, like my daddy used to carry me?" Not waiting for a reply, Joan hoisted him up easily onto her shoulders and started down the hall.

Hearing Matt's screams of delight, Ann smiled.

Minutes later the noise coming from Matt's bedroom subsided. Ann walked to her son's room and kissed him lightly. "Good night, Matty. Sleep tight."

Joan went to Matt's bedroom door. "I'll see you tomorrow, okay sport?"

Matt nodded sleepily, then snuggled into his covers. "'Night."

Joan accompanied Ann down the hall. "I guess I better be going home now. It's about time for me to get back to work." She stopped by the front door. "You take care of yourself, Ann, and don't let anyone start getting to you. And if you need anything, just let me know."

"Thanks, Joan, I really appreciate all your help." After Joan was out of sight, Ann closed the door and locked it for the night.

It was shortly after midnight when exhaustion finally forced Ann to bed. As she crawled beneath the covers, her body relaxed. She wriggled her toes, sinking deeper beneath the snuggly warmth of her cotton quilt. Her eyes closed easily. She'd just begun drifting off to sleep when the sound of her son's screams shattered the stillness.

Bolting instantly out of bed, Ann ran to his room. "Matt?" She switched on the light. The little bed stood empty, the covers tossed back.

Chapter Five

"Matt?" Her voice rose shrilly. Hearing a rustle below her, she took a step back. A moment later she saw something near the floor move. "Matt?"

"Mommy?" Her son's small face peered out from beneath the bed.

"Matthew, you scared me half to death!" As he crawled out, she grabbed him by the arms and pulled him toward her. "What happened? Why were you down there?"

"I was scared, Mommy. A ghost tried to open the window."

"Matt, *a ghost*?" She smiled at her son.

"Mommy, look!" he pointed to the window. It was open at least a foot. The curtains belled and fluttered gently in the breeze. "It did open the window!"

Someone *had* been there. She never left that window open at night. Ann examined the sill carefully, looking for evidence that it had been forced. She found none except the familiar scratches she'd made herself over the years. Since Matt's bedroom window was almost obscured by a large blue spruce, she'd occasionally used the window for access when she'd gotten locked out. She normally kept the screen unlatched and the window itself wasn't hard to unlock. All it took was a bit of experience and a coat hanger.

"Matt, there are no such things as ghosts," she said sternly. "Now tell me, did you open this window yourself before you went to bed?"

"No, Mommy. The ghost did it. Jimmy said that all our houses are haunted."

"Well, Jimmy's wrong." She stared at the open window. Suppressing a shiver, she turned to look at her son. "I've never lied to you, Matt, so you can believe me now. There was no ghost here tonight." She held out her hand to him. "Now come on. Tonight you can sleep in my room again." His expression brightened considerably as she led him down the hall to her bedroom. "No more talk about ghosts, okay?"

"Okay," he replied glumly as he settled between her sheets.

Ann switched off the light and pushed the door partially shut. Alone in the hall, she began to shake. Nothing could be allowed to endanger her son. She strode to the telephone in the living room and dialed the police.

Less than five minutes later she saw the flashing red-and-blue lights of a police vehicle through the living room window. She rushed outside onto the porch, not wanting them to knock and wake Matt. "Please come in, but be very quiet. My son is asleep again and I don't want him disturbed."

The officers listened to her story as they studied the window in Matt's room for signs of tampering. "The latch has been opened before from the outside, but you said you made those marks yourself. Are you sure you didn't leave the window unlocked or open tonight?" the shorter one asked.

"I'm sure," she answered flatly. "My son said he saw something out there tonight, officer. It's not like him to make up stories."

The officer glanced outside. "It's windy and drizzling tonight, Mrs. Dixon. Maybe a branch from that spruce rubbed against one of the window panes and frightened your little boy. Kids have very active imaginations."

"Matt would never have even heard a noise like that." She looked from one officer to the other. "It takes quite a bit to wake him up, believe me."

"That kid has been through a great deal in the past two days, Mrs. Dixon." The officer ran a hand through his thinning brown hair. "I'd say it's natural for him to sleep light for a while."

They weren't going to take this seriously. They were treating her as if she were a hysterical mother, and the realization angered her. "If you're not going to investigate this, then you might as well go. I need help, not sympathy."

"Ma'am, we realize this is a rough time for you, but if you're worried about your son, we suggest you consider placing security gates on your windows, or maybe changing the latches to something more secure." They stopped by her front door. "We'll patrol this area more frequently for the next few days, but that's all we can do. There's no evidence that a crime was committed here tonight. Nothing's been damaged or taken."

Ann heard the sound of someone crossing the driveway, then a second later Joan appeared in the circle of light from the porch. Her hair was damp from the rain and she looked as if she'd run all the way from her home. "Ann, I noticed the police car over here. What on earth is wrong now?"

Ann led the way into the living room, and she recounted the incident with Matt for Joan's benefit. "He was so frightened, but there's no evidence that anyone was there. They think I left the side window open."

"Where's Matt now?" Joan looked around anxiously.

"He's asleep in my room," Ann answered.

"I helped put that little boy to bed," Joan told the police. "I don't remember that window being open." She paused. "Well, I think I would have noticed . . ." Her voice trailed off.

"Ma'am, like we said," the officer nearest Ann told her, "you might try installing bars or changing the latches to make it harder for someone to open the window from the outside."

As the police officers started for the door, Ann stood in their way and blocked them. "I can't believe you're not going to do anything at all except give me security advice. My son could have been hurt tonight! I want you in there looking for evidence."

"*What* evidence?" the brown-haired policeman countered wearily.

As Ann started to argue further, Tom Keller appeared at the open front door. "What's going on here?" he demanded. "I got a call saying that you'd reported an intruder, Ann." He turned to the officers. "Did you find anyone?"

Another round of explanations ensued. Finally, Tom held up his hand. "Okay, I get the idea." He nodded to the officers. "Go ahead and increase your patrols, I'll handle things here."

The minute the two officers left, Tom walked down the hall to Matt's room and inspected the window. Ann and Joan followed him. "They're right, you know," he said quietly. "Matt could have imagined the whole thing or, if the window was already unlatched, opened it himself."

Ann said nothing, but she transfixed him with a glacial stare. He closed and locked the window securely.

"Okay, let's assume that someone tried to sneak into Matt's room tonight. Why do you think they'd do that?"

"I don't know, but I intend to find out."

"Look, Ann, I can understand how this has frightened you, but there's nothing that can be done now. It's been drizzling all night and there're no fingerprints out there. Why don't you try to relax and we'll talk more about this in the morning?"

Joan cleared her throat. "No matter what you decide, Ann, I think you should start watching Matt really carefully. You can't afford to take chances. Why don't you let him stay at home with me while you're off at work? I guarantee that he won't be out of my sight for one minute. At the day-care center he's just one of many kids. They can't give him the kind of attention *I* can."

Ann smiled and touched Joan's arm lightly. "You're one of the dearest people I know, but I can't take you up on your offer. You may work at home, but you have a job. Matt wouldn't let you get anything done. Believe me, I speak from experience. Every time you start to sit down to work, he'll divert you. By the end of the day you'd find yourself with a stack of work piled up, and a little boy who's still filled with energy.''

"Don't worry about that. I don't have any tight deadlines coming up these next few days."

"No, I wouldn't feel right about it," Ann said firmly.

Joan nodded, her expression downcast. "All right, but please, if you change your mind, just let me know. I'll be more than happy to take care of him." She stepped out onto the porch.

"Thanks, Joan."

Ann watched Joan cross the driveway and walk around the house toward the back gate. Then, closing the door, she bolted it shut and rejoined Tom. Ann lifted her chin and challenged him with a bold gaze. "I'm through waiting for the police department. No one has the right to threaten me and my son here in our own home. You may not be willing to look for answers, but I guarantee, *I will*!"

Tom's hands clenched and unclenched automatically. No one at the department questioned his orders. He could back down the best with one glance. But nothing he said made Ann back off. He admired her, but he also wanted her to accept that he knew best.

"What could you possibly do?" he managed to say through clenched teeth.

"I can research the newspaper accounts of Sean Jackson's murder. I can find out who some of his associates were, then go talk to them. That's as good a way to start as any."

"It's also one of the most dangerous things you could do," he argued. "If you go after them, they'll turn on you. The theft of your car and the intruder, assuming they are both connected to the murder, tend to indicate someone is looking for something they believe you might have. Then you have to take into account the person who spray-painted that warning to you. We don't know yet how sincere that threat is. If you go on the offensive, you're going to find yourself mixed up with some very nasty people."

"Then I'll have to rely on my charm." Ann smiled sweetly. "I'm a salesperson. I'm good getting people to cooperate with me." She shot Tom an annoyed glance. "All but the police, that is."

He glared at her wordlessly.

"You said so yourself, Jackson's associates must think I've got something of theirs. From their actions so far, I think it's safe to assume they're not prepared to be patient. We need answers fast."

Tom jammed his hands into his pockets. "So you're going to help us?" He rolled his eyes. "Look, I'm going to give you my home number. Before you do anything, at least give me a call?"

"I'll try, if there's time. Sometimes you have to act fast, you know."

He muttered something she couldn't quite hear and shook his head resignedly. "I better go home. I have an early morning tomorrow."

Ann watched Tom leave, then returned to her bedroom. In the stillness of her room she could hear the sound of her little boy's breathing. What did Tom expect her to do? Sit back and twiddle her thumbs? She was a capable person, and no one else seemed to be getting anywhere with the case. Besides, if things did get rough, she could always call Tom. Being a cop made him the best backup she could possibly have.

When the alarm clock rang the following morning, she felt as if she'd just closed her eyes. She groaned, realizing that Matt was already in the kitchen. She could hear him sliding a chair across the floor. With it, he'd be able to reach the counter and pour himself some cereal.

Ann showered and dressed, then joined Matt.

"Mommy, I got my own breakfast."

She smiled. "Yes, you did, didn't you?" There was cereal all over the counter, and milk had trickled from one end of the kitchen to the other. The half-eaten toast looked fine, except that the margarine on it was at least a half-inch thick.

Hearing the telephone ring, she reached over to the wall unit and picked it up automatically. To her surprise, her caller was her boss, and he didn't sound pleased. "Good morning, Jonathan."

"If you think it's good then you obviously haven't seen the so called 'exclusive' that appeared in that Denver scandal sheet."

A sinking feeling left her feeling weak at the knees. "The *Confidential*? They tried to interview me yesterday, but I didn't talk to them."

"They found a way around that. Let me put it this way. Did you find any traces of the intruder last night?" he asked acerbically.

"I should have expected this." She dropped onto a chair across the table from where Matt had eaten. "The moment I called the police, it became public record."

"Their reporter concocted quite a nasty story. He speculated that you were trying to drum up sympathy for your defense."

"What defense?" she challenged angrily. "I haven't been accused of anything! The last time I heard it wasn't illegal to find a body."

"Ann, I'm really sorry about this. Did you know that a Detective Glenn was here asking questions about you? He wanted to know who you were seeing socially and if there were any special clients you'd worked with these past few months."

"Oh, Jonathan, this is really embarrassing!"

"You're one heck of a real-estate agent, Ann, but things are getting out of hand. You've got to give the firm as well as yourself a chance. Take a few days off. Stay out of the public eye for a while. Also, you might consider letting me put your listings under my name. The commission will be split fifty-fifty of course, but it'll save everyone concerned a great deal of trouble."

"Yeah, everyone except me," she mumbled. "I've worked hard to build a reputation for reliability and trustworthiness. Isn't that worth anything?"

"Ann, if I thought you were guilty of any wrongdoing, I'd have already let you go. But, right now, you're a liability to the firm. The smartest way to play this is to use a little discretion."

Ann kept her temper in check. No one would hire her right now anyway, so quitting in anger scarcely seemed wise. Besides, this could turn out to her advantage. It would give her the time she needed to investigate and help the police clear her name. "Okay, Jonathan, we'll do it your way for the moment."

"That's the spirit. You'll be back in a week, you'll see."

Ann placed the receiver back on the hook, then considered her options. If she left Matt at the day-care center as usual, she could use the day to uncover some leads. Without hesitation, Ann picked up the receiver again and grabbed the phone book from the shelf with her other hand. First of all, she had to find a car-rental place that delivered.

Forty-five minutes later she dropped Matt off at the day-care center, then went directly to the library. Going through every Colorado newspaper for the past two days was time consuming. Slowly, she determined that everything Tom had said about Jackson was true. Two Denver papers had done lengthy background reports detailing Jackson's many arrests and prison record. His murder was no surprise, considering his life-style. But how had this man ended up in her driveway?

What she needed now were specifics, like his address, who his last employer was and so on. And there was only one place that was likely to have all that information on hand. Getting it, however, was bound to be tricky.

Ann drove to the police station and asked to see Tom. The officer behind the desk informed her that Lieutenant Keller was out. Instead, he directed her to one of Tom's associates in the Homicide section. "Just go to the third office on your right. I'll buzz and let him know you're coming."

As she walked down the hall, an overweight, middle-aged man came toward her. "Hi, I'm Detective Glenn. What can I do for you?"

"I'm Ann Dixon." She extended her hand. "It's about time we met. You've been asking a lot of questions about me."

He met her gaze without flinching. "I'm doing my job, ma'am."

She nodded. "The reason I'm here is that I need Sean Jackson's home address. Also, I'd like the name of his last employer," she said boldly. "I realize that you probably don't go around giving this information out to everyone who asks. But since he was found in my driveway and you all seem to suspect that I knew him, telling me shouldn't make any difference."

"Well, I see your reasoning, but I'm afraid I just can't—"

"Look, this is bound to be on record somewhere. I'll find it out sooner or later anyway."

"Ma'am, I don't know what I can do. My head would roll if I let you have information from our files."

"You're right about that, Glenn," Tom said, striding down the hall toward them. "What's going on here?"

"I was telling Mrs. Dixon that she'd have to go through channels," Detective Glenn explained.

Tom nodded. "Okay, Bob, thanks." After Bob went back into his office Tom led Ann to his own, then turned to face her. "All right, Ann, what the hell are you trying to pull?"

Chapter Six

"I've been straightforward about what I need," she answered, holding his gaze.

"I'm just not getting through to you, am I?" he asked. He didn't wait for an answer. "I guess I'll have to be blunt. Have you thought of what it'd do to Matt if you got yourself killed?"

The words hurt, but she refused to let him see it. "I'm aware of my responsibility to Matt. But if I do nothing, what you just said may happen anyway. Remember the message on the wall?" She stuck her hands deep into her skirt pockets so he couldn't see them tremble. "The police have to divide their attention between lots of cases. I can't afford to sit back and wait for you guys. Only people with very secure life-styles can afford to be that trusting."

Tom said nothing for several long moments. "You've had some difficult times," he muttered almost to himself. His gaze gentled. "Now you're seeing one of the reasons why I didn't want kids. I never wanted Jessica to go through what you have."

"It's true that I've faced some tough challenges, but Matt has given me the extra drive I needed to succeed. You may not understand this, but I need Matt as much as he needs me."

Tom retrieved several files from the cabinet. "You've always had the courage to reach out for what makes you happy. That's the mark of a strong person and it's also what makes you such a good fighter." He chuckled softly. "I re-member some of the arguments you used to have with War-ren. You'd never back down when you thought you were right, and Warren could be intimidating. Sometimes he'd bark an order at you, and you'd just fix him with that stare of yours until he'd back off."

She smiled. "It used to drive me nuts when you ordered poor Jessica around and she let you get away with it."

He grinned, a sensual smile that left her heart pounding. "I never said anything back then, but I always believed that we were all mismatched. Warren and Jessica belonged to-gether." He paused, then added, "Just like you and I."

Ann couldn't tear her gaze away. She felt acutely aware of Tom Keller. There was a powerful virility about him that made her feel weak at the knees. "That was then," she cau-tioned. She had to be careful. Otherwise, she and Tom could end up creating a bigger mess than the one they were at-tempting to resolve. "Will you give me the information I asked for about Jackson?" she asked insistently, refocus-ing on the business at hand.

"I'll do better than that," he answered. "I was about to go talk to Jackson's last employer. Why don't you come with me? I'll sign you up as my ride-along. Civilian observ-ers are common enough nowadays, since our police depart-ment started the new community-relations program."

"Great, but what if he recognizes me from the newspa-per pictures?" Ann stood and walked to the door.

Tom considered it for a moment. "Can you tie your hair back in a bun?"

She rummaged in her purse and managed to scrounge a rubber band and a few hair pins. "It'll be crude," she warned.

He studied the final product and nodded. "That's fine. You don't look so much like the newspaper photos any-more, but wait here. We need one more thing, then we'll be set."

Tom returned a moment later with a pair of eyeglasses. "Try these, they're plain glass, so they won't affect your vision. It's a prop one of our policewomen uses from time to time.''

Ann slipped them on. "I must look ghastly."

"No, you just look different. Sexy, too, in a cerebral way."

The words pleased her out of all proportion. "Thanks," she said with a smile, then added, "I think."

"Come on, let's go." He followed her outside.

"By the way, what kind of job did Jackson have?" Ann asked. "All the newspapers just said he was a salesman."

"He sold used cars at one of the least-reputable dealerships in the city," Tom replied. "We're always getting complaints about that place. Occasionally the guys working bunco manage to close them down for a while, but invariably they manage to reopen." He led her to his car.

"I bet I know the one you're talking about. I keep noticing it in the papers. Let me see...it's called Chuck's Auto Sales. Their ad always shows a salesman with a telephone daring customers to call the competition and try to find a better deal."

"That's the one," Tom answered, getting his car underway. "Jackson was Chuck's most successful employee. Now that should give you pause."

"I spent most of the morning at the library reading all I could about Jackson. He was a real winner, I'll say that for him," she answered cynically.

Twenty minutes later, Tom turned into Chuck's lot. He parked his sedan next to the brightly painted railroad car that served as an office. The converted boxcar was placed in the middle of the crowded lot filled with older model cars. Faded pennants were interspersed with light bulbs strung around the perimeter. "Stick close by me."

"In this place, you bet."

"I can't believe it. You're finally not giving me an argument."

"I know when to concede."

He smiled teasingly, then grew serious. "It's time for me to become a hard-nosed cop again." He took a deep breath, as if psyching himself up.

Ann thought he was incredibly stubborn and narrow-minded at times, but it was reassuring to realize he did care enough to worry about her safety. And now he was trying to be helpful. The thought warmed her. She strode across the parking lot, staying beside him.

As they walked through the wide doors to the office, they were met by a man with slicked back blond hair. Tom flashed his badge. "I want to see Chuck Adams."

"Well, officer, I'm Chuck. What can we do for you today? Can we interest you in one of our fine used cars?"

"Not likely. I'm here on business," Tom growled. "Where can we talk?" Tom glanced at a weary-looking middle-aged woman behind a small desk. She was discussing a transaction with a young couple probably still in their teens.

Ann tried not to look directly at Chuck, afraid he might read her thoughts. Whenever Chuck grinned at her, she had to suppress the urge to cringe. He had a lifeless smile that made her feel as if cold jelly were trickling down her spine.

"And who might you be?" Chuck purred.

"This lady is my civilian ride-along."

"Well, I can certainly see why the police are so eager to continue their public-relations campaign," Adams answered.

It took concentration, but Ann managed not to gag.

"We're both *extremely grateful* you approve. Now for the reason I came," Tom said firmly. "I need to ask you about one of your former employees."

With a patronizing smile, Chuck led Tom to the far corner of the room. "I don't discuss business matters with the police," he whispered harshly. "Go talk to my lawyers."

Tom transfixed him with a lethal glare. "We can do this the easy way, or we can play hardball." The edge in his voice was slowly growing in intensity. "By tomorrow morning, I can have the fire marshal down here checking the premises for safety or code violations. He has the authority to close you down. On Tuesday, some of my boys can come to browse, writing down the serial numbers of every car here. On Wednesday, we can start checking those numbers against every hot car reported in this state for the past two years. Who knows how many stolen vehicles we might end up finding?'' He grew quiet, having issued his challenge.

The man sighed with resignation. ''There's never any peace for the honest businessman,'' Chuck answered, looking over his shoulder to see if the others were listening, ''not with the police harassing us every moment of the day.'' He cocked his head and gestured toward his office, ''Come in.''

Tom grasped Ann by the arm and led her inside, staying between the other man and her. ''Now, tell me all you can about Sean Jackson.''

''There isn't much to tell,'' Chuck stated flatly. ''Jackson worked afternoons and evenings. I thought he had other action going, but as long as it didn't affect his business here, I really didn't care. He was one of my best salesmen.'' Chuck's grin was tainted with a malicious edge. ''He was particularly good with women.''

''Who were his enemies?''

Chuck laughed. ''You're kidding, right?'' Seeing Tom's impassive face, he stopped laughing and continued. ''That man had women everywhere. Married, not married, it didn't make any difference to him. My guess is that some jealous husband or boyfriend finally got even.''

''How did he get along with the others here? Did he make any enemies?''

''Naw, the other guys kinda admired him. I mean, why not? Most of them envied what he had going, and he wasn't messing with any of their women. Not that they knew of, at least.''

Tom asked a few more questions, but soon realized that he wasn't going to get anything else of value here. ''Thanks for your cooperation,'' he concluded, then started toward the door.

''You guys have any leads yet?''

Tom stopped and glanced back. ''Why do you ask?''

''He worked for me, for Pete's sake. Besides, I was curious how long it was going to take the police to sweep it all under the rug. He's not the type you're going to devote a lot of man-hours to.''

"You're wrong."

Tom walked back to the car with Ann. "You know, once the department's convinced that you had nothing to do with Jackson's murder, they might want to do what Adams said and that won't be good for you. As far as public opinion goes, it's my guess you won't be cleared until the real murderer is found."

"It sounds like you finally believe I'm innocent," she said, hoping she was right.

"Yes, you convinced me last night. When I arrived, you were as white as a sheet. No one could have faked that color. You were terrified." He paused. "If you'd been keeping something back, you'd have told it to me then. There's no way you would have taken the chance of endangering Matt."

Ann felt as if a great weight had been lifted off her shoulders. "Now that we've got that out of the way, we should be able to really join forces and find some answers."

They reached the police station and Tom pulled into an empty parking space near her rented car. "Ann, the reason I let you come with me today was so you could see the kind of people who filled Jackson's world. They're out to make a buck and they don't care who they hurt in the process. Just trust me to do my job, please. You and Matt will be fine."

"Tom, you can't guarantee our safety. The events are out of your hands. As it is, Matt and I are already in a great deal of trouble because of what's happened." She walked to her car, just a few feet away. "I have to do something to help myself, and looking into this is one way for me to do that. But don't worry, I'll be careful. And I'll keep you posted, okay?"

Tom watched her as she eased herself into the driver's seat. "Be *very* careful, Ann. When you start stirring things around, you never know what's going to come to the surface."

TOM DRUMMED HIS FINGERS on the desk impatiently. Waiting for the burglary section's records was taking forever. The department was small, with less than fifty field operatives at all levels. Crime had never been a big problem in Crystal, but things were changing. Their city was growing and with it, the crime rate.

He picked up the phone immediately when it rang. "Keller," he barked.

"Lieutenant," a man's voice blared from the receiver, "the computer's down and we're having a bit of a problem getting the printout you want. Also, the captain's okay is needed before you can take the file out of this section."

"Come on, Charlie, give me a break. This investigation crosses over into both our departments. If we stand on protocol, we're not going to get anywhere."

"Forget it, Lieutenant. I realize you like ruffling feathers, but I do what the boss says and it makes my life easier."

Tom slammed the receiver down. He'd been hoping to avoid meeting with the captain about this for a little longer. It would have been easier to approach the man with a case that offered more answers than questions. And if word that he'd known Ann in the past had already reached the captain, the going was bound to be tough. It was possible he'd be ordered to withdraw from the case completely. That meant he'd have to convince the captain that he was the one cop in the department best suited to solve this crime. Fortunately, the facts of the case would back him up.

Bracing himself, he strode to the captain's office and knocked on the open door.

"Keller, I've been meaning to talk to you. I'm glad you stopped by." Captain Howard Lambert was built like a soda machine with a head. He had no sense of humor and an enormous amount of energy that seemed incongruous with his massive frame. "Tell me, what have you found out about the Jackson murder?"

"Not much, except that I'm certain the body was dumped in Mrs. Dixon's car. There's some information I need about a case I worked involving a burglary ring two months ago, just before I was transferred back to Homicide. We had several leads that pointed to Sean Jackson. The ring was stealing collectibles, and the mayor's house was one of those hit. We were getting quite a bit of pressure to solve the case and then, just like that—'' he snapped his fingers ''—the thefts stopped.''

"So you think Jackson's murder is somehow connected to the burglaries?" Lambert leaned forward and picked up his pipe.

"It makes sense to me. There might have been a falling out among the thieves." Tom stood by an oak credenza holding framed photos of the captain and various city dignitaries.

"What about the Dixon woman?"

"So far we haven't found any motive or physical evidence linking her to Jackson. She has no record and has a solid reputation in this town. The case against her is purely circumstantial."

"Is it possible that you're letting her off the hook too easily? I've heard rumors that you two used to be friends."

Here it was. Tom forced himself to appear unconcerned. "We were neighbors once, sir, but I haven't seen her in three years. Besides, if you review my handling of this case, you'll see that she's received no special consideration. Detective Glenn has been backing me up on the leg work, especially with Ann Dixon's recent background. I've had him check her out thoroughly, trying to find some possible connection between her and Sean Jackson. But, from what we've learned, there isn't any."

Captain Lambert pressed tobacco deep into the bowl of his pipe with his forefinger. His face was furrowed with concentration. "Keller," he said at length, "I'm going to take you off this case. If you knew this woman before, there will be accusations of conflict of interest."

"There is no conflict, sir. I'm doing my job and following the best leads. Recently, there've been a few incidents that further indicate she didn't commit the murder. I have copies of the reports filed by the officers responding to those calls. Nonetheless, if I'm wrong and she is responsible for

Jackson's death, I'm still in the best position to find that out. I know more about her than any other member of this department."

The captain lit his pipe and stared at the wisps of smoke that trailed upward in hazy, circular patterns. "I don't know, Keller. I still have some reservations about this."

"Sir, if this *is* tied to the burglary ring we suspect Jackson was part of, I'm the logical person for the job. I worked on the case while I was still in Burglary. I know more about Jackson's background than any other officer here, and have the best opportunity to reconstruct his life. If anyone he dealt with was responsible for his death, I'll find out who."

"I'll tell you what. Uncover some evidence supporting your theory that Jackson's death was connected to the burglaries, and I'll keep you on. Fair enough?"

What choice did he have? Tom nodded. "I'll need your okay to get some of burglary division's records, Captain."

Lambert reached for his phone. "I'll give them a call and make sure they cooperate with you."

Tom returned to his office slowly. He had no intention of being pulled off the case, even if it turned out that the burglaries were not connected. He'd developed good police instincts in the past twelve years and right now they told him that Ann's troubles were far from over.

He'd learned his lesson the hard way in the past and to this day, he'd never shaken off the guilt. Oh, he'd reasoned it out, told himself over and over again that it hadn't been his fault. Yet, the feeling persisted. He should have kept his own counsel and not have allowed himself to be swayed.

This time, he wouldn't risk failure, not when Ann was involved.

By the time Tom got back to his office, the file he'd requested was on his desk. He glanced at the contents, refreshing his memory, and settled down to study the new information.

Once finished, he sat back for several minutes, mulling over the information before him. Finally, he picked up the telephone and dialed Ann's home number. He was still worried about her trying to investigate this on her own.

Perhaps that was the problem with being a cop. He'd dealt with criminals for so long that he kept imagining scenarios that Ann couldn't even begin to conceive. Relief flooded over him when Ann answered. "I'm glad you're home," he said, then clenched his jaw. The woman was making him crazy.

"Is something wrong?"

"No, but I need to talk to you," he answered honestly. He'd think of an official reason later. The fact was he just wanted to see her, but that was one admission he wasn't ready to make.

"I was about to leave to pick up Matt at preschool, but I should be back by the time you can get here."

He arrived at her house just as Ann was getting out of her car. Matt spotted Tom, then, with a smile, ran toward him excitedly. He stopped a few steps away. "Hi, 'Tenant Keller. Did you come for dinner?"

"No, just to visit, Matt," he answered.

"Will you be Mommy's new friend? She's always alone."

"Matthew!" Ann felt her face grow hot. "I have plenty of grown-up friends, so stop making it sound like I'm a lonely old spinster."

"What's a spinzer?"

"Never mind." She rolled her eyes. "Why don't you go get the mail for me?"

Tom grinned at her. "Don't worry. I'd never be able to see you in the role of spinster. You're too pretty, too young and too darn..." He shrugged and looked sheepish. "Never mind."

"Too darn what?" She was curious now and not about to let it go.

"Too darn sexy," he replied, and gave her a wink.

His words affected her as if he'd touched her bare flesh. She muttered a quick thanks to Matt as he rushed up and handed her the mail. Giving Tom a hesitant smile, she walked to the front door. It had been such a long time since she'd felt this electrifying rush of pure sensation. It was a wonderful case of grown-up lust. And perhaps something more, though she didn't dare try to define it.

As they walked inside, Matt ran to his room and emerged with a box of his toy robots. "'Tenant, want to play?'"

"Not now, Matt. I want to talk to your mom."

Matt looked slightly downcast, but then shrugged. "Okay, maybe we can all play together after you finish."

Tom waited as the boy settled in the den with his toys. Taking Ann's arm, Tom led her into the kitchen. "I've been checking Sean Jackson's background," he said in a soft voice. "We believe that for some time now he was part of a very successful burglary ring. I think he only had his job as a car salesman in order to hide his profits. Our intelligence report on his M.O.—method of operation—says that Jackson would case each home until he was familiar with the routines of the household. He'd then break in on a weekday morning after everyone had left the house. The same afternoon he'd fence whatever he'd stolen so that the merchandise was never with him for very long. The problem was that our department was never able to prove this or find his fence. He always seemed to know when he was being watched."

"So what was Jackson doing here early Saturday morning? That doesn't fit the M.O. you described. Do you think he changed his technique to throw the police off?"

"I don't think so. It's more likely it was a social call to a friend nearby. Maybe he spent the night with one of his girlfriends. Remember Chuckie's jealous-boyfriend theory? How well do you know your neighbors?"

"Well enough to tell you that no one around here is likely to have been having an affair with Sean Jackson," Ann said. "My neighbor to the left is married, works, and her husband is always home when she is. Joan, behind us up the path, probably hasn't had a date in two years. I don't mean anything unkind, but she's not the type men usually notice. Farther out, it gets even less likely. I doubt Sean was having a raging love affair with a seventy-year-old widow or with Mrs. Hammond, who lives at the corner. Mr. Hammond is an insurance underwriter with an office at home." She sat down at the kitchen table and with a wave of her hand, invited him to have a seat.

"The problem with this case is that we don't have a clear handle on what we're dealing with." Tom said. "That makes it nearly impossible to know what to expect. In line with that thought, have you given any more consideration to changing your locks? I don't want to alarm you, but if you did have an intruder last night, then that means someone felt it was worth the risk to break in here. You could be standing between the killer and whatever it is he wants, and that's not a good place to be."

The thought unsettled Ann, but she tried not to show it. She needed to prove to Tom that she could be cool and levelheaded despite outside pressures. That was the only way he'd ever come to trust her judgment. Eager for something to do that would mask her nervousness, she began to sort through the morning's mail. "I'll call a locksmith and get him out here as soon as possible."

She stopped and stared at the last envelope. It had no stamp or postmark. Her name was the only thing typed on it.

"What's wrong?" Tom walked to her side and glanced over her shoulder. "What have you got there?"

"I'm not sure." She tore the envelope open and extracted a small typed note. "Return what's mine," she read aloud, her voice wavering slightly, "or be prepared to face your worst nightmares."

Chapter Seven

Ann stared at the note aghast. "It continues on the other side. 'To return my property use the directions in the personal column of the morning paper. The notice will be signed "Artemis." '"

Ann sat very still. "I have no idea what he wants, but he's seriously misjudged me. He's declared war. The only way I'd hand anything over to him now is with a cop right behind me to arrest him." Her eyes flashed angrily.

Tom suppressed a smile of approval. The last thing he wanted her to know was how he admired that fire in her. It might encourage her to take risks. "I'd like to take the note and envelope with me to the station and have our lab check them for prints."

"Here." She pushed the papers across the table to him with her fingernails. "But, if you find out something, I want to know."

Before Tom could reply, Matt rushed into the kitchen. "Mommy, I'm going out to the backyard to play with my Rough and Tumble robots, okay?"

"Okay, Matt." She forced a smile. The little boy turned and ran back to his room to get his toys.

"Let's go through the house room by room. You can tell me about everything you've brought into the house recently," Tom suggested. "We've got to find out what Artemis is after." He grew pensive. "For instance, have you bought anything lately, or has something new been added?

Look at everything—the wall clock, the radio, even things in the drawers. Nothing's too trivial.''

"I'm not much for redecorating, Tom. After Warren died, I spent an entire year replacing the old furnishings with new things. I wanted to give our home a completely different look that wouldn't remind me of the past. I didn't have much money, so most of what you see came from neighborhood bargains and a few estate sales. Once finished, I considered the job done. I'm not the type who feels the need to periodically change the way my house looks." She glanced around the kitchen, then searched the drawers. "Nothing new here." They went to the next room.

"You still must buy things from time to time. We all do, even if they're nothing major." He stepped into her den. "Are any of the knickknacks you bought antiques or collectors items that could have a high value?"

"If they are, neither I nor the people I bought them from knew. We could ask Joan. She knows all about that kind of stuff. Besides, I've never liked to fill my house with things that couldn't be easily replaced if broken. I have enough to worry about with Matt."

"Okay, that sounds reasonable. What about purchases for your business? Or have you brought any important papers home lately?"

She stopped by her desk. "I'm always buying supplies, like ball-point pens and pencils." She extracted two unopened packages from her drawer. "The legal papers pertaining to my business are filed immediately with the title companies or other places."

He inspected the packages of office supplies, then placed them back in the desk. "Okay, what else?"

She walked around the den, then went to the living room and repeated the procedure. "This is hopeless. I'm telling you, if I'd purchased anything valuable or if anyone had added anything, I'd have known it."

"Let's keep looking. Maybe something will trigger your memory," he insisted. "Try to think back. Has anyone given you something to keep for them?"

She shook her head. "No, I'd already considered that. I even speculated that perhaps one of Matt's little friends or a neighbor had left something here."

"That's the idea."

"Yes, but it didn't pan out." She waved her hand around the room. "I don't know if you've noticed, but I'm really fussy about the way I keep house. I like everything orderly. I'm the kind who'll notice if a painting isn't hanging straight or if the items on the coffee table aren't in the same order I put them down in. My life's been chaotic at times and there's been very little I could do about that. Yet in my home, I'm in control. Everything has a place here and fills a specific need." She gave him a sheepish smile. "Now you're convinced I'm compulsive, right?"

"I think you've done very well for yourself and your son." He paused then grinned slowly. "So what if you're a little crazy about the housekeeping?"

She tossed one of the couch pillows at him, but he ducked and it sailed past him. "Skunk," she muttered, a trace of a smile on her face.

He handed the pillow back and watched her place it in exactly the same position where it had been. "Okay, let's get back to business. Besides groceries what other ordinary things have you brought into the house lately?"

She took a deep breath, then let it out again. "I've purchased some clothes for both Matt and myself, and a few toys."

"Why don't we take a look at those," Tom suggested.

A moment later, he placed her new clothes on the bed and checked the seams and pockets. "Nothing's here."

"I could have told you that. They're just work clothes I purchased through a catalog."

"Let's go take a look at Matt's things."

She walked to Matt's room and pulled out a couple pairs of jeans and two sweatshirts. "They're ordinary kid's clothing," she said. "If whoever's been harassing me is after these, we're dealing with a very desperate person."

Tom followed the same procedure he'd used on her clothes, then handed the clothes back to her. "What about toys?"

She went to the toy box and extracted several toy robots and one teddy bear. "This is it. As you can see, none is an original G.I. Joe worth thousands of dollars."

Tom inspected the toys, then searched through all the seams of the teddy bear. "Well, this stuffed animal hasn't been tampered with." He sat down on the edge of Matt's bed. "That leaves us with only one other possibility. Artemis must believe Sean brought something here."

"If that were true, either the police or I would have found it by now," Ann said cynically. "Of course, the note seems to indicate that Artemis thinks I have found it and kept it to myself. That might give me some leverage."

Tom cringed. "Don't even think about it," he groaned. "Look, for now, keep looking around the house and yard. Only don't tell anyone about the note or that we're looking for something, not even your closest friends. It's better to keep everyone in the dark about what you're doing."

"Okay. In the meantime I'm going to see if I can come up with a plan to go on the offensive."

"Ann, please don't do anything without talking to me first." It was like trying to control a loose cannon. Even as he spoke, he figured the odds were at best fifty-fifty that she'd confide in him before acting. Tom stood and walked to the door. "I'm going to take this note to the station now. The quicker we get some answers, the better off we'll be."

Ann rose and joined him. "Don't worry. With both of us working on this, we're bound to get answers soon."

"Will you try to remember that I'm the cop around here?" Seeing the nonplussed look on her face, he swore softly. "Why do I even talk to you? You don't listen."

"I do listen to you. And believe me, it's impossible not to hear you when you raise your voice. When you finally say something I agree with, I'll be glad to take your advice."

Tom groaned loudly. "At least you're going to change the locks."

"Of course. It's the only truly sensible thing you've come up with so far." She continued quickly, deliberately not giving him a chance to reply. "I'm also going to check about placing security gates on all the windows. I hate the thought of making my home look like a jail, but I'll do whatever's necessary to start feeling safe here again."

"If you even think that someone's breaking in, call the police. They'll be here in minutes, I promise you that."

"I need some kind of weapon," she said softly, as if to herself.

"Not until you learn how to use one. Until then, you'd be more likely to shoot yourself with a gun than an intruder. Those are the statistics, not my opinion," he argued.

He was right, but she couldn't resist teasing him for being so quick to assume she was wrong. He'd never liked having his authority questioned, so no doubt this would be a learning experience for him.

"I was thinking of mace, but maybe a shotgun . . ."

"Ann, have a heart, okay?" He turned and opened the door. "I'll see you later."

She watched him leave. He was so opinionated and bossy! She smiled, realizing that was exactly what he probably thought of her, too. It did give them something in common.

"Mom?" Matt tugged at her pant leg. "Want to play?"

She started to say no, but then recanted. She could sit at her desk and worry, but that would serve no purpose. "Sure, but in a while I'll have to go fix dinner."

"I'll help, okay?"

She suppressed a shudder. That cinched it. Now she knew what she'd be doing the rest of the evening. With Matt helping, dinner and the subsequent cleanup promised to be an all-night job. "Okay, you're on."

It was shortly after five when the doorbell rang. Matt started to go over, then stopped abruptly. "Mommy, want me to get it?"

"No, sweetie. Until the reporters go away for good, I'm going to be the one who answers the door, okay?"

"Okay." He returned to his circle of toy trucks.

Ann walked to the door slowly, hating her own reluctance to answer the bell. She peered through the peephole, teeth clenched, and was relieved to find Joan outside. "What's this?" she asked, opening the door.

Joan stood, holding two large boxes of pizza. "It's Matt's favorite kind, and I figured you could use the break."

Matt peered around the corner, then ran up to Joan. "Pizza!"

"With extra cheese, just like you like it."

"That's great, Joan. You're a life saver. To be honest, I wasn't looking forward to having to fix dinner at all." They all went into the kitchen. "You know, I'm not working, yet I'm more tired nowadays than I've ever been at my job."

"You should just put everything out of your mind." Joan lowered her voice. "But then again, I wouldn't be able to do that, either, if our positions were reversed. I noticed that detective was here again."

"Matt, there's a cartoon special on television right now. I checked earlier. Why don't you take a TV tray into the den and I'll bring you a slice of pizza? You can eat in front of the television set. How's that sound?"

"Aw-right!" Matt dashed into the den and switched on the set.

"I'll tell you how it sounds to me," Joan teased. "I'd say mom needs a grown-up to talk to."

Ann dropped onto the nearest chair. "And how! Do you mind?"

"What are friends for? Look, you just sit and relax. I know where everything is, so I'll get some milk for Matt and some colas for us. Then we can have a long talk."

"Thanks, Joan. I'm really bushed."

A few minutes later with Matt settled in the den with his pizza, watching the cartoon special, Joan and Ann sat down in the kitchen to eat. "You haven't been getting much sleep," Joan commented.

"I'm so angry about what's been happening!" Through the door she saw that her son was still engrossed in the cartoons. "I'd like to ask you a favor, Joan, if I may."

"Name it."

"Will you keep an eye on my house during the day when Matt and I are gone?"

"No problem. I'll even come down and check once in a while to make sure everything's okay. It'll be like old times. When I was a kid, my dad used to get me jobs watching the neighbors' homes while they were on vacation. I kind of miss those days."

"I didn't mean to put you to any extra trouble," Ann protested. "I thought you could just glance out your back window every once in a while."

"Don't give it a thought. It'll be like a stroll down memory lane," she assured. "You know, there's something I've been wondering about." Joan opened her mouth as if to speak, then clamped it shut again. "Never mind, I'm just being a nosy neighbor."

Ann laughed. "Go ahead. I've got a feeling I know what you're going to ask anyway."

Joan smiled. "Okay. So what gives between you and Lieutenant Keller? Am I wrong, or is he interested in you?"

"I knew him a long time ago, that's all. There wasn't anything between us back then, and there sure isn't going to be now."

"Why so certain?"

"Joan, if I ever get serious about any man again, it'll have to be with one who shares my views on life. I like kids and want to have more someday. Tom's feelings are exactly the opposite. That's why it wouldn't work between us."

"I can understand that. I'm looking for a man who values family life, too. Someone just like my father. He was always there for me." With a sigh, Joan looked down at her plate and reached for another slice of pizza. "But it's such a wasteland out there when it comes to suitable men."

"That's what I've heard, but to be honest, I haven't tried to date that much. At first I just wasn't up to it. For a long time after Warren died, I'd turn around and swear I'd just caught sight of him in the far corner of the room. Or I'd be playing with Matt and be sure that I'd heard Warren in the hall. Of course the second I'd look, he'd be gone. I know this doesn't sound logical, but I couldn't shake the feeling he was right there with us." Ann sipped her soft drink. "And for a while, that was enough. In a way, I still had both Warren and Matt." She leaned back in her chair and stretched her legs. "Then, as time went by, the focus of my life changed. Matt became the center of my world. He's such a terrific kid, and he needed my attention and my love."

"But now?"

Ann shrugged. "I'm very independent and I know I'm capable of providing for myself and my son. Yet, I can't deny that someday I'd love to find a man who'd want to come home after work and be a family with me and Matt."

As if on cue, Matt pushed into the kitchen. "I've seen this cartoon before, Mom. I'm going to play with some stuff in my room, okay?" He placed his empty glass and plate on the counter and dashed down the hall.

Joan looked down at the thin crust of pizza before her. "I suppose we're all raised to want a husband and a family sooner or later." Joan picked up her plate, then put it and Matt's in the dishwasher. "I'd better be getting back. I've still got some typing to do tonight."

"Thanks for coming over and bringing dinner."

Joan gave Ann a quick hug. "I'm always just a phone call away, remember that."

Ann saw Joan to the door, then headed for Matt's room. Matt was being too quiet. Her mother's sixth sense warned Ann it was time to check things out. As she entered the hall, she saw him sitting over the furnace grating with his toy fishing pole. With one tiny hand on the reel and the other gripping the pole, he was lowering the line through the opening in the register.

"Whatcha doing?" she asked.

"Fishing," Matt said seriously, his face furrowed in concentration.

Well, at least he was busy and out of trouble. Last winter he'd played in the hall constantly and parts of his toys had kept falling down the grate. The subsequent melt down released the most foul stench imaginable. Twice she'd had to turn off the smoke alarm when a plastic toy had ignited. Nowadays, because of the problems he'd caused in the past, he was forbidden to bring anything near the floor register except his fishing gear. In the summer, with the gas furnace off, there was no way he could hurt himself there. She smiled back at her son. "Caught anything yet?"

Matt gave her a big smile. "Nope, but I will."

"Well, if it's a shark, you better throw it back."

"I'm going to catch something neat, you wait."

Trying hard not to laugh at the solemn expression on his face, Ann returned to her desk and started to work. Even if she wasn't going into the office, there were still listings to review and weekly loan-interest rates to study. She stared at the sheets before her and realized she hadn't brought everything she needed from the office. Tomorrow, she'd have to pay Randall and Associates a quick visit. Despite her effort to concentrate on her work, she couldn't help but speculate on the kind of reception she'd receive.

At eight-thirty she put Matt to bed. Her little boy was thrilled to be sleeping in her room again. The arrangement suited her, too. There was no way she'd get any sleep unless he was right there with her. At least not until she'd had the locks changed and window gates installed.

In the morning, when her alarm went off as usual, Ann slipped on her robe and her favorite hippo slippers. It was impossible to take the world too seriously when she was wearing them, so they helped her put everything in perspective. She walked outside, picked up the morning paper and went to the kitchen. At least the reporters had stopped haunting her doorstep. Maybe they'd given up on her, finally. A quick scan of the classified section revealed no messages signed by anyone named Artemis. But maybe today either she or the police would finally find some answers. With that hope, she got Matt ready for school. After getting dressed for her own visit to the office, she called several locksmiths.

By the time she was ready to leave, her stomach felt tied in knots. She strongly suspected she wasn't going to be welcome at her own work place, and the realization made her fume.

After Ann dropped Matt off she went to her office, prepared for battle. She may have agreed to stop seeing clients, but she still had to keep up with the latest real-estate reports. If she didn't it would mean a further loss of income after everything was all cleared up.

As Ann strode into the office, Cindy's eyes widened slightly. "I thought that you weren't supposed to..."

"I'm here to pick up a printout of the latest listings," Ann replied crisply.

The receptionist smiled apologetically. "Sorry, I didn't mean to sound so negative. It's just that everything's been crazy around here. You won't believe how many crank calls we got yesterday. You'd think people would have better things to do with their time."

"I'm sorry they've been calling the office," Ann replied. "If there was anything I could do to stop it, I would."

Pat Miller strode into the reception area. Surprised, she stopped in midstride and stared at Ann. "What's it going to take to get you to stay away from the office? It's nothing personal, Ann, but the publicity surrounding you has really been affecting business."

"I'm here to pick up a few things, Pat." Ann fought the urge to be nasty. The woman was trying to protect her income, and she could certainly sympathize with that.

Pat exhaled softly. "I must sound like a witch, Ann, but it's really not personal. The competition here has always been good for both of us. It made us work harder. Sympathizing with you, though, doesn't make me worry any less about myself."

"Maybe it'll help if we *both* worry less about you," Ann countered smoothly.

Pat scowled, then glanced at her watch. "Time for me to go meet a client."

Ann walked to her desk, picked up the papers she'd come for and hurried out. By the time she reached her car, she was more determined than ever to speed up the investigation. This mess had disrupted her life enough. What she needed now was to learn as much as she could about investigative techniques. Her ingenuity and a little knowledge would make an unbeatable combination.

Ann stopped by the library, checked out several large volumes on criminology, then drove home. She'd study them, then devise a plan to uncover leads of her own.

Ann pulled into her driveway and walked to the front door, noting the absence of reporters and news cameras with satisfaction. The thought of spending a quiet afternoon in her nicely air-conditioned home seemed quite appealing. The temperature and humidity had soared and she was eager for the chance to be alone for a while and unwind.

As she walked inside, her breath caught in her throat.

Chapter Eight

Everything in her living room had been tossed around! The couch cushions had been thrown to the carpet, and the couch itself lay on its side. Dozens of books had been shoved off her bookcase and lay scattered all over the floor. The contents of the coffee and end tables now lay on the floor. Some things were broken beyond repair.

Ann stumbled across the debris into the kitchen, her mind in a whirl. This room was in no better shape. Every drawer had been emptied onto the floor. Cabinets that had once been filled with pots and pans now stood empty, their contents scattered from one end of the room to the other. Even a glass vase that had been filled with some fresh flowers from the backyard now lay broken on the floor. Shards of glass lay scattered about like silent witnesses, attesting to the destruction.

She picked up one of the overturned chairs and collapsed onto it. From where she was seated, Ann could tell that the den had received similar treatment. No doubt the bedrooms were wrecked, as well.

Feelings of inadequacy and frustration engulfed her. She bit her lip, struggling against the urge to cry. Feeling sorry for herself was certainly not going to accomplish anything. What she needed to focus on was the healthy dose of anger swelling inside her. More than anything, she wanted to catch whoever was doing this to her and make them pay.

As she took a deep breath, she heard the back door swing open. Ann catapulted out of her chair. She was frightened, but the urge to confront her mysterious adversary was too powerful to resist.

When Ann reached the open back door, there was no one in sight. The door was damaged, and she realized it had been forced open. She stepped quickly outside and caught a glimpse of someone moving through the underbrush just beyond her back gate.

Ann dashed after the figure. The stubby heels of her office shoes sank into the ground, making running difficult. If she could at least get a good look at the person, then the police would have their first solid lead. She was determined not to give up the chase.

The area behind her house was thick with trees and shrubbery, making it impossible to see far ahead. Ann dodged through the underbrush at a jog. From the sounds, the intruder was about fifty feet ahead of her traveling hastily parallel to the ditch. Dodging toward the clear spots where she could gain some ground, Ann tried to head him off.

Finally, she came to an abrupt stop by the drainage ditch. She could no longer hear anyone moving up ahead. She strained to see in front of her, but the massive thicket lining the ditch made that impossible.

Hearing twigs snapping only inches from where she stood, Ann turned to look. Strong arms suddenly grabbed her from behind and shoved her down the steep embankment. As she tumbled into the ditch, she caught a glimpse of a face distorted by a stocking mask.

Ann sat up slowly. The murky water, only a few inches deep, had soaked her thin skirt, making her feel soggy and uncomfortable. She'd had her chance and she'd blown it. She slammed her hand down against the water in frustration.

Sore, Ann struggled to her feet in the moss-slick stream bed. She'd have to find a way to climb out. Going up the sides was bound to be difficult. The dirt there had been softened by the recent rains.

Ann tried to get a toe hold, but the muddy embankment collapsed under her weight. Grumbling under her breath, she moved a little farther down the ditch. Using one of the wild plants that had taken root there as a hand hold, she tried to pull herself out. She was halfway up, when the plant suddenly uprooted and she slid back down again on her knees.

Ann stared at the steep ten-foot bank. Refusing to be intimidated, she dug her fingers into the soil and placed her feet sideways to the slope. Slowly, she started to inch upward. The second the ground gave way, she stepped up quickly, grabbing whatever was available to steady herself. Five minutes later, covered in mud and dirt, she collapsed at the top of the ditch.

Ann sat up slowly in the damp grass and tried to collect her thoughts. She'd climbed up the side of the ditch away from her home because it was dryer there. Now Joan's home was closer than her own. She'd call the police from there. The sooner they arrived, the better.

Ann walked briskly, too tired to run, and made her way through the thicket to her neighbor's yard. She weighed all the events of the last few days. Someone had searched her home. Her car had been stolen, her house trashed. She had nothing else left . . . except Matt.

The possibility made her go cold all over. Fear became a palpable, breathing entity that took over her mind and body. Ann sprinted forward using energy reserves she hadn't known she possessed. The second she reached Joan's back door, she began knocking furiously on the glass.

Only a minute or so passed while she waited for a response, but to Ann it seemed like a lifetime. She peered through the glass, desperately, and knocked louder. If her friend wasn't home, she'd have to run even further to get to a telephone. "Joan!"

A moment later, Joan stepped into the kitchen. She was in a robe and, from her damp hair, had obviously just come from the shower. With a shocked look on her face, she opened the door quickly. "Good heavens! Ann, what happened to you?"

"I'll explain later. Joan, I've got to use your telephone right now." Without waiting for permission, she dashed inside, grabbing Joan's kitchen phone from its wall mount. "I've got to make sure Matt's okay," she explained, dialing quickly.

"Do you think something's happened to him?" Joan's voice rose.

"I—" Ann started to reply, then switched her attention to the woman on the other end of the line. "This is Ann Dixon. Is my son all right?"

"Hello, Ann," Allison answered. "Matt's fine. Why? What's wrong?"

"Are you sure, Allison? Have you seen him in the last few minutes?"

"I'm looking at him right now through the window. He's out in the playground outside my office. He's on the jungle gym. From the looks of it, I'd say he's having a really good time."

Ann let out her breath slowly. "You must think I'm crazy, but you wouldn't believe what I've been through today."

"Ann, relax," Allison said gently. "You know it's impossible for any strangers to get into our grounds. The playground faces away from the street and is enclosed by an eight-foot fence. The kids are perfectly safe."

"I'd really like to talk to him," Ann said, feeling sheepish as she said it. "I need to hear his voice."

"Well, sure. Hang on. I'll call him."

A moment later, Ann heard Matt's familiar voice. "Mom?"

"Hi, sweetie." A rush of love quickly soothed her bruised body and spirit. "I just wanted to talk to you. How are things going?"

"I almost won. Jimmy and I were seeing who could hang on the jungle gym the longest. But then you called and I lost."

Hearing the trace of anger in his voice, she smiled. One thing about her son, he did have a temper, though it didn't surface often. "I'm sorry I ruined your game, honey. Why don't you go back outside and ask Jimmy for a rematch?"

"Okay!"

Ann heard the phone land with a clank and the muffled patter of sneaker-clad feet.

"Ann?"

"Thanks for letting me talk to Matt, Allison. I'll pick him up at the usual time."

Ann placed the phone back, then smiled sheepishly to Joan. "I'm turning into a hysterical mother."

Joan laughed, clutching her robe tightly around her. "My mom and I were the same way whenever my dad came in late from an errand. He worked at home a lot and we weren't used to him being gone." She grew serious. "You should see what you look like, Ann. Are you going to tell me what happened?"

Ann glanced down at her dripping clothes and muddy shoes. "Yipes, I've tracked gunk all over your floor!"

"Don't worry." Joan laughed. "It's easy to clean up."

Ann bent over and removed her shoes. "All I'd planned to do this afternoon was read. Would you believe it? Instead, I was out there trudging in mud like a marine." She told Joan what had happened to her house, and then went on to describe the chase through the woods.

"Did he hurt you?" Joan walked to the door and glanced outside.

"No, and I think he's long-gone by now," she answered.

"I'm going to call your friend at the station. What's his name, Tom Keller?"

"Yes, he really should be notified. In the meantime, I have to get back to the house and you have to finish drying off. I must have pulled you out of the shower. You're as soggy as I am right now."

"Don't worry about me right now. That should be the least of your concerns." Joan picked up the receiver. "Don't touch anything at home, Ann. They may want to look for fingerprints."

Ann nodded then started back down the path leading toward her house. An intruder had been in her home, and that made her feel sick to her stomach. Knowing Matt was okay made things easier to bear.

If only one of the locksmiths she'd called had been able to come sooner. The earliest anyone had been able to promise was sometime tomorrow.

Ann reached her home, then walked around to the front porch to wait for the police. If she went inside she'd start organizing everything. There was so much to do before she left to pick up Matt later this afternoon. There was no way she was going to bring her child home to this.

Less than three minutes later Tom pulled up, followed by two patrol cars. He rushed up to her. "Joan told me that the intruder knocked you down. Are you hurt?"

"I'm fine, but my home's a wreck." Her voice broke and she cleared her throat to disguise it. In a monotone, she described what had happened.

Tom questioned her at length as the other officers checked with the neighbors and searched the outside of the house.

"You're undoubtedly going to find some fingerprints," she said when he'd finished. "There's no way he could have avoided leaving some. Wait until you see the way everything looks."

The two officers continued searching outside, while Tom went into the house alone. He returned a few minutes later. "We're going to have to go through everything. The officers will take photos of the damage on the back door. That should tell us something about the intruder. Then we'll check the places we believe fingerprints would have been left."

"As soon as you finish with one room, will you let me know?" She stood up wearily. "I've got to get busy straightening the house, then shower and change. There's no way I'm going to let Matt see his house, or me, looking like this."

Tom nodded somberly. "Sure, I'll let you know when you can start. In the meantime, I'm going to need an accounting of everything that's missing. That might help us narrow down what he came to get."

"Well, it's obvious he didn't find anything. The search included the whole house." She stopped. "That is, I think it did. I never made it as far as the bedrooms and the garage.''

"The whole house has been ransacked, but the garage was untouched. I don't think the intruder had time to check it out. There doesn't seem to be any major damage, though. Your television set and other valuables are still there. Personally, I don't think it was a thief. The worst of it seems to be Matt's room. That's been completely tossed and his toys are scattered everywhere. Will you be able to tell me if anything's missing in there?''

She smiled and nodded. "I have to clean that room practically every day. Believe me, I know it by heart."

"Good. If he took anything, I want to know what it is." He paused then gave her a long speculative look. "By the way, right near the front door I found a stack of books on police procedures. Where did those come from?''

"Well, the crook didn't bring them, that's for sure," she muttered.

He cursed softly. "Ann, you can't become a detective by reading books. Give it up."

"Forget it. When they picked on me and my son, they made it as much my business as it is yours. You might as well get used to the idea that I'm going to work on this. I'm reading the books to learn what the rules are and how to avoid duplicating police efforts. If you accept my help, which I would advise you to do, then I'll be glad to let you know what I'm doing. If not, I'll work on my own."

"You *advise* me to take your help?"

"Like it or not, you're not finding answers. It looks to me like you need all the help you can get."

"You're the most exasperating woman I've ever met." He glared at her, but then looked away when she didn't flinch. "I'm going back inside the house where I can do some good."

She watched him go through the front door. Why was he being so unreasonable? There was no doubt in her mind that if the situation was reversed, he'd be doing the same thing she was.

Twenty minutes later, Tom came back outside. He had the grace to apologize for his earlier temper. "The officers are going back out on patrol. I'll stay and help you clean up this mess. You're going to need a second pair of hands to put some of that stuff back where it was."

Straightening the furniture and discarding the broken odds and ends was quite a task. Yet it was seeing her son's room in shambles that was practically her undoing. With Tom's help, she pushed away all the toys strewn in her path, placed the mattress back on the bedframe and remade the bed.

With effort, she swallowed the lump in her throat, determined not to break down in front of Tom. "This person is deliberately undermining the sense of home I've worked so hard to give Matt. I wanted him to feel secure here, to know this was the one place in the whole world he could always feel safe." Her voice trembled but she tried to disguise it by clearing her throat.

Tom went to her side. "I don't know what to do with you," he said, drawing her against him. "One moment you make me angry enough to want to shake you, then the next, I want to be here to take care of you." His voice was husky. His gaze held hers for an instant, then he slowly dipped his head downward. His lips moved over hers in a gentle, persuasive dance.

Feeling his desire inflamed her own and for a moment Ann allowed herself the luxury of feeling instead of thinking. She returned the pressure of his mouth, drinking in the taste of him.

His muscled chest felt taut beneath her palms. Though his arms offered comfort, the fiery pleasure that sizzled through her was scarcely that. She wanted it to go on forever, but with a strangled cry, she pulled away. "It would be wonderful to be able to lean on you right now. Sometimes the pressure seems overwhelming, but what you have to offer doesn't include Matt, and he's at the center of my world."

"You misjudge me, Ann. It's true I never wanted children, but I'm just trying to avoid hurting Matt. I know how vulnerable kids are, and Matt in particular. He's looking for a father figure. It wouldn't be fair of me to take that place. Matt needs a man who'll be around for him and who wouldn't stop coming to visit if things didn't work out with you."

She nodded, understanding. It would imply a kind of commitment Tom hadn't made. She couldn't blame him for that. At least he'd shown the presence of mind and the sensitivity to want to protect her son. For a man without a family of his own, he seemed extraordinarily attuned to the emotions of a child in Matt's situation. "Did you lose one of your parents when you were young?"

"Let's not get into that now." His tone betrayed a pain he was unable to disguise. "We still have to get the rest of the house in shape," he said. "You have to pick up Matt sometime before six, right?"

She nodded. There was so much she didn't know about Tom. He made it very difficult for anyone to get past the barrier he'd erected around himself. Yet, she'd glimpsed pain behind the veiled look in his eyes and that was one emotion she was too familiar with not to recognize.

It took the rest of the afternoon to restore a semblance of order to her house. Outwardly, at least, things looked much as they always had. Closets and drawers, however, that weren't in Matt's room, had been filled hastily. She walked from room to room surveying her work. "I don't think Matt will notice anything," she said satisfied. "And as far as I can see, there's nothing missing."

"Are you certain?"

"I'm not infallible, but I do know my home. If something has been taken, it's so insignificant that it makes no difference to the way things look." She wiped the perspiration from her brow, then glanced at her watch. "I'm going to take a shower now. Washing up wasn't enough after that tumble I took earlier today."

"Can I use your telephone and desk? I have to call the station and get an update on several other cases Bob Glenn and I have been investigating."

"Sure, make yourself at home."

Tom watched her go, lost in thought. These past few years he'd avoided getting involved with anyone. He knew he wasn't able to provide a woman with what she'd want most, security and a family. The first simply wasn't to be found in the life of a cop. The other would have required he become completely hardened to everything he'd learned as a kid. Now of all the fool times, he was becoming increasingly attracted to a woman who already had a son. He should be grateful Ann had pulled away from him. Cursing softly, he picked up the phone.

It took about ten minutes to finish his briefing with Glenn. Hearing Ann still in the shower, he went to the back door and inspected the damage.

A few minutes later, he walked to Ann's bedroom and knocked on the door. "Do you have a hammer and some nails? I'm going to see what I can do about that back door of yours."

"In the garage," came her reply. "The keys are on the hook in the kitchen."

Locating the tools he needed, he did his best to fix the door. His thoughts, however, remained firmly fixed on Ann's predicament. If his guess was right, the people she'd become mixed up with were not through with her yet. If he was to continue to be of help to her, though, he'd have to keep his guard up. He knew that personal feelings had a way of obliterating objectivity. The problem was Ann had an absolute gift for weaving her way past his defenses. She was the first person he'd ever met who actually made him want to talk about his past. He'd been sorely tempted to share a part of himself with her he'd never opened to anyone before.

"You look like you're a million miles away," Ann said, interrupting his thoughts.

"That was fast," he said. His eyes darted over her in a quick but thorough gaze. "You look beat." He fought the urge to step forward and pull her into his arms.

"I am. I thought a shower would renew my energies, but it had the opposite effect." She glanced at his repair work. "I see you fixed the door so it'll close again. Thanks."

He checked his watch. "It's time to pick up Matt. Why don't you let me drive you over? Maybe you can catch a quick nap on the way."

She hesitated. "I'd like to take you up on your offer," she admitted. "I'm really tired and I know Matt's going to be loaded with energy. He usually is." She smiled. "But you've already done more than your share around here today."

"I wouldn't have offered if I hadn't wanted to do it." He hadn't planned to say that. Her gaze, and the warmth he sensed lay beyond, could make a man do almost anything. In self-defense, he moved away from her. "My car's parked out by the curb."

As he drove through the rush-hour traffic, Ann leaned back, settling into the cushioned seat. "I'll just close my eyes for a few minutes," she mumbled.

Despite his efforts to concentrate on the road, his gaze kept drifting to her. Her breasts, full and sweet, rose slowly, and drifted down again in the lazy rhythm of her breaths. She was made to be loved. The desire that coiled in his gut was as fierce as it was sudden.

He forced himself to concentrate on the road. He'd kill them both with thoughts like that. Ann wasn't his nor likely to ever be. And a one-night stand wouldn't help the situation any. Ann wasn't the kind of woman a man could make love to and then walk away from. He gripped the wheel tightly. Damn it all! The woman had woven a spell around him with her violet eyes! He rolled down the window. Summer was getting hotter all the time.

He struggled to concentrate on something else as they neared the day-care center. When he saw what was in the parking lot, he reached over to waken Ann.

Ann's eyes snapped open. "What's going on?" She leaned forward. "There's a police car at Matt's school!" Her heart lodged in her throat. "And what's that fire engine doing there?"

As they approached the school, Tom slowed down. Without waiting for the car to come to a full stop, Ann leaped out and rushed toward the onlookers. They were crowded around the burned-out shell of a car. Quickly glancing around, she spotted Allison speaking to one of the police officers.

The moment their eyes met, Ann knew something was wrong. As Allison drew near, Ann's chest constricted painfully and her blood turned to ice. "Oh, please, God, don't let this have anything to do with Matt!" Her soft words were lost in the tumult of the crowd.

Chapter Nine

"I've been trying to reach you for the past twenty minutes. Then I realized you must have been on your way here," Allison explained, her voice taut. "I just don't know how to tell you this."

"The car," Ann managed to say, her voice taut, "Matt wasn't in there."

Allison's eyes widened. "Oh, Ann, no! Of course not!"

Ann started breathing again. "You scared me half to death, Allison!" she retorted angrily. "I thought something had happened to Matt!"

"Something has," the young woman replied gently.

Ann couldn't breathe. Everything around her seemed to slip out of focus, as if she were viewing the world from the wrong end of a telescope. "What..." Her voice broke.

"Someone threw a fire bomb into the car. The explosion really shook the building. The kids were scared half to death and it was chaotic. In the confusion, Matt seems to have disappeared."

"Disappeared? What do you mean?" Was her son frightened and hiding somewhere inside? "Have you looked for him?"

Tom came up and stood beside her. "Police officers are searching the grounds now. If he's hiding someplace, we'll find him."

The thought of her son, frightened and alone, sent a stab of pain ripping through her. The need to find and protect him became such an urgent driving force, Ann could barely stand still. "I'm going inside to look for him."

Allison nodded. "Okay, but the staff is already in there. We've been checking every possible hiding place—"

Ann didn't wait for her to complete the sentence before dashing toward the building. Mercifully, it wasn't a very big school, but nonetheless, hiding places abounded. She searched closets and beneath desks, ignoring the others who claimed they'd already looked there. With each failure to find her son, Ann's anguish grew.

Fifteen minutes later Tom found her outside, searching the grounds. "Ann, I need to talk to you." He took her arm and gently led her away from prying eyes. "We've spoken to the other kids. Matt was seen getting into a car."

"What car?" she blurted. "Did someone take him home?"

Tom could see that the implications of what he'd said weren't reaching her. For the first time since he'd know her, she looked fragile and almost at the breaking point. Even Warren's death hadn't devastated her to this degree. Taking a deep breath, he hardened himself for what he had to do. "There's a strong possibility that Matt's been kidnapped."

She stared at him, her face as pale as the white blouse she wore. "You can't be sure of that. Maybe a friend or neighbor saw him wandering about and picked him up. It's possible, isn't it?"

Her struggle to hold on to some shred of hope tore at him. He couldn't bring himself to dash it with harsh realities.

"Don't you see? It doesn't make sense," she insisted. "Artemis searched everything I own. By now he must realize I haven't got anything he might be interested in."

Allison rushed toward them. "The press is here, Lieutenant. What shall I do?"

"Tell them about Matt," Ann interrupted. "If everyone knows, then the person who picked him up will be able to bring him back home."

"No, Ann, you can't," Tom contradicted gently. "Listen to me. I want to be wrong, believe me, but if Matt has been kidnapped, you don't want the press involved. They could interfere with your chances of finding him." Shock and confusion were evident on her face. His heart wrenched inside him. *Understand, Ann, please! You have to face the truth. I would give anything to shield you from this, but I can't.*

"I— Do whatever you want." Ann walked away from him and stood alone near the swing set. Aimlessly, she pushed one of the swings and watched it sway to and fro.

After instructing Allison to keep Matt's disappearance from the press, Tom turned to watch Ann for a moment. She looked defeated and utterly alone. If only he could have foreseen this, but he, too, had believed Matt would be safe at the school, in a crowd of other children, and several adult supervisors. Even if he'd considered kidnapping as a possibility, he would have still reasoned that Matt was in greater danger at home with only Ann to guard him.

He placed his hand on her shoulder and gently guided her around. "Let me take you home, Ann. There's nothing more you can do here."

She said nothing as she walked back to the car with him. Her eyes darted around, hoping against hope to catch a glimpse of Matt somewhere.

Her silence worried Tom more than anything else. She had withdrawn into herself. Throughout the entire drive, she never even looked at him. As he parked in her driveway, Joan came rushing toward them.

"Do you want me to get rid of her?" Tom asked, taking Ann's hand and giving it a gentle squeeze.

"It doesn't matter." Ann shook her head as if trying to clear her thoughts. "No, wait. It does. She might know something. If Joan had seen Matt, she'd have picked him up. Or maybe someone else we know did and they've called her." She stepped out of the car and met Joan.

"Ann, I just heard about the fire in the parking lot at Matt's day school. Is Matt okay?" She glanced inside the car, then quickly back at Ann. "Where is he?" she asked frantically.

As she recounted the details, Ann's voice broke and she began to tremble. "I've got to find him, Joan. I'm going to start by calling everyone I know."

"My men will keep checking the school neighborhood, trying to match the vehicle descriptions we managed to get."

"Were they all different?" Ann asked Tom.

He considered the question for a moment. Admitting how little they knew at this point made his gut twist. It would hurt Ann more, but she deserved the truth. "Kids that age don't know about a vehicle's year and model. What they do is compare it to what their parent's car looks like and to the colors they know. From the descriptions we got, a 'grown-up' wearing a hat and driving a 'regular'-sized car, picked up Matt. Even the color seems to be open for debate, though most of them agreed it was a light color, probably either dirty white or a pale yellow."

Ann unlocked the front door and went directly to her telephone. "Maybe someone's left a message with my answering service." She sounded more like herself, now, as if direct action made her feel more in control. As she started to dial, Tom and Joan walked back outside.

Joan returned a few moments later. Seeing Ann replace the receiver dejectedly, Joan placed a hand on her friend's shoulder. "Tom's going back to the day-care center. He'll return in about an hour." She led Ann to the couch. "Don't panic," she said quietly. "I'm sure Matt's okay."

Joan fixed them both a cup of tea and tried to keep Ann's spirits up. Nonetheless, the minutes passed with agonizing slowness.

The sun had begun to set when the doorbell finally rang. Ann shot out of her chair and raced to the door. Seeing Tom there, alone, made her heart sink. "He's really gone, then," she managed in a thin voice.

"Ann, we have to talk." Tom led her back to the den, dreading what he was about to do.

Ann sat down on the sofa beside Joan, while Tom chose the chair across from them. "You're going to have to face the likelihood that Matt's been kidnapped."

"But why? It doesn't make sense."

"There are two possibilities. If Artemis thinks you have something of his, he'll try to use Matt as leverage to get it back." He felt lower than a snake as he saw her eyes water with tears of fright. "There's also the chance Matt was taken by the person who threatened to get you for killing Sean Jackson."

Her breath came out in a shallow gasp. "But why my son? I'm the one they have a quarrel with."

"Perhaps they each want to lure you to come to them on their terms."

Ann pursed her lips. "Whatever their terms are, I'll meet them," she replied flatly. "You better understand that right away. Once Matt's safe, then I'll go after them. I'll spend every bit of money I can spare to hire people to track them down. One way or another, I'll make sure they end up in jail."

She was showing the same stubbornness and determination that had seen her through her husband's death. "Your priority should be getting Matt back. I understand and agree with that completely, but you can't let them call all the shots. You can't trust a person who'd do this type of thing. You have to play it smart."

"Oh, that's really easy for you to say," Joan interrupted. "It's not your kid we're talking about here. If the kidnapper says no police, why on earth should she gamble by bringing you guys in? You can't guarantee that everything will go right just because you're there. And what is it that they want from Ann, anyway? My father always said—"

"Joan, this is a police matter," Tom interrupted in a harsh voice. "I think you'd better leave." Tom stood as if to walk her to the door. "I'm experienced in this kind of thing, you're not." His thoughts drifted to the last time he'd dealt with a missing minor and he felt his skin grow cold. "The last thing Ann needs now is someone who's going to add to her confusion and fear."

"I'm not going anywhere until Ann tells me to leave. In fact, I think you should leave and let us handle this by ourselves."

"Ann, this is your decision. I've got experience dealing with this. If you let the kidnapper play on your fears, it'll give him the advantage. You've got to find a way to stack the deck in your favor. At least for now, let me help you. You can get rid of me anytime you want, if you feel involving the police is working against your interests."

Ann took a deep breath, then let it out slowly. "Okay. That's fair enough." She stood up slowly and gave Joan a nod. "I'll be all right, Joan. Thanks for caring."

"You call me anytime, day or night. I'm always there for you and Matt. In fact, would you like me to sleep here tonight?"

Ann shook her head. "I'll be fine." She walked with Joan to the door. "I'll let you know as soon as there's any news. And please don't tell anyone what's happened, Joan. I don't want the press involved in this. They'll just make a bigger mess of everything."

"Okay." She gave Ann a quick hug. "Let me know if I can help."

"You made the right decision, Ann," Tom said as she returned to the den. "Two Colorado Bureau of Investigation agents will be coming by soon. My captain called Denver for state help in finding Matt and we can request the FBI's involvement, too, after twenty-four hours, though they won't automatically step in unless there's evidence Matt was taken out of state. I don't want you to worry. I'm going to stay right on this, too."

"I appreciate that," she answered. She stared absently out the window, in the faint hope that Matt would find his way back home. "You know, Warren felt the same way you do about people in dangerous professions having kids. Yet I'm in a fairly routine job. The biggest worry I've ever had was predicting income. Despite this, my son is in more danger now than he ever was because of his father's work." She turned around and gave Tom a sad smile. "Life never has any guarantees, does it?"

"I wish to hell I could do something to bring him back to you right now." Tom's voice was low and soft but the cold determination there reverberated in the quiet of the room.

"What I can do, though, is give you my word that I won't give up until Matt's back home."

"At this point, I don't even know how I'm going to get through the next hour without knowing—" The doorbell rang, and she dashed to answer it without finishing her sentence.

Tom caught up to her in the hall. "It's probably the CBI. You can't let your hopes soar like that every time the doorbell rings. You won't last five minutes that way." He placed a comforting hand on her shoulder, then opened the door.

Two men, dressed in light summer suits, stood in the doorway. They flashed their badges and introduced themselves.

When they were done, Tom nodded to them and extended his own hand. "I was hoping you two would be helping on this case." He stepped back to let the men come inside. "Ann, this is Special Agent Denis Arteaga and Agent Bill Murphy of the Colorado Bureau of Investigation."

"We need to ask you quite a few questions, Mrs. Dixon, so where will you be most comfortable?" Arteaga, a slender, dark-haired Hispanic man asked.

"The den." She led the men through the house. Ann sat on the sofa and folded her hands on her lap to keep them from trembling.

"What was Matt wearing when you last saw him?" Arteaga asked. Murphy, a huge, red-haired, athletic-looking man, began taking notes on a legal pad.

"Jeans and a white Samurai Squirrel T-shirt."

The questions seemed endless, but Ann continued to answer as quickly as they could ask them. In response to their request for a recent photo, she walked to the bookcase and pulled out a bulging album. She leafed through the pages and finally extracted one. "This was taken less than two months ago, when he first got his guinea pig." She stared at the photo and felt her aching emptiness rise to overwhelm her.

"Mrs. Dixon," Denis Arteaga confided, "I have a four year old boy myself. I know what you're going through. Believe me, we'll work round the clock until he's back."

Denis glanced at Tom. "What I'm still not clear on is your connection here. Why are you so certain the boy's been kidnapped?"

Tom explained everything that had happened since the murder. "It's my guess that it's all connected, but I have no evidence yet to prove that." He clenched his jaw, then forced himself to relax. "What convinced me that we were dealing with a kidnapping was the way everything was orchestrated. The Molotov cocktail thrown into the car was a classic diversion."

"We're going to need access to all the police files on these incidents," Denis said, "and Mrs. Dixon's description of the person she caught in the house."

"You've got it." Tom paused, and was silent for a moment. "Denis, I know this is your case, but since we're going to be working on this from two different angles, I'd like to make a deal. If you'll keep me posted on what you learn, I'll do the same."

"Done." Denis signaled his partner. "Mrs. Dixon, we'd like to place a tape recorder on your phone to monitor any possible calls from the kidnapper."

"What if he suspects you're listening?"

"That's always a possibility, but even if he does, you can't afford not to do it. By recording the call, we might be able to pick up valuable clues. For instance, the background noises might allow us to pinpoint the area of town where he's holding your son."

"All right, but I have to warn you. I'm taking this one step at a time. I'll tell you what I've already told Tom. I don't care about police procedures. My only concern is for my son."

"I don't understand." Denis turned to Tom. "What does this mean?"

Tom explained Ann's concerns. "It's her prerogative, Denis."

Ann stood. "Can I get you all some coffee?" She needed something to do. Inactivity and waiting were torture to her.

"That would be great," Denis answered.

"Don't underestimate her, Denis," Ann heard Tom saying softly behind her. "She'll use every advantage she can get to turn the odds in her favor."

Ann started filling the coffeepot. He was right. She'd do whatever it took to get her son back. She'd become as hard and as cunning as she had to be. Matt was depending on her, and she wouldn't let him down.

Tom peered into the kitchen. "You okay?"

"Fine. Coffee's almost ready. Let me get some cream." She tried to keep her voice steady. The more controlled she appeared, the more inclined they'd be to let her in on everything. Fighting to keep her worries masked, she walked to the refrigerator to get a pint of cream.

Ann opened the door, then jumped back with a startled scream.

"What's wrong?" Tom rushed to her side. Placing his arm over her shoulders, he followed her gaze. A framed photo of her and her son had been placed on the refrigerator shelf. Directly below it was a typewritten note.

Ann started to reach for it, but Tom stopped her. "Don't touch anything. Wait."

He brought the note out gingerly by the edges and set it on the table.

Denis and Bill stood behind Tom. "Damn!" Denis muttered under his breath. "I'd hoped they'd use the telephone." He studied the note. "Short and to the point.

"'I have something of yours, you have something of mine. Trade while the offer still stands. I'll be contacting you. Artemis.'"

Denis glanced at Ann. "Any idea what this Artemis character is talking about, Mrs. Dixon?"

She wanted to scream, to grab Denis by the collar and shake him until he rattled. "No, I don't." Her voice sounded unnaturally calm. "If I did, I'd turn it over to him in a second. Nothing is worth more to me than my son."

"Easy, Ann," Tom said quietly, then glanced at Denis. "She let us take the other note. It's being analyzed by our lab people here. Shall I send it over to you?"

"Have the department send a report and the note to the state crime lab when they're done with it. Between our experts and yours, we're bound to find something." Denis walked to the telephone and made several quick calls. "The crime scene unit from the local police department will be arriving shortly. They can gather the physical evidence here and send it by courier to our state labs. We'll check for prints and see what turns up. In the meantime, we still have to find out how the person got into the house."

"Probably the back door has been forced again. We were unable to make anything but temporary repairs earlier," Tom explained.

Ann tried to control her mounting temper. "It's useless. If it's the same person who broke in last time, you're not likely to find anything. The police already tried that once and failed." She glanced at Tom. "You never said anything more about it, so I assume I'm right."

"You are," he admitted reluctantly. "We're still hoping we'll find the tool that was used to break in. If we do and can link it to a person, then we'll have some evidence. We should be able to match the marks on the door to whatever was used to pry it open." He rubbed the back of his neck with one hand. "That's another reason why I think we're dealing with a professional associate of Sean Jackson's. This person is not only determined, but good."

An hour later, Ann watched the men from the crime scene unit leave. They'd found a few fingerprints on the picture frame and the refrigerator door. More than likely, however, they'd turn out to be her own. The experts would check for a match against the set they'd taken from her the day of the murder.

"Mrs. Dixon," Denis said as he came up and sat down across the table from her, "we're going to be leaving you now. The recorder Bill attached to your phone will activate every time you get a call. We'll be close by, but we don't want anyone to get the impression you're surrounded by police. The less visible our involvement is the better off you'll be. You can call us directly at this number, anytime, night or day." Denis handed her a card with a number written on the back. "The back door had been forced open again. I jammed a chair under the knob for now. But you should have a locksmith put in a deadbolt as soon as possible."

"There's a man coming to take care of that tomorrow," she replied.

The thought of being alone in the house filled her with an oppressive heaviness of spirit that nearly overwhelmed her. She started to ask Tom to stay, but then stopped. As a police officer, it was possible his presence would deter the kidnapper from making contact. The risk was too great to take.

Almost as if he'd read her mind, Tom came up and stood beside her. "I'm not leaving yet, Ann. The person who took Matt must have been watching you for quite a while. It's a safe bet that he's seen me here with you before. I think he'd really be suspicious if I left you in the midst of a crisis."

Ann and Tom returned to the den and Ann sat at her desk, watching the telephone.

"Try to relax. It may be a while," he cautioned.

"I can't. All I can think of is Matt and how frightened he must be. If only I'd anticipated this!"

"You had no way of knowing. Neither did I." He walked down the hall and emerged a few minutes later with two pillows. "Here, lie down on the sofa. I'll put the telephone closer to you."

"I can't lie down." She stood and started pacing.

"Ann, please, you're not doing yourself any good. This is far from over and you've got to conserve your strength." He watched the struggle going on inside her, then crossed the room in three easy strides. When he tried to pull her against him, however, she pushed him away. "I'll face this on my own, Tom. Believe me, it's much better for everyone if I do. It's my problem and I'll deal with it."

"I can't feel what you're feeling no matter how hard I try to empathize. But you need a friend right now, Ann. At least let me be that to you," he asked softly.

Her gaze met his, and she felt her facade of toughness collapsing like the house of cards it had been. "I'm so scared, Tom. I loved Warren very much, but when I lost him, I took comfort in knowing my son needed me. If anything happens to him..."

He lifted her off her feet, then placed her gently on the couch. "Nothing's going to happen to Matt. It's not him this person wants. He's just a tool to get to you. Harming Matt would defeat his purpose."

She struggled to hold on to the logic of Tom's words. "I won't fall apart," she said, for her own benefit as well as for his. "I'll fight as hard as I can to get my son back. And no one is going to stand in my way."

Tom said nothing for a moment. That intense fire in her eyes bothered him. He'd seen it before in people who thought they had nothing to lose. "You're upset right now. You're going to have to think clearly," he warned in his best cop's tone. "This is not a time for gambles or heroics."

"I have no intention of relying on either. Whatever I do from this point on will be well thought out, I assure you."

"Don't kid yourself. You may think that you're acting on intellect alone, but you won't be." He searched her eyes. Would she try to go off on her own to get her son back? "Cops are trained to think in crisis situations. Yet, even so, it's policy never to let an officer handle a case that involves a relative or close friend. There's a reason for that." He sat on the edge of the couch beside her. "Ann, for Matt's sake, work with the CBI and with me on this."

She sat up slowly, unable to remain lying down. "I won't do anything foolish," she answered calmly. "You said once that you believed I was a strong person. Trust me now." She tucked her legs beneath her and eased herself on the cushion beside him. "I'm not going to turn into a vigilante, so don't worry. But no one is going to make all the rules for me, not the kidnapper, and not the police. I'll be making my own as I go."

"Lady, you're scaring the hell out of me. I guess I expected you to fall apart and I was ready to help you through that. But I'm not sure what I can do now."

"Your support is what means the most to me." She sank into the cushions.

"Ann, why don't you try to relax? You look exhausted."
He pulled her against his side, his arm draped around her
protectively. Taking the remote control, he switched on the
television. "We'll watch a mindless movie while we wait.
Maybe it'll help you doze for a bit." He switched through
the channels then finally stopped. "Ah, here we go. This is
a musical about a lawyer who becomes a world-famous
chef."

They watched television for hours before she finally
drifted off to a restless sleep with Tom's arm still around
her. Tom glanced at her, noting how perfectly she fit against
him. He resisted the urge to brush a kiss over her forehead.
The more time he spent with her, the stronger his feelings for
her became.

He remained still, hoping to avoid waking her. Aimlessly, his gaze drifted around the room. The furniture didn't
have much in common with his, but there was a comfortable homeyness about it that made you feel relaxed. The
whole house, in fact, had the warm, pleasant feel of an old
patchwork quilt. It was the perfect place for a family. For
an instant, he pictured himself as a part of it all, Matt as his
son, Ann as his wife. Pleasing images flitted through his
mind. Aware suddenly of how much he was enjoying the
daydream, he jolted his thoughts back into line.

The decisions he'd based his life on were still valid, perhaps now more than ever. Ann had been right when she'd
pointed out that life held no guarantees. But there were ways
to decrease the uncertain factors, and he still believed those
were of paramount importance whenever a child was concerned.

Tom gathered Ann gently into his arms and carried her to
her bed. She stirred, but didn't wake as he laid her down
gently.

He watched her sleep for a moment longer, then walked
out into the hall. If he was certain he was making such a wise
decision, then why did his own life seem so empty whenever he was away from her? He stood in the corridor for a
moment and considered what he should do next. Knowing

how much she needed someone with her tonight, he couldn't bring himself to leave. He'd spend the night on her couch.

Tom slipped off his tie and rolled up his shirt sleeves. He would have rather slept next to her, if only to keep her in his arms all night long.

With a groan, he kicked off his shoes and laid on the couch. Since his divorce he'd convinced himself he could live without women. That was the best way to avoid the complications they'd bring. This was his punishment. He stared into the darkness. It was going to be a very long night.

ANN WOKE UP SLOWLY as dawn peered through the open curtain. Had it all been a dream? She rushed to Matt's bedroom. His little bed hadn't been slept in. Tears came to her eyes as she picked up his teddy bear and hugged it tightly.

A bitter, empty feeling stabbed through her as she reluctantly placed the stuffed animal back on the bed. She would not cry again. Matt needed her to stay in control. With new determination, she started toward the kitchen.

Ann stopped halfway down the hall, remembering the first note she'd received from Artemis. Rushing outside, she searched for the morning newspaper. It wasn't on her porch or in the driveway! Suppressing a scream of sheer frustration, she searched the yard frantically. Moments later, she found it beneath a bush near the porch.

Ann rolled the rubber band off and immediately opened the newspaper to the classified ads.

Chapter Ten

The town's local newspaper was thin, making it easy to skim through the classified ads. By the time she reached the door, she had confirmed that there was no message from the kidnapper.

Disappointment, like a slow poison, sapped her strength. She sat down heavily on the porch steps, void of energy. It made no sense that he hadn't contacted her. A thought slowly formed as she stared at the newspaper in her hands. It would take two or three days to have a message inserted into the paper. Artemis would need more time to contact her. She would have to wait.

Feeling disappointed but oddly relieved, she walked into the kitchen to fix herself some coffee. As she reached into one of the cabinets, she caught a glimpse of Tom stretched out on the sofa. She walked to the den and stood there for a moment watching him. A day-old beard shaded his face, and locks of dark hair fell over his eyebrows. His half-opened shirt was coming untucked from his pants, giving him a crumpled, endearing look.

So he'd spent the night. She had been so obsessed with finding the paper that she hadn't noticed his car parked along the curb. She smiled slowly. At least now she knew why she'd woken up fully dressed in her own bed.

Quietly, she returned to the kitchen and started fixing breakfast. She wasn't hungry, but Tom probably would be.

She'd just broken the eggs for an omelet, when Tom padded into the kitchen. "How are you feeling?" she asked.

"I was about to ask you the same thing," he muttered, running a hand across the stubble of beard. "I see you checked the paper already." He glanced at the classified ads, folded back on top of the other pages. "Nothing yet?"

"No. I was afraid at first, then I realized it would take a few days to place an ad."

"What are you fixing?" he asked, hoping to change the subject for a few minutes.

"Breakfast. Is a cheese omelet okay?"

"Yeah, thanks." He smiled. "I'm glad to hear that you're planning to eat something." He walked to the counter and poured himself a cup of coffee.

"Actually I was fixing this for you," she answered. "I figured that a night on that horrible couch deserved something special." She gave him a sheepish, halfhearted smile. "It's great for sitting on, but not as good as a bed for sleeping."

He rolled his neck, hoping to work out the kinks. "I've had better nights."

"I hope so. Otherwise I'd have to feel very sorry for you," she said in an attempt at lightheartedness.

Tom chuckled softly, then stood. "I'm going to go into the living room and use your telephone. I want to call Denis and the station to see if there're any new leads. I'll also call the newspaper and ask them to let us know if Artemis places an ad. When I'm done, I'll give you a hand in here."

"Don't worry about it. I've got this covered. After you make your calls, there are a few things I want to discuss with you."

He gave her a worried look as he slipped on his shoes and straightened his shirt. "I won't be long."

Ann paced around the kitchen, coffee cup in hand, waiting for him to finish. She needed to get her son back. The police and the agents from the Colorado Bureau of Investigation had procedures and rules to follow—rules that might slow things down. She was reluctant to request that the FBI get involved in the case, afraid things would get even worse. Yet surely there were things she could do that the authorities couldn't. She owed loyalty to no one except Matt and herself.

By the time Tom returned to the kitchen, she had formulated a theory and a plan. But first she had to find out what Tom knew. "What have they learned from the fingerprints?"

"Nothing," he admitted reluctantly. "They only found a child's, presumably Matt's, yours and a few others that were too smudged to identify."

"What about the note? Couldn't they get anything from that?"

"The note was typed on a current-model electric typewriter, so that doesn't tell us much. As a point of interest, someone looked up the name Artemis. The name a person selects can sometimes give us a clue."

She nodded in approval. "I hadn't thought much about it. What does it mean?"

"Artemis was a Greek goddess of the hunt. The name means giver of life, and preserver of health, but the goddess could also be cruel and destructive. I think it's meant to scare you and act as an implied threat." He picked up the paper to double-check the ads.

Ann remained quietly pensive as she lifted the omelet onto a plate. "Finding the object Artemis wants might give us a clue to his identity."

"Maybe you can find out what it is when you're contacted," Tom suggested.

"That's one way, but I'm not just going to sit around in the hope that'll happen. I've got a theory. It's possible Jackson might have been carrying something valuable on him the day he was murdered. Knowing he was about to be killed, or even as he was dying, he could have managed to hide it." She placed the omelet in front of Tom. "I'm going to search the woods behind the house, and the area where Jackson's car was found. I know your people checked there already, but you never know, they might have missed something."

"Ann, I know waiting by the telephone is difficult, but if Artemis tries to contact you and you're not here . . ." He let the sentence hang.

"I've already thought that out and I've got it covered. I'll take my cordless phone out in the yard with me. And, I'll have my answering service discontinued and switch back to my answering machine for when I'm out of cordless range. The kidnapper won't want to have other people involved in this. And, in case I have to do more driving to follow up leads, I'll get a rental car with a mobile telephone and leave that number on the machine. Then he'll have a choice. Either reach me in the car, or leave a message on the machine. I don't think having his voice recorded is going to spook him. If he's as smart as he seems, he'll realize that he could have never guaranteed I wasn't doing that anyway." She appeared self-possessed and in control, yet in reality she was neither. "I'm not sitting around here and letting the kidnapper snap my leash whenever he feels like it," she added flatly.

Tom couldn't find it in himself to argue with her. "Denis and Murphy might have a very difficult time monitoring a mobile telephone," Tom warned.

"They'll have to depend on my memory then, or figure out a way to get it done."

"I'll tell Denis what you're planning," Tom said after a moment. "I don't blame you, Ann, but I wish you'd just stay home. Then at least I'd know you'd be safe."

"If this was your child, would you stay home?"

He met her gaze. "No," he admitted. "I'd move heaven and earth to get him back." He toyed with the food before him. "But, Ann, knowing he's *your* child is enough. I won't stop searching, you have my word on that."

His voice held such conviction that the emotions behind his words touched her deeply. "I'm glad you're my friend."

"And Matt's too," he said in a barely audible voice. He finished the last of his food as someone knocked on the back door.

Ann rushed to open it. Her hopes fell as she saw Joan, clad in a jogging suit and sneakers. "Good morning, Joan."

"I came over to see—" Spotting Tom sitting at the kitchen table, she stopped. "Maybe I should come back another time."

Tom gave her a nod and got up from his chair. "I'm on my way out," he said. "Don't leave on my account." He stopped by the front door, then glanced back. "Thanks for breakfast. I'm going home to shower and shave, then I'll be at the station if you need me. If I'm not in, ask them to reach me on the radio. I'll call you back right away."

Joan joined Ann in the kitchen and helped her pick up the breakfast dishes. "Anything new about Matt?"

"No, but I could sure use your help if you can take a few hours off from work."

"Of course I can. For you and Matt, anything. What do you need me to do?"

"I'll let you know in a minute. Go pour yourself a cup of coffee while I make a quick phone call."

Joan seated herself, while Ann called and made arrangements to trade her rental car in for one with a phone. As she started to hang up the receiver, a sudden thought jolted her. Jackson had used that phone the day he'd stopped by! With trembling hands, she unscrewed the two ends of the handset. She was disappointed to find nothing that wasn't supposed to be there.

Discouraged, she went to the kitchen table where Joan sat looking at her curiously. Saying nothing, Ann poured herself a cup of coffee and sat down. "I need you to stay here this morning. The locksmith is due and the car-rental place is sending someone over to bring me a car with a mobile telephone. Would you answer any calls I get while I'm out, in case the kidnapper phones with instructions? I won't be far and I'll take the cordless with me. But if I don't pick it up by the second ring, assume I'm out of range."

"I'll get it in time, don't worry. But where are you going to be?"

"I'll be searching the wooded area between our houses, up and down the drainage ditch. Maybe I can find something there that will help us identify the person who broke into my house." She wanted to trust Joan and tell her everything, but Tom was right about not confiding in anyone. Getting Matt back was the most important thing right now. Joan would understand, once Matt was home and Ann was able to explain everything to her.

"Look, I have a better idea. I'll go search the woods and you stay here and get your business done. The idea of getting a car phone is great. That way you won't go completely crazy sitting around, worrying and waiting for the kidnapper to call." She pursed her lips thoughtfully. "Hasn't anyone contacted you yet, Ann? It seems to me you should have heard something by now."

"I've told you all I can, but believe me, I still have no idea why Matt was taken. We're no closer to finding him now than we were yesterday."

Joan nodded slowly. "Ann, let me give you a piece of advice. Don't trust the cops too much. Remember, to them it's only a case."

"That would apply to the majority of them, but Tom cares, Joan, he really does. I have no reason to trust the police in general, or the folks from the state bureau of investigation who Tom's boss called in to help. But I do trust Tom."

Joan nodded slowly. "You've got good instincts about people, but remember that no one has as much at stake here as you do. Don't let them talk you into anything that could end up putting Matt at risk."

Ann gave the other woman a level look. "I'm not going to allow anyone to influence my judgment on this, Joan."

Joan finished the last of her coffee, then stood. "I'm going to go through every square inch of those woods. If there's anything there, I'll find out and bring it back here. Then it'll be up to you to figure out whether you want to turn it over to the police."

"Thanks, Joan. That's exactly what I want."

Two hours went by. The locksmith arrived, shook his head at the damage, then went to work. He was just leaving when the car-rental representative came to the door. Soon, he'd made the switch and she was able to add the car-phone number to her answering machine message.

As she waited for Joan, Ann paced back and forth, too restless to sit down. The silence in the house grated on her nerves. Forcing herself to calm down, she picked up the books she'd checked out of the library. They covered everything from surveillance to questioning techniques, so any knowledge she could gain from them would give her an added advantage.

It was close to eleven when Joan returned, holding a small paper bag. "I scoured the area back there and collected whatever I could find. In detective novels you always see them picking up matchbooks that solve the entire case, but all I found were a bunch of those lift tabs from cans, a bra—" she smiled and rolled her eyes "—one tennis shoe that has obviously been chewed up by a dog, and a pen that doesn't write anymore." She placed the bag in front of Ann.

Ann exhaled softly. "You tried, and that's all any of us can do. Thanks."

Joan sat across the sofa from her. "I see you got the locks changed. That was a good idea. Have you heard anything more about Matt?"

Ann shook her head.

Joan stared across the room absently. "So now what?"

"I'm going over to the station. Tom hasn't called, and I want to know what they've been doing to find my son."

Ann walked Joan to the door. "If you need someone to talk to, I'm always home."

Ann said goodbye, then returned inside. She'd take a quick shower before going to the police station. If Tom wasn't in, she'd wait there until he came back.

Less than an hour later, she was ushered into Tom's office. He rose as she walked in the door. "Are you okay?" he asked softly.

"I'm fine." Ann saw the concern in his eyes and wondered if she looked as bad as she felt. "I came over to find out what kind of progress you'd made."

He gestured to one of the chairs, walking around his desk toward her. "There've been no new leads, but one of my men is out interviewing Jackson's known associates. If anyone's keeping something back, he'll know. He's one of the department's top men." Tom stood in front of his desk and leaned back against it.

"I've gotten the mobile phone." She handed him a piece of paper with the phone number. "So now the kidnapper will have his choice. He can either catch me in the car, or leave a message on my machine. I'll be calling the machine periodically and checking for messages. Also since the CBI is recording and monitoring all the incoming calls, I'm sure they'll let me know right away if we hear anything." She shrugged. "But let's face it. It doesn't look like Artemis plans to contact me that way."

"True," Tom acknowledged. "Either way, you can trust Denis and Murphy," he assured her. "They're working hard on this. I spoke to them earlier and found out that they've been questioning people who live around the day-care center. It's possible someone saw something that might be useful to us. They're also showing photos of Matt to the residents of the area in case any of them have seen him, though they're withholding his identity." Hearing a knock at his door, Tom glanced up.

"Sorry to bother you, Lieutenant, but we have a problem out here with an arrest report. Could you come take a look at it?"

"I'll be right back," Tom said, and strode out the door.

Ann waited until his footsteps had faded down the hall, then stood and glanced down the now-empty corridor. It was time to use a little resourcefulness. If she found a lead worth pursuing, she wouldn't be hampered by all the legalities Tom was bound by. It could help her find Matt that much faster.

Walking around to the front of Tom's desk, she began searching through the files stacked there. Names had been typed on each label. Finding one with Sean Jackson's name, she opened it and studied its contents. Ann copied down Jackson's home address. Then, hearing voices, she stuck the information in her purse and quickly placed the file back where she'd found it.

She finally had a starting point! Excited, she walked to the doorway and saw two uniformed officers engaged in a conversation at the end of the hallway. Tom was nowhere in sight. She considered staying until Tom returned, but there seemed little point in waiting now. Ann scribbled a note to him explaining she had another appointment and strode out to her car.

Jackson's apartment wasn't too far from the station. Maybe she could learn something from the neighbors if she approached them as a prospective tenant. Also, there was a chance she'd be able to get inside the apartment. What better place was there to look for leads than inside Jackson's home? The police had probably searched it. Yet, maybe an amateur, who viewed things differently, could spot something they'd overlooked.

Ann parked near the entrance of the building and walked inside. Within five minutes, she'd located Jackson's fourth-floor walk-up. She stood before the door and stared at the yellow-tape police seal that crisscrossed it. She'd never be able to get in this way.

A little discouraged, she looked around. The only sound that reached her in the empty hallway was the hum of the fluorescent lights. She knocked on several doors, but no one responded. Realizing that most of the tenants probably held day jobs, she walked to the window at the end of the corridor and studied the building's layout. Orienting herself from that vantage point, she returned outside.

The long branches of an old Douglas fir touched the tiny balcony of Jackson's corner apartment. If she could make it onto his porch, forcing the lock on the sliding glass door would be easy. The biggest problem would be climbing the tree. She hadn't done that in years.

Making up her mind, she started toward it. Suddenly fingers clamped over her shoulders like a vise.

Chapter Eleven

"Do you realize the trouble you'd be in if you got caught breaking in there? Of course, that's providing you didn't break your neck scrambling up that tree!" Tom said angrily.

Ann stared up at him aghast. "How could you have known where I was? I didn't tell anyone..."

He glowered at her. "I noticed some papers were sticking out the side of the Jackson folder. I always tap each file against my desk so that the contents don't spill out like that. Coupled with your hasty exit, it wasn't hard to guess what you were up to."

She stared back at him defiantly. "We need a break in this case. Now I grant you that I'm not a trained investigator, but it's possible I could find a clue the police have overlooked."

"It's not likely. We've been over that place with a fine-tooth comb."

"Let me put this another way. As of right now, you have no leads. What I propose is a gamble, but don't you think it's worth the effort?"

"You should have been a politician," he muttered under his breath.

Sensing he was still reluctant, she added, "Keep in mind that if you force me to leave, I might just return later. On the other hand, if we both go in now, you'll know exactly what I touched and what I found."

Tom realized that he was grinding his teeth, so he forced his jaw to relax. "If the department finds out I'm letting you in there, they'll barbecue my fanny."

"They won't find out from me."

He rolled his eyes, then shrugged. "All right, I give up. Come on. Let's get this over with."

They went upstairs to Jackson's apartment. At the door, Tom stopped and glanced at her. "This seal has been broken." He lifted one corner. "It's just resting there against the door knob. See where it's been cut?"

"I came up here less than five minutes ago and it was intact then," she whispered.

"Until you tried the door knob," he countered in a harsh whisper, "right?"

"Wrong. I was tempted, but I didn't. Someone must have been here after I left."

Tom tried the handle, but the door failed to open. "It's still locked," he said quietly. "Maybe it's just kids messing around." He pulled a key from his pocket. "I'm going to slip inside and take a look. Stay here."

She heard the muted click as the door opened and then an instant later, Tom crept inside. Ann waited for him to get several steps ahead, then followed him silently. Even if there was somebody inside, she was well behind Tom, who was armed. And surely she was safer with a cop who had a gun than standing alone out in the hall. She saw Tom go through the bedroom door and edged in after him.

He stood by the window, checking the lock there. Suddenly, there was the sound of door hinges creaking in the living room. Tom spun around and practically collided with Ann. "I told you to stay put!" he roared. Realizing that someone else was in the living room, he rushed past her.

Ann followed. As she traversed the living room, she caught a glimpse of the open closet door. Someone must have hidden in there when they'd come in.

Tom headed for the stairwell at breakneck speed and Ann, determined to keep up, raced along behind him. They descended the stairs at a run. Then, without warning, Tom stopped. Unable to slow down in time, Ann collided with him, knocking him forward a step. Tom reached out, steadying her and himself, then motioned her to be quiet. "Listen, there's no sound of anyone running ahead."

"You're right, but where..."

"He must have slipped through the doorway leading to the third floor." Without hesitation, Tom ran back upstairs.

Ann started after him, but then stopped. The intruder was undoubtedly heading for the stairs at the other end of the building. The best way to help Tom was to continue downstairs until she reached the first floor, then make a dash for the rear exit.

As she spurted forward, she tried to figure out how to cut the intruder off. She'd need to find some way of holding him until Tom could catch up. Reaching the bottom landing, she dashed down the hall toward the rear lobby. There wasn't much time. She could hear the sound of running footsteps coming down the stairwell.

Glancing around, she spotted a trash can in one corner. Ann picked up the large metal container, then rolled it across the floor on an intercept course with the staircase. An instant later someone appeared. Tom's familiar features registered a split second too late. There was no time to even yell out a warning.

Tom cursed expertly as he tried to sidestep the large metal can. In a last-ditch attempt, he hurtled over it, then dove toward the door.

The realization that they'd been too late and the intruder had eluded them made Ann's heart sink. Fighting the desperation that swept over her, she followed Tom outside.

He was several yards ahead of her, his eyes trained on a black van speeding out the far end of the parking lot. Its tires screeched as it maneuvered around the corner, making its escape.

Tom swore softly. "I didn't get a plate number. It was obscured with mud, probably on purpose," he said, returning to where she was. "You didn't help matters much, either. What the hell were you trying to do with that trash can?"

"I thought I'd beaten the intruder to the back stairs. When I heard running footsteps, I was certain it was him. I was going to slow him down until you got there."

Tom shook his head slowly but didn't say anything. "I better radio in a description of that van. Maybe one of the patrol units can pull him over. I'll be right back."

When he returned a moment later, his face was void of expression. "Let's go back upstairs."

She led the way inside Jackson's apartment and glanced around. "If he was searching for something in here, he either knew where to find it or was extraordinarily neat."

Tom walked to the open closet, then crouched down before it. "Now what's this?" he muttered, almost to himself.

Tom pulled out a framed oil painting of a landscape and held it up so they could both see it. "Take a look at the right-hand corner. It's been peeled back." Using the tip of his pen, he lifted the canvas away from the backing. "What's beneath looks like an original comic-book art panel." He brought it closer and switched on a table lamp. "It's Manstalker. I used to buy comic books featuring him when I was a kid. The series has been out since the late forties." He studied the artwork. "Unless I miss my guess, this sketch must belong to one of the earliest versions. Look at the style of dress."

"Is it valuable?"

"I don't know. It might be older than we are." He put the painting under one arm and walked around the room, studying the walls. "The person we surprised must have come to get this. He had a key, probably, and he knew where to look." Tom stopped by the hallway leading to the bedrooms and turned on the light. "I think the painting was probably hung right there." He gestured at the wall in front of him.

Ann could see a couple of faint marks on the wall and a hole where a small picture hanger had been. "There was certainly something there before," she replied.

"I have photographs of the apartment and a complete inventory of everything that was here. I'll check it once I get back to the office." He locked the front door, then walked downstairs with her. Careful not to smudge possible prints, he carried the oil painting outside. "I don't dare leave this, the guy might come back for it if it's worth a lot." He gave her a hopeful look. "This is a good lead."

Ann walked with him to his car, parked a few feet behind her own. "So it's a good thing we came."

"The burglar must have been waiting for the police to clear out and seal off Jackson's apartment. He just hadn't counted on you." Tom stood outside his vehicle, radio mike in hand, and gave the dispatcher the details. Then he asked, "Have there been any reports of stolen comic-book art panels recently?"

They waited for about three minutes, then one of the detectives from burglary called him back. "We had a break-in about four weeks ago that seems to fit. A former publisher, living in Denver, had his personal collection stolen. The seven panels that are missing are worth up to twelve thousand apiece. The whole set is worth even more." The voice was punctuated with static, but was loud and audible.

As soon as Tom completed his conversation, Ann spoke up. "I wonder if that's what the kidnapper's been looking for?" She stared at the pavement, lost in thought. "Yet, if he's searching for one or more art panels he believes Sean Jackson had with him at the time of his death, he can't be the killer. The person who murdered Jackson would have looked before dragging him into my car."

Another possibility dawned slowly over her. If what she'd reasoned was accurate, she'd finally stumbled onto the most important clue of all. Only, it was imperative she keep Tom out of it. Though it wasn't particularly dangerous, the legality of what she was about to do was questionable.

"All good points," he said, considering her theory. "That means we're dealing with more than one player."

"They're undoubtedly working separately, though. Whoever has Matt must believe that I killed Jackson and kept the art he wants. It might even be the same person who left the graffiti for me at that property I've been trying to sell. Remember? He said he'd get me if the police didn't,'' she said, her voice rising slightly.

"Wait a minute. We have scores of degenerates on the streets who could have left that message for you. You're correlating two things that don't necessarily follow. I agree that whoever has Matt must also believe you murdered Sean. Only, so far, his actions have been radically different than those you'd expect from whoever left that spray-painted message for you. The kidnapper hasn't shown any interest in you personally. Rather, he's been very single-minded about getting back something of his he thinks you have. He took Matt because he wanted leverage against you and he thinks you're holding out on him."

"If that's right, then at least my son's not with a killer,'' Ann said in a shaky voice. "I don't think I could cope with that."

"You can handle anything, Ann. I'm beginning to realize that about you."

"Don't kid yourself,'' she admitted. "You've been more of a help to me than you can possibly know."

His eyes lit up with a peculiar, intense quality. "I'll be right beside you as long as you need me,'' he said in a husky voice.

Ann felt her pulse quicken, and a warmth too penetrating to be comforting coursed through her.

The sound of an incoming radio call broke the mesmeric spell. "Is that for you?"

He glanced back, then shook his head. "Someone else can take that call. You and I have to go back to your house. We should take another look around now that we know what we're searching for."

"We've done that, and believe me I'd have noticed something the size of an art panel. Besides, it couldn't be inside the house. The only time Sean Jackson came in was when he made a call, and he didn't have anything big enough with him then." She paused, then without meeting his eyes added, "I'm tired. I'm going to go back home and lie down for a while."

Tom's eyes narrowed. "I'll follow you home. It'll be a big help if I can stay and use your telephone while you take that nap."

He knew. Somehow he'd guessed that she was up to something. "You'll keep me awake if you're talking," she protested.

"Okay, then I'll catch up on my paperwork. I need a little time to unwind, and in another twenty minutes I'll be off duty."

"Tom, I really want to be alone," she insisted, hoping he'd give up.

He hesitated for a moment, then nodded. "All right, Ann. If that's the way you want it. I'll head back to give Denis the number of your car phone in case he needs to contact you."

"Please don't worry. I'm just tired, that's all. I'll call you later."

Rushing off before Tom could change his mind, Ann went to her car and drove directly home. It was time to test out her theory. If she was right, she'd find one or more of the stolen art panels and be able to trade them for Matt. She felt guilty about keeping her theory from Tom, but she wasn't sure that what she planned to do was legal.

Once Matt was safe, she'd confide in Tom and explain how she'd arrived at her answers.

Ann parked in her driveway then rushed through the back gate into the wooded area. After crossing the small footbridge, she stopped and studied the ground. There were no signs that the earth had been disturbed there. Perhaps farther into the woods, near the path, she'd find her answer.

Ann spotted a small mound of loosely packed dirt, then crouched down to inspect it more closely. If it was an animal home, the last thing she wanted to do was disturb it. She separated the bush directly behind it, trying to see if there was an open hole below.

"What are you searching for, Ann?"

The voice was unmistakable. With a start, she turned around. Tom looked like an enormous rampart towering above her. Desperately, she tried to think of what to say. The truth was out of the question. "I'm looking for clues," she hedged. At least that wasn't a complete lie.

"Ann, you're after something specific. I've been following you all this time. I'll give you another choice. Either tell me what you're up to, or I'll take you in for questioning. In the meantime, I'll have a team of men go over this area, searching the ground for any fresh holes someone might have dug."

"You reached the same conclusion, didn't you?" she observed, her shoulders slumping dejectedly.

"It was obvious. Either Sean Jackson didn't have any art panels on him the day he was killed and the kidnapper was wrong, or Jackson managed to hide them before he met up with his killer. If that was the case, there's a chance the panels might still be in these woods. Of course, the killer might also have retraced Jackson's steps and retrieved them himself."

"It's possible, but they're still worth searching for. If he hid them, my guess is that he wrapped the panels in something to protect them and then buried them out here. Judging from the dimensions of the one back in his apartment, the hole wouldn't have had to be any larger than legal-size paper."

"Why didn't you tell me what you were thinking before, Ann. Don't you trust me?"

She stood up and faced him. "Tom, the police wouldn't have given me any of the art panels to trade for my son. I didn't have a choice." She accepted defeat with as much grace as she could. "Is the search team on the way over now?"

"No." He met her eyes with a level gaze. "I wasn't worried about the department cooperating with you because I'm certain they would have. It's Denis Arteaga's boss I'm not sure of. I was afraid he might have wanted to give you forgeries in the hope of tricking the kidnapper."

"So you didn't tell anyone!" she concluded. Ann threw her arms around him and hugged him with all her might. "Tom, thank you!"

He held her tightly against him. "You forget that I care about you, lady." He hesitated for a moment. "I also care about Matt, Annie. He's a part of you, and because of that, he's included in my feelings for you." Burying his fingers in her hair, he tilted her face up. He'd meant the kiss to be slow and easy, but he hadn't counted on the force of his own need. The moment his mouth claimed hers, desire turned his blood to fire. His tongue rushed forward, mating with hers and filling her mouth until she moaned softly.

That small cry pierced his soul. "Trust me, Ann," he whispered. "I will look after you and Matt."

He continued to hold her, but did not try to kiss her again. His control had been pushed to the limit and he didn't want to do anything to hurt her. Ann was vulnerable right now and her needs had to come first. Comforting was all she'd wanted and he wouldn't force something more on her.

Tom released her slowly. "Let's take a look at what you've found here." He crouched on the ground.

She knelt beside him. "Be careful. It could be a squirrel hole or something."

Soft, rapid footsteps through the brush made them both glance up. Through a maze of trees, Ann glimpsed a small boy running clumsily through the woods. Rays of sunlight filtering through the pines made his blond hair sparkle with a golden glow.

She bolted to her feet. "Matt?" Without hesitation, she sped off after him.

Chapter Twelve

Ann yelled out Matt's name, but the boy didn't slow down. Was someone else chasing him? She glanced behind her but saw no one. "It's all right, Mommy's here!"

Running after him at full speed, she narrowed the gap between them quickly. Finally she managed to capture his tiny shoulder and whirl him around. "Sweetie, it's me, it's okay!"

It was only when she saw his face that she realized it was someone else's child. He looked as if he were about to cry.

Her hopes plummeted. "I'm so sorry! I thought you were my little boy," she explained.

Wide brown eyes peered back at her. Unwilling to trust a grown-up who'd chased him, the child began to back away warily.

The ache in her chest grew. The boy looked so frightened! The thought that she'd caused it made her almost ill. "I'm sorry, honey, but what are you doing out here all alone?"

"I'm not supposed to, but I went exploring out through the loose board in the fence. Only then I couldn't find the bridge to get back across the ditch."

"Where do you live?" She could see Tom out of the corner of her eyes. Too humiliated to turn around, she avoided looking at him at all.

The child pointed at a two-story house barely visible through the trees at the foot of the hill. "Over there. The house with the green roof."

"All right, then. I want you to go back home. It's dangerous for a little boy to be here all alone. The bridge is back that way and to your left." She pointed in the right direction and saw the boy off.

Ann watched him as he dashed through an outcropping of trees then continued down the incline. She folded her arms over her chest, hugging herself and trying not to cry.

"Ann." Tom placed a hand on her shoulder from behind. "It was a natural mistake. The boy does look a lot like Matt."

She shook her head, unable to talk without betraying herself.

He knew she was struggling to keep control and tried to support her efforts. "Let's get back to what we were doing. That mound of dirt turned out be the entrance to a rabbit hole."

They divided the area into sections, then explored it thoroughly. An hour later, they'd still found nothing. Ann, more composed now, stopped and glanced at Tom. "This isn't going to work. These woods are too large for just the two of us to cover. It would take days to check every foot."

He nodded. "Yes, I thought that might turn out to be the case, but it was worth a try."

"You might as well make it official and call some officers in." There was a hollow pain in her chest as she spoke. "They might be able to find something we missed."

"Try not to worry, Ann. If they do find something, I have a feeling everyone will cooperate with you. If the department or the CBI was to pull a fast one with a ransom payment and it failed, the press would have a field day with them." He walked beside her, occasionally offering her a hand when she needed it. "My biggest concern is that there'll be delays because of the red tape. There's bound to be some arguing between the department and the state people about who takes charge of what. If that happens, I'm going to have to do something to speed them along."

"Like what? There'd be nothing you could do," she said dejectedly.

"Trust me, I know how to get around them. A rumor that the press has learned that paperwork is holding us up would be enough to get some action," he responded. "Of course, it's also possible our guys won't find anything out here, either. Remember, so far we're operating on a theory."

"You know what scares me? What if they're there, but no one finds them?"

"Let me tell you something about investigative work. Stick to the facts and the probabilities. The what ifs are mind games that can defeat you."

She remained quiet for a few moments. "Thanks for being my friend at the time when I need one most," she said at last. "When Matt comes home," she continued, mentally affirming his return, "I hope you'll come by and visit often." She led the way back inside the house.

"Maybe after Matt's home, you won't want to see me," Tom observed quietly. "I'll be a reminder of a very unpleasant time in your life. It happens, you know. Things change and people with them."

"Not in this case," she replied confidently. "You'll always be welcome here." But one thing remained unanswered between them. He'd acknowledged Matt's special needs. Would he really want to enter her life and be a part of it after the case was over? Or would the friendship he offered exclude her son? Perhaps that was not the kind of commitment he would ever be able to make.

"I'm going to call the station and ask for a search team." He walked to her desk and began to dial.

The police team arrived half an hour later. Tom stood in Ann's driveway and directed the men. He was about to go back inside when another car pulled up. As Captain Lambert emerged from the unmarked car, Tom's body tensed. The captain didn't normally get involved with cases out in the field. Over the years his job had become strictly administrative.

"What brings you out here, Captain?" Tom asked, coming to meet him.

"I heard you requested a search team, so I decided to take a look at what was going on."

Tom made a full report, omitting the fact that Ann and he had done a partial search already.

"What prompted you to go to Jackson's place? There was nothing at that point to indicate stolen art panels," Lambert asked.

Out of the corner of his eyes, Tom caught a glimpse of Ann standing less than ten feet away. From the look on her face, he was certain that she was prepared to back him up and shift the blame away from him if necessary. A powerful urge to protect her drummed through him. Yet the knowledge that he'd evoked a similar passion within her filled him with a fierce sense of pride.

As the captain shifted, Tom's attention moved back to him. "I went over there on a hunch," he answered. It was at least partially the truth. "I needed to prove my theory that the robberies, the murder and the kidnapping are all connected. Jackson seemed right in the middle of everything so I took a chance. I thought that Jackson's apartment might hold some answers."

"Good instincts, Keller," the captain replied. Ann followed the two men as they walked to her backyard. There, they watched the police officers as they searched their way down the hillside. "By the way, as of today, you're off the case."

The news took Tom completely by surprise. He could see Ann staring at them both, her mouth open. "Why's that, Captain? You don't approve of the way I've been handling this so far?"

"Not at all, Keller. You've done a commendable job, considering all the curves this case has tossed you." The captain stared at the search team, hands thrust deep in his pockets. "But the latest events indicate that Mrs. Dixon is not Jackson's killer. As far as I'm concerned, that now makes his murder low priority. Off the record—" he lowered his voice so Ann couldn't hear "—the man was scum. I don't want too many man-hours wasted on this."

"So we're going to drop the investigation altogether?" Tom asked, trying to figure out where all this was leading.

"Not exactly. I've handed it to the burglary division." Lambert was still speaking softly. "What you found at Jackson's apartment makes it clear that he was part of the theft ring we've been tracking. The burglary-division detectives will be able to uncover more clues than you could at this stage as they try to catch up with the rest of the team."

"And if they uncover something about the murder?" Tom asked. "What then?"

"If they do find something conclusive, you'll check it out. Until that time, though, it's pointless to keep you on this. You'd be tripping over the burglary people at every turn. There are still two unsolved murders that have been on our books for quite a while. Solving those cases would give us some very good publicity. That's where I want you to concentrate your efforts."

"Captain, Jackson's murder plays a prominent part in Matt Dixon's kidnapping. I believe the kidnapper is after the art panels and he's convinced Ann Dixon has them." Tom explained how he'd arrived at that conclusion.

"The kidnapping is the Colorado Bureau of Investigation's headache now," Lambert insisted in a low, clipped tone. "That's why I called them in. If anything goes wrong, we'll have someone to share the blame with. You should thank me. I'm making sure *this time* things will be different."

Tom could feel the blood draining from his face as the old memories came flooding back. He clenched and unclenched his fists as he struggled to remain outwardly cool. "You're making a mistake taking me off the case. Time is crucial in something like this, and we've only just begun to scratch the surface. I could help the CBI considerably."

Lambert noted with satisfaction that his reference to the past had hit its mark. "My decision stands. You've been working on the Jackson case intensively. I don't think you're aware of how involved you've become. You're losing your perspective, Keller. I think your personal ties to Ann Dixon are responsible for that." He held up a hand before Tom could answer. "Don't bother to deny it. You know I'm right."

"It looks like they've finished one quadrant," Tom commented in the most casual tone he could muster.

"I'm going to go up there. If they've found something, I want to know." The captain opened the back gate to Ann's yard, then stopped. "You should explain to Mrs. Dixon that you've been reassigned. Assure her, however, that the CBI is very much on top of the investigation of her son's kidnapping and that she has no reason to worry. She's in capable hands with them."

Tom watched Captain Lambert as he strode away. Once again fate was giving him a choice. He could either follow orders or go with his own instincts. He made his decision quickly.

"Is it true?" Ann's voice broke through his thoughts.

Tom faced her as she came up to him. By now he knew that nothing would deter her own investigative efforts. Yet he wanted to hear her say that she needed him to stand by her. He wanted to matter to her, to be the man she counted on, and not just because through him she had access to the police investigation. "What are you asking me? Do you want to know if I'm so personally involved with you that I'm no longer of value to the investigation?"

She shook her head. "I know differently. But what do you plan to do now?"

"Officially I'm off the case," he answered.

Her shoulders sagged. "Will you still come around?" Her voice wavered, but she cleared her throat and went on speaking. "Understand, Tom, I'm not begging for your friendship. That's something that can only be freely given. I just need to know what to expect."

Their eyes met. There was a dignity about her that got under his skin and touched his heart. "I'll be around," he said quietly. "I'm going to continue working on this on my own time." Ann's smile made his heart pound against his ribs. "I couldn't walk away from this now, even if I wanted to."

"Because of me?"

He nodded slowly. "You're a big part of it, Ann. I could never leave knowing you needed my help. You're too special to me." His voice was deep and as smooth as a heady wine.

"But there's more, isn't there?" she insisted.

He turned away and watched the men making their way into the wooded area. "There are some things that are too personal to share with anyone, Ann."

"But I'm not just 'anyone.' There isn't much of a friendship between us if you still don't feel comfortable enough to trust me."

"I've never let you get close. I've allowed you to assume things that were, at best, only partially true." His voice was barely more than a whisper.

"Like what? I don't understand."

He gave her a wry smile and shrugged. "For instance, you think that my reasons for not having kids stem only from logic. But that's not so. You see, I've never wanted a child to experience what I went through as a kid." His voice became strained. "Both my parents were cops. When I turned eight, my mother was killed on duty."

"I'm so sorry. It must have been very difficult for you, particularly at that age," Ann said gently.

He nodded. "It was. At first I missed her terribly and all I could think of was how badly I wanted her back. Then I started getting panic attacks. I'd become terrified that something would happen to my dad, too. What frightened me most was the thought of being alone in the world with no one who cared about me to look after me. Ironically, my father rejected me, as well. To him I was just a reminder of the life he'd shared with my mother and lost."

"But it doesn't have to be that way," Ann protested in a kind voice. "Look at the life I've made with Matt."

"That's true, but it's hard for a kid to reason fear away. Ann, I don't want a child of mine to ever experience the terror of wondering if life will take away the one parent who's left. I lived with that for too many years before I finally was able to handle it."

"So Matt's the other reason you're staying on the case," she observed thoughtfully. "You realize how much he's been through already since you've experienced something like it yourself.''

"He must feel very alone and scared,'' Tom answered quietly. "But I still haven't given you the whole story,'' he admitted candidly. "My reasons for staying on this case are complex, Ann. They're not something I can explain in just a few minutes.''

She nodded slowly. "Okay, I can accept that. You've trusted me with this much. You'll tell me the rest when you're ready. Only there's something I want to say. Your circumstances with your father were very harsh. I can understand how it affected your decision not to have children. But your father—''

"Taught me a great deal. Don't knock it. I learned back then that the key to survival is never to let anyone get too close. Only people who really know you have the power to hurt you deeply.''

"Or heal you,'' Ann said softly, remembering Matt's fears.

"That, too,'' Tom admitted with a gentle smile. He wanted to gather Ann into his arms and just hold her, but the captain and the searchers were starting to work their way down the hillside toward them. In another half hour, they would be finished. "When the captain gets here, let me handle him. I know you're as curious as I am, but he's more likely to talk freely with me than with you.''

"It isn't really fair, but you're undoubtedly right,'' she said with a scowl. "Let me know as soon as you can, though, okay?'' She turned and walked back into the house.

Chapter Thirteen

Tom approached the captain. "Did they turn up anything?" he asked casually. He wanted it to seem like nothing more than professional curiosity.

"No, sorry to say. With all these men, it's doubtful that we've missed anything. We swept the whole area twice." Lambert wiped the sweat from his brow. "I'm going home," he muttered, heading through the side gate to his car.

Tom waited until everyone had left, then started toward the house. Ann was waiting for him by the door. "They didn't find anything," he said, responding to her silent question.

In her eyes he saw a kaleidoscope of pain, sorrow and anger waiting to burst out. Yet the control she held over herself did not diminish. "Let's go have a talk," he said.

Ann nodded, leading him to the kitchen table. Sitting across from Tom, she opened her hands in a silent gesture, urging him to continue.

"I'm not going to defend the captain; he and I have never had much use for each other. But right now, I think he's being pressured to take me off the case. I know he's got several big names in this town that are working to jump him past the chief to the job of commissioner of public safety. Having me solve one of the other murders in our active files would give him a lot of good publicity. Those cases involve innocent citizens. Solving Jackson's murder, on the other hand, would accomplish almost nothing.''

''And my son? Doesn't he count for anything?''

''You're forgetting that the CBI is in charge of that, not us. There's something very odd going on here, Ann. Lambert's kept burglary division working on the thefts. But he doesn't want us to actively investigate the murder. It sounds like he wants the stolen property recovered but he doesn't want us to look too closely at the rest of the case.''

''Is there any way you can prove or disprove that?''

''Not at this time. But for now, you and I need to concentrate on finding Matt. And since that's going to require us to keep following Jackson's trail, we'll have to watch our step.''

''Now that you're officially off my case, your time during the day will be taken up with other police business. If you'll tell me what to do, I can pick up the slack. From now on I'll take care of all the leg work.''

''There are some things you could check out. But you have to stay in contact, and if you ever think you're in danger, call me or Denis. Don't take chances.''

Ann couldn't promise she wouldn't take chances, not if taking them would get Matt back safe again. ''If I learn anything, I'll get in touch with you right away.'' Wanting to divert him quickly, she continued. ''By the way, Agent Murphy called while you were outside with the captain. They want to ask me more questions.''

''That's to be expected. This Artemis character doesn't seem to be worried about moving fast. He's calculated and very cool. That means the CBI's going to have to dig deep. It'll entail knowing everything they can about Matt, what he likes, what he dislikes, how sharp he is, whether he's likely to try to engineer his own escape, and so on.''

''Matt has quite a temper. If he wants to go home and Artemis is preventing him from doing that, he's going to do his best to get away. But if he's scared, then it's hard to predict what he'll do.'' Ann stared across the room, disconnected from everything except her own thoughts. ''Nature endows children with very strong defenses. Like you, they find a way to cope with situations that seem practically overwhelming. Matt might turn this into a game and envision himself fighting bad guys.''

Tom nodded, remembering how easy it was for children to escape into a world colored by their own imaginations. ''I'm supposed to meet Denis later this afternoon. I'll have to let him know that officially I'm off the case, but don't worry. Denis is a buddy of mine. I don't think we'll have any problems getting him to pass on any new information they get. Of course, we'll have to do the same for him.''

''Fine.''

''I'll call you after I've seen Denis.'' Throwing his jacket over one shoulder, Tom walked slowly to his car. Something very odd was happening to him lately. He was starting to feel more at home at Ann's than he was at his own apartment.

As he drove away from Ann's neighborhood, his mind replayed the captain's reference to the past. The emotional wound, which had never healed, reopened easily. This time, though, it would be different. He was no longer a rookie detective. Experience would give him an advantage and no one, including Lambert, was going to stand in his way. Matt would be returned safe and sound to his mother.

Only what then? Tom wondered about the future and what it would hold for the three of them. Matt had blessed Ann's life with a richness he envied. There was much to be said for having a family to love and be loved by. But was it something he could not afford to have.

THREE HOURS LATER, after a shower and a short nap, Tom pulled into the parking lot of Harry's Place. The bar, known for its rough clientele, was where Denis had elected to meet him. The choice still puzzled Tom, but he was willing to play along.

He left the car and started for the entrance. He was wearing comfortable jeans, worn boots and a Western shirt. He'd fit right in.

As he strode across the parking lot, Denis drove up beside him. ''Hold it a minute. I want to talk to you first.''

Tom walked over to him. "How's it going, buddy?" he said as Denis emerged from the car. "Nice choice," he added ruefully, cocking his head toward the bar.

Denis laughed. "Hey, what can I tell you? It's the only place my informant likes to meet."

Tom walked with Denis toward the entrance to the bar. "So who are we meeting here?"

"His name is Victor Naranjo. He and Sean Jackson were drinking buddies. I caught up with Naranjo earlier today, and he said he had some information about Jackson to sell. I figured you'd want to be in on this."

"Thanks, buddy. I owe you one."

Denis chortled. "One? You wish. Try several hundred." He stopped for a second near the doorway of the crowded bar and gauged the atmosphere. "He'll be in one of the corner booths. Let's go."

Loud, forced laughter surrounded them. Both men waited a moment just inside, their eyes struggling to adjust to the near darkness of the room. Two heavily made up ladies started to move toward them, but Denis waved them away before they approached. Denis and Tom reached the booth a moment later, and Denis slid in beside Naranjo.

"Hey, what are you pulling, Arteaga? I do you a favor and you bring an audience?"

Tom sat across from them but said nothing, letting Denis set the pace.

"There's a bonus for you in here," Denis said, slipping an envelope beneath the table, "so lighten up."

The man placed the envelope in his jacket with a subtle, fluid motion, like a pickpocket in reverse. "You can't blame me for being nervous. Jackson was tied to some very nasty people, so they say."

Not bothering to introduce Tom, Denis prodded Naranjo. "So what's this information?"

"You asked me to get whatever I could on Jackson, right?" The man didn't wait for an answer. "Well, I got something. It seems Sean was on a lucky streak lately. He'd pulled off a string of burglaries without tripping any alarms or being seen. From what I hear, some of the houses he broke into had some heavy-duty security systems, too. Everyone's trying to figure out how he managed to find an inside man at each of the places he hit. My guess is that he didn't. He just cased cach place long enough to learn all he needed about the particular alarm system. What do you think?''

Denis said nothing, allowing the moments of silence to drag on.

Aware of Denis's interrogation tactic, Tom waited, knowing the quiet would be uncomfortable for their informant.

"I tried to get the name of his fence for you, but no luck. Personally, I think it must have been someone in the Denver area who deals in antiques and collectibles. There's no one like that around here.''

"So far you haven't earned your money, Victor. Don't make me regret giving you that envelope,'' Denis growled.

"Okay, okay. How about this? Jackson had a live-in girlfriend.'' Seeing the quick look the two men exchanged, Naranjo smiled. "Yeah, I *knew* the cops didn't know about her. No one had been asking questions.''

"What's her name and where is she now?'' Denis urged.

"Her first name is Lenora. I don't know the last. She's a tall, hefty blonde. Built like an Amazon, I hear. Not a real looker, but doesn't exactly bay at the moon, either.''

"Address, Victor, address.''

"She's hiding out, man, what do you think? She doesn't want the police asking a lot of embarrassing questions.''

"Okay, Naranjo, keep me posted.''

Tom followed Denis back outside. Alone near Tom's car, they both finally relaxed. "I'd say your stoolie earned his money,'' Tom commented. "That's some news flash.''

"You mean your department had no idea there was a woman living with Jackson? How the hell could you guys miss that?''

"There was no evidence of any woman spending time there at all.'' Tom rubbed the back of his neck. "I should have guessed, though. Our reports all mentioned that he loved the ladies. A man like that would have had women over as often as possible. We should have found earrings, perfume or makeup somewhere in there. Now I realize why the apartment was so clean. His lady must have been real busy lately, covering her tail."

"Okay, that's it for my part, buddy." Denis grinned. "Now what have you got for me?"

Tom filled him in on what they'd learned about the art panels. "The problem is that I'm now officially off the case." He gave Denis the details, then explained how he and Ann had devised a way to get around the situation.

Arteaga's eyes narrowed in a pensive manner. "I seem to remember a case involving a rookie detective—"

Tom held up his hand, interrupting him. "You and I go back a long time, Denis. I'm not going to try and kid you. That case still keeps me up nights, but that's not the only reason I'm not going to drop it."

Denis nodded. "I thought I sensed something between you and Ann Dixon."

"What you sensed was nothing more than friendship," Tom answered. "But I'm not saying it couldn't be more someday. We may or may not be right for each other. I'm not ready to close the door on the possibilities."

Denis said nothing for a moment, then shrugged. "As long as you keep me up on whatever you find, I see no reason why we can't continue to exchange information. We'll keep it out of our reports." He leaned back against Tom's car. "But you're talking about letting a civilian get involved. Have you thought that through?"

"I couldn't keep her out of it if I tried." Tom briefly recounted what had happened up to then. "Believe me, the only way I'm going to be able to stop her is to arrest her. This way, I can direct her efforts and maybe keep her out of any major trouble." Tom rubbed his hand over his face. "She's a mother looking for her kid, Denis. There's no stronger motivation, and no one's going to keep her from doing that."

"You're right. God knows it wouldn't be the first time we've had to contend with family members who want to help." He stepped away from Tom's car. "I'm going to start tracking down Jackson's fence. The notes Ann Dixon has received all claim that she's got something the kidnapper wants returned. If you're right about the art panels, then that means the kidnapper knows what kind of merchandise Jackson was dealing in. That makes him either one of Jackson's associates or his fence.''

"I'll try to track down Lenora. As soon as I've got something, I'll give you a call."

Denis started to walk away, then stopped and turned around. "Tom, I'm your friend, so I'm going to give you a little friendly advice. Forget what happened years ago. It wasn't your fault, and you've got nothing to blame yourself for.''

"Yeah, right," Tom muttered.

"I mean it. Put it behind you once and for all."

"I would if I could, buddy," Tom replied tonelessly.

Tom reached his apartment twenty minutes later. In contrast to his desk at work and Ann's meticulous housekeeping, his place was a disaster area of major proportions. It sneered at him and defied his best efforts to keep it clean. The problem was, he was never here. To him, the apartment was a place to sleep and change clothes. The rest of his time he spent out in the field, working. Dead plants and the yellowish light coming in from the streetlight outside enhanced the gloomy picture. He turned on the lamp, but instead of improving matters, it seemed only to give the room an even deeper yellow cast. He swore softly. It had never mattered before.

He walked to the kitchen and searched the refrigerator for something to eat. There were two slices of bologna left, one slice of bread and a jar of what had once been mayonnaise.

He made a sandwich on dry bread and finished it in two bites. It was close to eleven. He wanted to call Ann. Would she be asleep? His telephone rang and he picked it up before it could ring again.

"Tom, is it too late to call?"

He smiled. The room seemed less yellow now. "I'm glad to hear from you. I was just wondering if I should call you." His mouth was dry. There was nothing to drink in the refrigerator, so he glanced around the kitchen. Reaching for the open can of beer on the counter he jiggled it in hopes of finding some trace of liquid inside. The swallow of flat beer would normally have made him gag, but even it didn't seem so bad now.

"I'm in front of the convenience store near my house, so you don't have to be afraid to talk," she assured him. "I was going to wait until I saw you tomorrow, but I couldn't sleep. I wanted to know how your meeting with Denis went."

"Ann, you shouldn't be standing out in a phone booth at this time of night," he countered harshly. "It's dangerous."

"I won't be here long."

"Look, I live only fifteen minutes away from you. I'll come over."

"No, I'm already out," she countered. "I've got your card. You scribbled your address and telephone number on it, remember? I'll be there in ten minutes." She hung up before he could protest.

Tom glanced around the room and cringed. She had a thing about order. If she saw his place, she'd die of a heart attack. He grabbed the three pizza boxes from the top of the counter, folded them forcibly in half and fitted them into a plastic trash bag. Dashing across the living room, he retrieved a coffee cup with one dead fly in it, and a small pile of clothes that he had dropped several days ago.

Tom tossed everything in his bedroom, then shut the door just as he heard a knock. "Coming." The place looked a lot better now. At least one could see the color of the sofa.

Ann came inside, then glanced around. "Nice," she said, wondering how he managed to avoid depression in such a barren apartment. "Your plants are dead," she observed, picking up one dead vine from a hanging pot, then dropping it again.

"It saves on water," Tom joked halfheartedly.

She sat down on the sofa, but not before checking the cushion suspiciously. A thin sprinkling of crumbs and either dust or whole-wheat flour covered the surface. "Now tell me about your meeting with Denis."

Tom brought her up to date on the pertinent details. "Tomorrow morning I think you should go back to Jackson's neighborhood. You can question store owners and restaurant employees in the area. Try to find out where he ate and shopped, and anything you can about Lenora. If possible, get a more accurate description of her. Also, see if you can find out where she could be staying. Her name is unusual, so that may jog their memory."

"I'll do that first thing. Will you be coming over tomorrow after work?"

"Maybe even before." He smiled and shrugged. "We are allowed breaks, you know." He wondered what she thought of his place. "Can I get you something to drink?" he asked, then remembered that he'd taken the last swallow of beer.

"No, I better be going," she answered. "You need to get some rest." She gave him an apologetic smile. "I'm sorry I barged in on you."

"It's fine, but you didn't give me much of a chance to get things fixed up." Of course fixing this place up would have taken a miracle, but it seemed like the polite thing to say. "You see, I usually get in late at night, dead tired, and leave in a rush the next morning. To be honest, I never really looked at the apartment until tonight."

"Because of me?"

"Yeah," he muttered grudgingly. He couldn't tell if she was made pleased or uneasy by his admission. "Let me walk you to your car," he said, quickly changing the subject.

Two minutes later he watched her pull out of the parking lot and disappear down the street. He hadn't wanted her to go. He'd wanted to take her into his room and make love to her all night long. Only he hadn't been certain he could find the bed under the pile of clothes he'd tossed over it. Then again, she'd have probably taken one look at the state of his bedroom and run out screaming.

He exhaled softly. Being a bachelor sometimes wasn't all it was cracked up to be.

ANN WOKE UP EARLY the next morning. Today she'd find Lenora. Saying a prayer for her little boy, she forced her fear back. Her son was fine. She had to believe that. Yet, more than anything, she wished that the kidnapper would contact her and let her speak to Matt. She wanted desperately to hear Matt's voice, not just to assure herself but because her heart demanded that contact.

As she showered and dressed, Ann wondered about her growing relationship with Tom. Worry for her son had become a constant ache inside her. Yet, there seemed to be room in her heart for Tom, also.

The danger sign was impossible to ignore. Tom was all wrong for her. With a job like his, even something as insignificant as being a little late could take on frightening overtones. She'd lived through that once with Warren. Surely she wasn't going to welcome that into her life again.

Ann left her bedroom and strode down the hall. She'd put off checking the newspaper for a message from the kidnapper, afraid of being disappointed again. Not knowing for sure allowed her the luxury of hope. But now she couldn't delay it any longer. She started to go outside, then noticed an envelope stuck beneath the bottom of the door.

Her heart froze and for an instant she couldn't move. That hadn't been there last night before she'd gone to bed! Ann rushed forward and retrieved it. With shaking fingers, she tore it open and pulled the contents free.

Chapter Fourteen

As a new instant photograph of Matt dropped into her hand, she realized the kidnapper had thrown a curve ball. He'd led them to expect something in the newspaper, but had done this instead.

Tears of relief mingled with longing as she looked at her son's face. Matt was standing against a bare white wall, holding a clock. He looked tired, but was obviously unhurt. Fumbling nervously, she opened the note that accompanied the photo and read it.

> Time is running out. Find the cassette I want or get it from the police. Go to Fremont Park alone at 11:00 a.m. and bring the cassette in a brown lunch sack. Sit on the far swing and read the instructions taped on the bottom. If you say anything to the authorities or listen to the cassette, I'll know and your son will never come home.
>
> Artemis

Ann stared at the note in confusion. Cassette? What cassette? She and Tom had been certain he'd wanted the comic-book art panels. And how was she going to get what he wanted? Without asking the police, there was no way she'd learn if they'd found a tape in Jackson's possession.

Ann heard her car phone ringing. She dashed to the driveway and picked it up. "'Lo?"

Tom's voice was plain over the receiver. "Hi. I figured you'd be on your way to Jackson and Lenora's neighborhood by now. I just wanted to check and make sure all was going according to schedule."

Did he have ESP or something? "Everything's under control. As soon as I have something on Lenora, I'll give you a call."

"You sound confident. That's good."

"We're due for some good luck," she mumbled. "I hate to hang up, but I have to get some questions ready for the store owners."

"Your questions will have to be phrased carefully, but it's your approach that'll determine how successful you are. Remember, you're trying to get them to help you, so act friendly. Also, Ann, put up your hair. You don't want to be recognized from the papers."

"Okay." She hesitated for a moment. "Tom, I could really use your help. Would you mind if I tried out my approach on you first? I could drop by your office for a few minutes." She needed his help, that was true, but that wasn't why she was going over there. Using subterfuge with Tom made her stomach feel queasy.

"No problem. Only use the side door. That way you won't be walking right past the captain's office, okay?"

"I'll be there in about twenty minutes."

As she hung up she felt a pang of conscience. Maybe she should have told him the truth. She trusted Tom. But the kidnapper had said that he'd *know* if she brought the authorities in. It was possible he had a contact somewhere within the department. There was no way she could afford to take a chance.

She collected her thoughts quickly. The only cassettes in her home belonged to Matt. Had the police confiscated a tape important enough to induce murder and kidnapping without knowing its value? If it had appeared to be an ordinary music tape, they probably wouldn't have listened to it at all.

Almost absentmindedly she pinned her hair up and put on the glasses Tom had loaned her. Then she locked the house and drove to the police station. Using the side door, she walked directly to Tom's office.

Hearing her approach, he glanced up and smiled. "That cerebral look becomes you," he said pleasantly, then ushered her in.

"Thanks." Ann didn't want to spend any time on trivialities, but there was no way around it. Unless she used some finesse she'd arouse his suspicions for sure. "I've been thinking I'd approach the store owners as someone who went to high school with Lenora. What do you think?"

"You'd have to know more about her for that," he answered, shaking his head. "Your best chance is to be somewhat vague. Don't volunteer information. If they want to know why you're looking for Lenora, say that her family asked you to look her up when you came to town. Since she wasn't at her apartment, you thought you'd check around the neighborhood."

"You know, I wonder if we're going off on a tangent by investigating Lenora. Maybe we're missing something that's been in front of us all along. Are you sure the police didn't find anything, even seemingly innocent, on Jackson's body or in his car, that might furnish a clue?"

"No, I would know about it. I've been over the list countless times and there's nothing." Tom pulled a file from the stack on his right. "Not even a giant stretch of the imagination could make anything out of this list," he added.

Ann forced herself not to jump out of her chair. Calmly, she walked behind him and glanced over his shoulder.

"The only things they found on Jackson was forty-nine cents in change, his wallet with a driver's license and fifty dollars in cash, a pen, a handkerchief and a comb. As far as keys, he had an ignition and trunk key that fit the white Chevy, a key to his apartment and finally, a mailbox key. We tried them all."

"What about in his car?"

"Nothing that shouldn't be there. Just hand tools and a jack."

"What about papers or special equipment like a CB radio or a tape player?" Ann wanted to disguise her real question among the rest.

"We found registration papers and a few candy wrappers. As for equipment, he had a standard radio, nothing else."

She returned to her chair. He wasn't keeping anything from her. She'd read the list herself. "Have they searched Jackson's apartment again?"

"Yes, but no other art panels turned up," Tom replied patiently. "Ann, we're pursuing the best lead we have by trying to find Lenora."

"Would you let me take a look at the inventory of things found at Jackson's home?"

Tom narrowed his eyes warily and he leaned back in his chair. "This is starting to sound like you've got something very specific in mind." He gave her a long, speculative glance. "What are you up to now?"

She gave him a halfhearted smile, then shrugged. "Nothing. I was just looking for another lead that would make me feel I'm really doing something to get Matt back," she answered somberly.

"You are, believe me," he assured confidently.

She stood. "I better get to work then. Will you stop by later?"

"Count on it."

She met his eyes, and then quickly averted her gaze. She'd have to be careful. She'd almost given herself away. If the choice had been hers, she'd have handled things differently. But she was working for the kidnapper now.

TOM PACED AROUND his office. The tug at his scalp and the strange prickling of his skin were clear signs that something was wrong. His instincts never lied.

He'd seen Ann studying the list detailing Jackson's possessions. And her questions had all been very directed, as if she'd been looking for a particular item. She was up to something. Only what? He was fairly certain she hadn't been contacted by the kidnapper yet. It was too early for her to have received her mail, and he'd checked the newspaper ads himself. There'd been nothing there. The newspaper was supposed to let him know, but perhaps Artemis would change his name to throw them off. Or he could have left a note again without using the newspaper. Denis would have called immediately if Ann had received a call. The CBI man had promised to do that.

Had Ann come up with another theory she was keeping from him? Tom's nerves grew cold at the thought. This time she could be rushing headlong into danger without any way to defend herself. He adjusted his shoulder holster and hurried after her. How ironic that the qualities he loved most about her, her independence and her strength, were the very things that were driving him crazy.

As ANN DROVE BACK HOME, she tried to go over everything she'd seen at Jackson's apartment. The furnishings had been sparse. There was a nice TV, she recalled, but no VCR or tape player, much less tapes.

There was only one thing to do. She'd take Artemis an audio tape with a message of her own recorded on it. She'd plead for her son's life, explaining that neither she nor the police had the missing tape. She'd assure him that no matter what she had to do, she'd find it and get it for him. But first he had to tell her whatever would help her locate it. If he wanted the tape even half as badly as she wanted Matt, he'd give her the information.

A short time later Ann placed her own tape in a paper sack. It was time to go. She'd made an arbitrary choice on the cassette size and prayed the kidnapper would listen to her message. Her hands were shaking as she reached for her keys.

Fremont Park was less than ten minutes away. She had just started out to the garage when she heard a knock at her door. She was tempted to ignore it, but didn't dare. Hurrying, she went to answer it.

Joan smiled brightly at her. "I came to see how you were doing and to ask if there's been any more news."

Ann tried to hide her impatience. "There've been no new developments." Taking a new house key from a pocket in her purse, she handed it to Joan. "I want you to have this. It's a spare. If Matt manages somehow to get away or if he's returned, he'll need a way to get inside. If I'm not home, he'll go to you. Here's my mobile number, just in case." She handed Joan a piece of paper. "Please, if you see him . . ." Her heart felt as if it were tearing in two, and her voice wavered.

Joan gave her a hug. "Don't you worry. If Matt comes back while you're gone, I'll find a way to get ahold of you immediately."

"Thanks, now I've got to get going. I've got an appointment." Saying a quick goodbye, Ann locked the doors and hurried to her car. It was time to get her son back. More frightened than she'd ever been, she started the engine and got underway.

TOM FOLLOWED ANN, keeping at a safe distance. He remembered how she'd spotted him tailing her before.

Her actions this morning continued to puzzle him. He noticed the small paper sack she was holding as she'd emerged from the house. It looked like an ordinary sandwich bag. Only what was she doing with it, and why wasn't she out questioning people about Lenora?

Filled with questions, Tom followed Ann to a small neighborhood park. He sat in his car down the street from where she'd parked, and waited, watching her in his rearview mirror. His eyes never left her as she walked to a small swing set in the center and sat down. Did she miss her son so much that she'd come here to a place where he'd played to remember happier times? His heart twisted, feeling her sorrow.

She moved from swing to swing, trying out each, then finally settling on the last one. He saw her lean forward for a moment, then stare at her hands. Was she holding something? He grabbed the binoculars from the seat, but the angle was wrong and he couldn't see. He started to get out of the car for another look when she stood up, dropped the paper bag into the trash bin, then walk slowly to her car.

She'd made a drop, either that or changed her mind about lunch. This had gone far enough, it was time to confront her. He followed her until they were a block from the park, then gunned the engine and pulled up beside her. "I want to talk to you. There's a school parking lot ahead. Go in there."

Ann's face went white. "No, not there. Follow me." Not giving him a choice, she pressed on the accelerator.

With a short but expressive oath, Tom sped after her. He toyed with the idea of asking a patrol car to head her off, but then changed his mind. Ann was his concern. Too bad she didn't know it.

Five minutes later she pulled into the parking lot of a shopping center, emerged from her car and waited for him to approach.

"You have some heavy-duty explaining to do," he growled.

"I did what I had to." She told him what she'd done.

"You mean you didn't even tell Denis what you were doing?" He ran one hand through his hair in a gesture of sheer exasperation. "Don't you realize he could have had several guys with telephoto lenses ready, and maybe learned the kidnapper's identity?" Tom ran to his car. "Maybe it's not too late." He picked up his radio microphone, but Ann rushed up and placed her hand over his.

"Can you be certain that the kidnapper won't spot anyone? And what if he has a contact working for the police?"

"That's exactly what he wants you to believe."

"Tom, think about that park. There's only a handful of young trees and they're clustered at one end. How's anyone going to hide there? One slipup and I could lose my son."

He put the radio mike down. "You're going to have to make up your mind, Annie. Do you want to face this alone, or will you trust us? Remember that you're dealing with someone who seems to know all the angles."

"It's so simple for you, isn't it?" she countered angrily. "You know what should be done and exactly how to go about it. You don't have to contend with real emotions like fear. There are thousands of missing children out there, Tom. My son could end up one of them. I love him and he's been taken from me. Can you even imagine a love so strong that without it a big part of you will be lost forever?"

Tom remained silent for a moment. What she'd said had cut him deeper than she'd ever know. "There are a handful of people who can hurt me. My son may not be the one who's in danger, Ann, but your pain is my own." His whispered voice resonated with emotion.

"Tom, I'm sorry." She covered her face with her hands. "I'm scared, tired, and half the time I'm not sure if I'm doing the right thing. I'm trying to hold myself together, but I feel like a rubber band that's about to snap."

Tom pulled her close and held her against him. "You don't have to accept my help. My friendship is not conditional on that. Only, I worry about you, so I'm not sure that I'm going to be able to stay out of it completely."

She laughed softly, blinking back the tears. "We'll work together from now on. I'm sorry, Tom, I probably should have trusted you more."

"Will you trust me now and let me tell Denis what's happened?"

She took a deep breath and stepped away from him. "I don't suppose there'll be any harm in it now," she said almost to herself. "Okay. Do it."

"You'll trust me, but only if I tell you what I'm thinking and you happen to agree," he added wryly.

"It's not personal. I just happen to believe that two heads are better than one."

"Some things never change," he muttered, then gestured to a phone booth at the corner. "I'll use that. It'll involve fewer people. Then we'll head to your house."

As Ann walked with him to the telephone, Tom said, "I wonder what that missing tape contains and where it could be? We need to find the connection."

"And pray that meanwhile the kidnapper listens to my message and understands," Ann added quietly.

TOM STUDIED HIS OWN handwritten copy of the note Ann had received. The house was quiet now. Denis had come and gone, but his anger at Ann's actions had been evident. He'd sent Murphy and others over to the park, but they hadn't found the paper sack nor any witnesses who had noticed anyone hanging around. Finally, he'd gone to the park himself to see if there was anything further they could do there.

"If there's any way to do it, Denis will find out who this Artemis is. He's very thorough and most of all, he's one determined son of a gun," Tom said as he set the copy of the note down on the kitchen table. "What we need to do next is find out about the Jackson investigation. Now that I'm off the case, getting up-to-date information without having the captain find out is going to be tricky. I'm going to use your telephone; the CBI recorder only monitors incoming calls, so it'll be okay. I need to arrange an unofficial meeting with some friends of mine who are working on the burglary case. I think they'll help."

"That's good. While you take care of that, I'll head on to Jackson's neighborhood and see what I can learn about Lenora."

Tom glanced at his watch, then shook his head. "This wouldn't be a good time. The shops are starting to close and the restaurant owners and employees are busy getting ready for the dinner crowd. You'll have to wait until tomorrow." He dialed his friend's number, then waited.

Ann stepped out of the room, giving him greater privacy. She hoped he'd hurry. It was hard for her to wait with nothing constructive to do. A moment later he called out to her. "Would you like to go with me?" He smiled hesitantly.

"I'd love to. Are you sure they won't mind?"

"Having you along will show them that I trust you. That could come in handy later."

"Then let's go." She grabbed her purse from the table.

They headed past the college campus, toward an older, more run-down part of town. The neighborhood was filled with crumbling houses that screamed for upkeep beyond what the residents could provide. Old brick warehouses, formerly the sites of banks, hotels and well-established businesses, surrounded the section, once the pride of Crystal.

Tom turned through an alleyway as the setting sun came out from behind a cloud for one final burst of light. Squinting in the glare of the yellow-red glow, Tom approached the end of the narrow roadway.

Suddenly, a vehicle appeared before them, blocking their path. Menacing black figures leaped from the car, hazy silhouettes against the light of the sun.

Chapter Fifteen

Ann gripped the door handle, ready to make a run for it.

"It's about time, you guys," Tom yelled at the pair through the open window. "I thought I was going to have to drive around all night." He glanced over at Ann. "I'm sorry, did they scare you? These are my friends, Joe Garcia and Dan Rainer. I guess this was their idea of a joke."

Ann's glare was lethal. "Some joke. I thought we were going to be attacked."

The men got into the back seat of Tom's car. Both were dressed in worn jeans and dirty jogging shoes. The dark, Hispanic man was wearing a faded Broncos sweatshirt with the sleeves torn off, and his blond companion, a ragged blue T-shirt. To Ann they looked shifty enough to steal the hubcaps off a car.

"Hello, buddy boy. What's this about a favor?" Joe asked.

"I told you, I need the latest on the Jackson investigation," Tom said.

"You're not still working on the murder, are you?" Dan Ranier asked.

"No, let's say I've got a more personal stake in this."

Joe took a long look at Ann, then nodded. "Okay, but you never heard any of this from us. Captain Lambert would go through the roof on this one. Particularly if you ended up stepping on the toes of the CBI, *comprendes*?"

"You got it," Tom answered without hesitation.

He pulled several photocopies from his hip pocket. "Here's background data we collected on comic-book art when we went to talk to dealers about the stolen panels. It should give you a fairly good idea of the market value for original art of this kind. Jackson hit the jackpot with this stuff. And we've now linked Jackson to at least twenty residential burglaries."

"Hey, guys, I owe you one."

"Don't worry, we'll collect," Joe shot back. "Next time we need to have a roomful of stolen merchandise inventoried and catalogued on Friday or Saturday night, we'll know who to call."

Tom groaned. "Thanks. Your generosity is underwhelming."

Joe started to slide out of the back seat, then stopped and placed his hand on Ann's shoulder. "We're pulling for you and your little boy, ma'am. And don't worry, Keller's not much on personality, but he's a damn good cop."

Tom turned around. "Get back to work, you slug. Is this what the city pays you for?"

"Oooh," Joe said in a falsetto. "Isn't our language getting nasty. You'll be hearing from my union."

Tom watched the men return to their car and, in a squeal of tires, speed away. "Now, if by chance someone saw us meeting, they'll think it was either a police shakedown or a drug deal. Either way, they'll leave it alone."

"Your friends are nice, but—" Ann fumbled for the right word "—peculiar."

Tom laughed loudly. "I'll be sure and tell them. They'll love that."

Ann shook her head. Good-ole-boy humor. She'd never understood it.

They drove to Ann's house in silence as night slowly enveloped them. Ann tried to ignore the cold, empty feeling going home created within her. "I used to look forward to evenings at home with Matt. Now I dread the nights." She suppressed a shiver. "Tom, what do you think the kidnapper will do when he hears my tape? Do you think he'll even stop to listen to what I said?"

"That, I'm certain he'll do. He'll be curious, if nothing else. For all he knows, you've got the cassette he wants and you're negotiating a more favorable exchange."

"And once he hears it?"

Tom paused. He didn't want to lie to her. "I'm not sure. My best guess is that he'll either let Matt go or force you to search for the tape and take all the risks." He reached across the seat and took her hand. "But no matter what he does, Ann, I'll be right beside you to help you through it."

"When you answered the homicide call at my home that morning, you sure ended up with more than you bargained for," she observed wryly. "You've never wanted anyone to become dependent on you. When people got close, you pushed them away. Now you've ended up with precisely what you've been trying to avoid."

Tom pulled the car into her driveway and parked. He shifted to face her. "Maybe I'm not trying to avoid it anymore," he said slowly.

"Maybe? You're not sure?"

"It's not that simple for me. I like being a cop, and I'm aware of the uncertainties of my profession." He stared into the darkness, searching for the right words. "You and Matt deserve security and a life-style a cop could never provide. If we tried to make a go of it and something went wrong, Matt would be hurt the most."

"You're right." She sighed, then gave him a hesitant smile. "But you're not the only one with reasons for not wanting to get involved. After Warren's death, Matt and I grew very close. Someday, I know, he'll grow up and away from me, but right now we have a very special relationship. I'm not sure I'm ready to share that."

"Do you think Matt wants a new daddy?"

"He says he does, but I don't know if he's aware of all the changes that having one would make in our life. He dreams about a fantasy father he could be very close to. But not all men want that kind of relationship with somebody else's little boy."

The moments of silence stretched on. "It's all so logical. So why do I think I'm falling in love with you?" Not giving her a chance to protest, Tom gathered her against him and took her mouth with his own.

Tom groaned when instead of resistance, he felt her melt against him. He tore his lips from hers and rained small, warm kisses down the soft column of her neck. He claimed her mouth again a heartbeat later, as if wanting to memorize the taste of her forever.

He felt an urgent fire raging through him. It had been a mistake to kiss her this way. He'd wanted her before, and now it was worse.

"Did you mean it?" she said, her breath coming in uneven gasps.

"I am falling in love with you," he answered, knowing what she meant.

"But it doesn't make sense. It's no good between us," she protested.

Imprisoning her in his arms, Tom used his lips to rub hers apart. His kiss took everything, but gave everything in return. He drew her tongue into his mouth, then sucked it gently until she was shivering uncontrollably in his arms.

Then, without warning, he released her. "Don't tell me that it's no good between us! The problem is that it's too damn good!"

Breathless and wanting, Ann moved away from him. "It's wonderful physically," she rationalized for both their benefits. "It's an explosion of hormones."

"Really?" he countered. "Is that why I stopped? And is that why finding your son and taking care of you seem to have become the two major concerns in my life?"

"I—" She snapped her mouth shut. He was right, but she wasn't about to say anything else. "I better go."

"I'll walk you to the door."

A minute later, she was inside her home. Tom remained on the porch, viewing her through the screen door. He had calmed down somewhat, but his body still felt taut with desire. He wanted to change the subject. "What are your plans for tomorrow?"

"I'm going to spend the morning tracking down Lenora."

"Good. I'll review this file tonight, and pass it on to you before I return it. Then we'll see what sort of plan we can come up with."

Their eyes met for one brief instant, then wordlessly Tom turned and walked back to his car. It was going to be one hell of a night. Maybe after a cold shower he'd feel better. Then again, maybe not. Swearing eloquently, he switched on the ignition and pulled out of the driveway.

BETWEEN WORRIES ABOUT MATT and thoughts of Tom, Ann's night was restless. When morning finally came, she was eager for a chance to get started and divert her thoughts.

She set out, wearing a pair of leather walking shoes with soft soles and comfortable slacks. The search for Lenora was bound to be difficult and Ann wanted to be prepared.

Hours later, after walking for miles in Jackson's neighborhood, she'd discovered nothing new except the pain of aching feet. It was nearing the end of the lunch trade, and she wanted to check one more restaurant before she took a break.

The national-chain steakhouse she was going to next did a brisk lunch business. There were a large number of cars still in the parking lot, even though it was approaching two o'clock. She stepped through the heavy wooden door as two businessmen were leaving, and stopped by the counter in the small lobby. No one was behind the cash register or even in the room, so she went to look for the hostess who seated the customers.

The dining area was much more dimly lit than the outer lobby, and after the bright sunlight outside, Ann was almost blind. Standing still for a few seconds, she gave her eyes a chance to adjust. The diners were separated into individual booths by translucent gray Plexiglas partitions.

Walking around the aisle, she finally noticed a well-dressed young woman with a pad and pen assisting an older couple to their table. Ann waited until the woman left the table and began walking toward her.

"Excuse me," Ann said cheerfully, "are you the hostess?"

"Yes, ma'am. I can find you a table right now. Thanks for waiting."

"Actually, I'm looking for a friend of a friend named Lenora. She wasn't at her apartment when I dropped by, and my friend mentioned she sometimes comes here for lunch. She's tall and athletic looking, with long blond hair."

They walked back toward the lobby. "Let me think a minute, her name sounds familiar." The hostess stopped and looked down a side aisle at four booths. "I think the lady you're looking for is seated at the end booth, alone. She's changed her hair recently. It's dark now and much shorter than it used to be."

"Thanks very much," Ann managed to say, her heart beginning to race. She wanted to run to a phone and call Tom immediately, but she noticed the hostess watching her expectantly. Turning, she walked toward the last booth in the rear. Ann approached the dimly lit area slowly, wondering what she'd do or say.

As she stepped past the partition, she froze. No one was there, only the empty dishes and silverware of a just-completed meal. Ann picked up an almost empty water glass by the very bottom, and poured the remaining ice and water into the plate. Gently, she lowered the glass into the center compartment of her purse. As she zipped the pocket shut, she noticed two young men at the booth across the aisle watching her curiously.

Smiling at them, she hurried back toward the lobby. Maybe Lenora, if that had really been her, was still in the area. As Ann reached the main aisle, just steps from the lobby, she saw the hostess pointing back at her. A tall, dark-haired woman in black slacks and a green blouse was looking her way.

Ann broke into a run, but the woman spotted her then and rushed to the door.

"Lenora, wait," Ann cried out, dashing past the surprised hostess. The heavy door slammed in front of her, and she hit it hard with her arms, bouncing back a step.

"What's going on?" the hostess demanded.

Ann, halfway out the door, barely heard her. As she emerged, she spotted Lenora running full speed down the opposite sidewalk.

"Wait," Ann yelled, starting out after her. Dodging behind a passing car, Ann ran across the street. When she reached the sidewalk on the other side, Lenora was half a block away.

Ann hurtled down the sidewalk, sidestepping pedestrians and customers emerging from stores.

Ahead, Lenora was gaining ground. Obviously determined to get away, she was sending those in her path crashing to the sidewalk or bouncing off parked cars. Ann tried to avoid those who'd been knocked down, apologizing as she ran.

Then Lenora turned left around a corner and disappeared from sight. When Ann reached the corner a few seconds later, Lenora had vanished. Making an arbitrary decision, Ann sprinted down the side street. As she reached the spot where the alley joined the street, a massive delivery truck pulled out in front of her. Unable to stop, Ann collided with the cab of the truck, stumbling up onto the running board and slamming against the passenger's door.

"What the hell!" the shocked driver exclaimed.

"Sorry." Ann rubbed her shoulder, which she'd banged against the truck, and stepped back from the vehicle.

Impatient to resume the chase, she started to dash around the front of the truck. But the driver, impatient, too, had started to move forward. The truck rocked as he slammed on the brakes again.

The driver stuck his head out the window, his face red with anger. "Damn it lady," he roared, "stand still so I can hit you!"

"Sorry again," Ann shouted as she ran on.

Glancing farther down the street, she could see no sign of Lenora. Realizing she'd lost the woman, Ann returned dejectedly to her car. At least she now had the woman's fingerprints. Perhaps the CBI and police would be able to learn more about her.

Remembering her collision with the truck, Ann checked her purse. The glass she'd taken from the table had broken into three large pieces and several tiny ones. Her heart sank, but she tried to hold on to the hope that perhaps finger-prints could still be collected.

Ann called Tom from the car, but he wasn't in. Dialing Denis Arteaga, she related the events, concluding that Lenora must have mistaken her for the police.

"Not necessarily," Denis answered. "She might have recognized you from the newspaper photos. Why didn't you call Tom or me first?"

She explained the situation at the time. "I've still got the glass, though it is in pieces."

"My temporary office is at the state police building. Bring it here. I'll interview the restaurant employees, especially the hostess. Then, I'll speak with Tom."

Twenty-five minutes later, after dropping off the glass, Ann started the drive back home. Her spirits were leaden. It had been over twenty-four hours since the kidnapper had last contacted her. Fear, like an ice-cold dagger, stabbed at her soul. She swallowed back the tears she felt building. She needed to hold on and not slack up on her efforts to find Matt.

She was near the house when her mobile telephone rang. "Hello?"

"Ann, it's Tom. I've got an idea and I'm going to take the afternoon off so I can pursue it. Can you be ready to go to Denver with me in a half hour? There's a comic-book convention there. It starts this evening, and I've been told any-one who has anything to do with comic-book collectibles will be there."

"I'm ready to go whenever you want," she replied flatly. "Just tell me where to meet you."

"I'll come pick you up, then you can tell me how it went for you today. Denis called a few minutes ago and said you almost met up with Lenora. I want to hear what hap-pened."

"There's not much to tell," she warned with a sigh.

Ann pulled into her driveway and parked. Her eyes focused on the mailbox as she rushed up the path to her door. Perhaps today... But there was nothing out of the ordinary there. Taking the mail with her, she walked inside. A moment later, all the possibilities had been checked. No message had been left on her machine or under either of her doors. Her heart plummeted.

Ann curled up in one corner of the sofa and hugged herself. Not knowing was the worst part. She rocked back and forth and wished Tom had already arrived. It seemed easier to be strong when he was around.

She stood and forced herself to get busy. It was inactivity that always got her into trouble. Ann walked to the kitchen and fixed a fresh batch of lemonade. She'd just finished when she heard a car pull up outside.

Ann didn't wait for Tom to come inside. Instead, she went out to meet him. She was about six feet from the car when she stopped in midstep and stared at the stranger before her. A thick black mustache practically obscured his face, and his eyes were shielded by dark sunglasses.

"Hey, it's me. Relax," a familiar voice assured her.

She stared at him for a moment, then when he took off his sunglasses, she smiled. "Good grief. I didn't recognize you!" As their eyes met, she felt overcome with awkwardness. After yesterday, this was the last thing she'd ever expected to say to Tom. "Why on earth are you disguised like that?"

"It's added insurance, that's all. I brought some stuff for you, too. We're going to be posing as amateur investors with money to spend. A buddy of mine on the force has a brother who's a collector. He's agreed to meet us at the convention and introduce us to the major dealers." He handed her a small gym bag. "Here. This is so they won't recognize you from the papers."

She picked up the auburn wig in the bag by one strand. "Ugh. This is a great color for a horse, but I'm not sure it fits a person." She went back inside the house with him.

"It'll look great. One of our police-woman decoys with your coloring uses it, and believe me she gets offers!"

"Wait, you mean a woman posing as a prostitute uses this?" Ann's voice rose an octave.

"Calm down," he said, laughing. "You're not going to be wearing the rest of the clothes she uses on her assignments. And you can use the prop glasses, too."

Ann returned a few minutes later. "Try not to wince," she cautioned. Long locks of auburn hair framed her face and fell softly over her shoulders.

Tom whistled appreciatively. "Hey, you look great."

She gave him an incredulous look. "Ugh. Get glasses, will you?"

"I mean it."

She picked up her purse from the table and walked to the door. "Come on, and quit staring. I feel self-conscious enough as it is."

Ann looked good no matter what she was wearing. Her shyness made her all the more tantalizing and provocatively sexy. Tom made a mental note not to let her out of his sight. "Tell me all the details about your encounter with Lenora. Denis and Bill are out in that neighborhood looking for her now."

"I hope they find her. Maybe she can identify Artemis or give us a clue that can help us find Matt." She shook her head. "I tried so hard to catch her. I almost got myself killed, but I still failed."

Tom stopped abruptly. *"Almost got yourself killed?"* he roared.

She gave him the details, and then noticed his silence as he walked around to her side of the car. "Say something," she insisted.

His eyes blazed. "I'm doing my best to keep you safe, but you keep going headlong into danger. What are you trying to do to me, woman?"

"To *you*?" Her voice rose. "Do you think it was fun for me? Instead of yelling, you could try comforting me a little."

"And who's going to comfort me if something happens to you?"

For the first ten minutes of the journey, neither spoke. Finally, Tom broke the silence. "I'm sorry I yelled at you."

"Do you finally understand that I didn't have a choice?"

"Don't push it," he warned. "I said I was sorry."

She smiled.

Another fifteen minutes elapsed. "No word from the kidnapper still?" he asked, glancing over at her.

"No, I checked as soon as I got home. You know, I try not to hope for it. I swear to myself that I'm not, but then when I check and there's nothing, it just about kills me."

"Try to remember that the waiting game is meant to unnerve you. Keep in mind that it also gives us more time to find him."

She leaned back against the seat, fighting the weariness that came from repeated disappointments. "Tell me about this convention we're going to. What do you expect or hope to find there?"

"I'm not sure. I want to check out people who deal in art panels. If we can find someone who specializes in locating specific items for collectors, that might give us a lead. With the kind of money that's involved in this, some of the middle men may not care how they get the merchandise."

The drive to Denver, out of the foothills of the Rockies, was pleasant. By the time they arrived, Ann was eager to get started. The hope that they'd be able to find something that would bring her son back had slowly renewed her energy.

Tom paid their admission fees, and they went inside the grand ballroom of the turn-of-the century hotel. Tom glanced around, then led Ann to a booth manned by three comic-book artists. Each of the men were working up sketches of their famed Super Slug, the wormly crusader against crime. Fans clustered around, waiting to purchase the work.

"Jerry?" Tom looked at the two men managing the cash box.

"That's me," one answered.

"I'm Tom Hastings," Tom said, using a prearranged false name, "your brother's friend."

"Gotcha," Jerry answered, then turned the cash box to the man beside him. "Come on. I'll introduce you around."

Hundreds of people hurried about, and their enthusiasm charged the air. The crowd was comprised of an odd assortment of youngsters and adults. Some were looking for comics essential to complete their collections, others for assorted paraphernalia ranging from T-shirts to sketches. Smaller rooms beyond the main display area held discussion groups of artists, writers and enthusiasts.

Three hours later, tired and frustrated at having turned up no new leads, Tom and Ann left and began the drive back to Crystal. Ann was silent, staring at the gloomy darkness encasing the car.

"Ann, I'm sorry. I wish we had discovered something. But it wasn't a total loss. We did get a feel for what interests people associated with the comic-book industry. Remember Jerry told us *Detective Comics No. 27*, which originally sold for a dime back in 1939, is now going for as much as twenty-five-thousand dollars because it marks Batman's first appearance in a comic book. Collectors can sure become obsessed with getting the editions they want and that drives the price way up. When the money's this high, it transcends a hobby.

Tom glanced at Ann, then focused back on the road. "When Jackson broke into that publisher's house, he took a virtual gold mine. The one-of-a-kind art panels he stole marked the first appearance anywhere of Manstalker. The original art is worth much more than a mint-condition copy of the issue it appears in. Ironically, someone told me the artist who did that issue eventually lost his job and committed suicide right in front of his family. And a tragedy like that makes the panels worth even more to the collectors. Can you believe it?"

Ann finally spoke. "But what's a tape got to do with any of this? And where's Matt? And why hasn't the kidnapper contacted me?" she asked in a whisper-thin voice.

"I wish I had the answers, Ann. All we can do is continue to work on the leads we have."

"So what's next?" she asked wearily.

"If Jackson's fence has the contacts needed to unload stolen art panels, some of the local comic-book vendors must have heard of him. Let's see if one of those merchants can lead us to the man. Fences are very cautious. They like to *know* the people they do business with. It's quite possible Jackson's fence will be able to tell us about the tape."

Hearing his call sign come over the radio, Tom picked up the hand-held mike. In one brief sentence he acknowledged the code, then placed the microphone back in its holder. "There's an interesting turn of events," he said. "Your car's turned up."

"That's wonderful! Were they able to get any prints from it?"

"No," he answered flatly. "It's been burned to a crisp."

Chapter Sixteen

The next morning when Tom pulled into her driveway, Ann rushed out to meet him. "Can we go see my car now? I still can't believe they actually burned it!"

"Slow down. It's not going anywhere," he answered with a rueful smile.

"I know." She grew somber. "But Saturday's always been my special day with Matt," she explained, "and to be honest, I can't stand to be home right now."

He reached over and gave her hand a squeeze. "We'll find him soon, Ann. Just hang in there."

It took almost a half hour before they arrived at an area outside the city where people sometimes dumped trash. "This place used to be really nice once, only nowadays it's a mess."

"There's Denis, near that ridge." She gestured just ahead.

"I see he's got the crime-scene unit out here. Let's see what else they turned up."

As Tom and Ann walked up the dirt track, Denis met them. "I hope you guys turned up something interesting at that convention," he muttered.

"Nothing specific," Tom answered. "We did meet quite a few vendors, though. Maybe we can track down Jackson's fence through them."

Ann stared aghast at the burned-out wreck down the slope from them. "Is that my car?"

Denis nodded. "Our people made the ID based on the serial numbers found on the engine block. We figure that whoever stole your car drove it out here, ripped through the seats and upholstery, then torched it."

"Do you think there were at least two people involved, one in a second car?" Tom asked.

"It would have been easier, but much more conspicuous, too. It makes just as much sense to say the thief came here alone and walked back to town. The closest bus stop is only a mile down the road, by the gas station. We'll question people who use that stop, and the bus drivers. Maybe they noticed a stranger, or someone who looked suspicious."

"Have you turned up anything more on my son?" Ann asked, knowing the answer yet unable to keep from asking the question.

Denis's gaze was sympathetic. "We've interviewed several of the joggers who frequent the park where you left the tape, and several of the local residents. So far we haven't turned up any leads, but you never know. All it takes is one person."

"But what about the notes I've received, or the ads Artemis said he'd place? Surely you've found something there," she insisted.

Denis shook his head. "I'm sorry, no. The notes were all typed on different typewriters on a common brand of white paper. There were no latent fingerprints, only yours. Whoever delivered them must have been wearing gloves or handling the paper only by the edges.

The knot in Ann's throat turned the size of a tennis ball. She didn't trust her voice. Wordlessly, she nodded.

"What about Lenora, Denis?" Tom asked. "Have you guys turned up anything there or been able to get fingerprints from the glass Ann gave you?"

"Well, she certainly was in Crystal yesterday. The hostess confirmed her identity, but she didn't know her last name. The woman paid in cash, so there are no checks or credit cards. As for the glass, we got a few good fingerprints and are trying to rule out the restaurant employees." His gaze shifted to Ann. "But even if we find hers, it's no guarantee we'll get any further. Unless she's got a record or has been printed before, we still won't know much."

Denis glanced at Tom. "We've started a statewide search, checking all of Jackson's known associates. Someone's bound to know more about his girlfriend."

Denis loosened his tie, uncomfortable in the heat. Seeing the look on Ann's face broke through the impassiveness he tried to project as a professional. "I know this is very hard on you, but don't lose hope. The kidnapper wants something from you so, believe it or not, you do have some leverage. We'll make it work for you."

If she hadn't blown it all already. The thought depressed Ann so much she turned away from both of the men and walked back to Tom's car.

Tom joined her several minutes later. "I'm going to meet Denis at his office in an hour. He's going to use the modem there and link up with the CBI's computer. Maybe it'll have some information that will help us find Jackson's fence." He glanced at her as he switched on the ignition. "Ann, you look like you're ready to collapse. I know you don't want to go home, so how about if I drop you off at my apartment? You can watch some TV there and maybe try to relax." He started the drive toward Crystal.

"I'm going to go with you and help."

He shook his head. "This time I have to say no. It's not my office or people we're working with. Denis is a friend, but he likes to stick to the book on his cases." He stopped the car at a red light.

Once again, a faint ray of hope broke through her anxiety. "Then I'll go home and see if the kidnapper has tried to contact me. Maybe he'll give us something to work with."

"Ann, you're getting your hopes up again," Tom cautioned. "You can't give this person that much power over you."

"He already has infinite power over me. Don't you understand? The kidnapper is the only link I have to my son. He's got me exactly where he wants me."

Silence stretched between them as they traveled to her home. Tom pulled to a stop in the driveway, then turned to face her. "Will you be all right?"

"I won't be okay until my son's back," Ann answered, "but I'll handle it."

"If you are contacted, call Denis's office." Seeing her nod, he continued. "After I finish there, I'll be going to the station. I can get some work done on the case today. The captain isn't there on Saturdays. If you need me for anything, call."

"All right, thanks." Ann left his car and walked up the drive.

Gathering the morning paper from her front yard, she hurried inside. Ann rushed first to the answering machine, then to the kitchen table to study the personals. Once again, there had been no message from the kidnapper. She bit down on her lip.

Suddenly the telephone rang and she jumped.

"Ann? It's Cindy from the office."

She recognized the voice. Why was the receptionist from Randall and Associates calling her? "Hello, Cindy. What can I do for you?"

"A man phoned and left a message for you here. He said it was urgent and that I should pass it along to you as soon as possible."

Her fingers clenched around the receiver. "I'm listening."

"His name is Chuck. He said you'd know who he was."

So he hadn't been fooled after all when she'd visited him in disguise earlier with Tom.

"He wants to have a private conversation with you about Jackson. You're to meet him at twelve-thirty sharp at his other business location, a warehouse called Chuck's Service Center." Cindy gave her the address, then added, "Ann, if it was me, I wouldn't meet this guy alone."

"Don't worry. I know what to do." Ann could feel her body shaking. She'd meet with him, of course. She couldn't afford not to. But she'd let Tom and Denis know exactly where she was going and why. With them close by, she wouldn't have anything to worry about.

Ann grabbed her keys and purse and rushed outside to her car. It was close to noon. By the time she arrived at the warehouse, it would be twelve-thirty. She picked up her mobile telephone and dialed Denis's number. A civilian operator informed her that he was on his way to the office. Tom also hadn't arrived there yet.

"Please tell Special Agent Arteaga that Ann Dixon called. I'm on my way to Chuck's Service Center. Chuck has some information for me about his former employee."

Dialing again, she called the police station. Maybe Tom had changed his mind and decided to stop there first.

Detective Glenn answered. "He's not here, Mrs. Dixon. Would you like to leave a message?"

She considered her words carefully. No one in the department was supposed to know Tom was still working on the Jackson case. "Tell him that I'll be over at Chuck's Service Center for a private business meeting. If he could meet me somewhere in the area, I'd appreciate it."

"Ma'am, the owner of that service center is not very reputable. You really shouldn't go over there alone."

"I'm a real-estate agent, Detective Glenn," she said, trying to mask her real reason for going. "This is what I do for a living. I can take care of myself."

He didn't comment. "I'll pass this on to Tom as soon as he calls in."

She was scared and excited. Maybe she'd finally be able to find a lead that would take her to Matt. She tried to will her hands to stop shaking. She had to go to this meeting looking cool and very confident, so her emotions couldn't be used against her.

Ann arrived at the warehouse a short time later. A small sign overhead read:

CHUCK'S SERVICE CENTER
The Birthplace of Fine Used Cars

She drove inside the large, fenced parking area and pulled into an empty spot. A number of older-model cars were parked nearby. As she approached the door marked Office, she could smell the strong scent of oil and automobile exhaust.

She knocked, and the door swung open slightly. "Chuck?" she said as she walked inside, hearing the hollow sound of her voice and her heels clacking against the concrete floor. "Hello? Is anyone here?"

She glanced around the garage area. Suddenly a man stepped out from behind a stack of barrels. "Tsk, tsk. What's a pretty lady like you doing out here all alone?"

She stepped back instinctively as the man approached. "Where's Chuck?"

A second man appeared behind her, blocking her escape. "How nice of you to join us," he said softly.

Ann realized with sudden clarity that she'd walked right into a trap. Her heart pounded against her ribs. She tried to run, but one of the men grabbed her. Pinning her arms at her sides, he held her against him. "Now don't panic," he said, tightening his hold. He reeked of tobacco and sweat.

"Let go of me." She suddenly relaxed her body, then stepped down hard on her captor's instep. The man let go as he bent over, yelling an obscenity.

Ann made another desperate dash for the door, but two more men appeared, standing in her way. She tried to dodge past the short, balding one, but he grabbed her arm and twisted it painfully behind her back. "Feisty little thing," he whispered in her ear, then laughed harshly.

She tried to aim a kick backward, but he shifted away from it and pulled her to his side. When she continued to struggle, he brought his mouth close to her face and said, "Keep it up and I'll rearrange your pretty face."

He dragged her over to a desk where the eldest of the four men stood. "We really *don't* want to hurt you. All we want you to do is phone Tom Keller and ask him to meet you here. But if you let him know that anything's wrong, you'll be the first one to regret it."

"I'm not calling anyone. If you want him here, call him yourself."

The man by the desk gave her a lifeless smile. He pulled a large folding knife from his pocket, then flipped the six-inch blade open. "We can do this nicely, or make things very unpleasant for you. It's your choice." He took the cold steel blade and pressed it flat against her face.

"Why do you want him here?" she choked out, trying not to move. She needed to play for time. Maybe Tom *was* on his way over. If he wasn't and he still hadn't received her message, she was in big trouble.

"Our reasons don't concern you." He moved the blade to the other side of her face, then slowly dragged the point across her skin.

Ann screamed as loud as she could, and the knife was drawn back as someone clamped a hand over her mouth.

"If she keeps this up, someone's bound to hear her," the man behind Ann warned, almost choking her with his sweaty hand.

"Gag her," the one with the knife ordered. "And Al, find a spot near the door and keep a lookout."

She jerked her head from side to side trying to prevent them from putting the oily rag in her mouth. Her efforts were useless, and a moment later she nearly choked on the foul taste.

She struggled against the man holding her prisoner as the eldest of the men stood at her side again, blade open. Grabbing Ann by the hair and holding her steady, he showed her the saw-toothed top edge of the blade, then ran that side of the knife downward along her cheek. It was under enough pressure to scratch, but not enough to cut. "What a shame it'll be to leave scars on your pretty face."

Her eyes were watering from the tug upon her hair, but she didn't dare try to move.

"Get away from her." Tom's voice echoed clearly from the door to the warehouse. A second later, he stepped into view, gun drawn.

She couldn't shout a warning. Helpless, she saw Al, the men's lookout, come up from behind Tom swinging a length of pipe. In a desperate gambit, Ann stared wide-eyed, right past Tom.

Alerted, Tom jumped to one side. Although he evaded the blow, the pipe caught the tip of his gun's barrel. The weapon spun out of his hand and across the concrete floor. Unarmed, Tom faced his adversary.

"It looks like Keller followed her here anyway, so we got him right where we want him," the eldest man said. The other men laughed, their attention diverted. "Good thing Al was over there. Losing that firepower is going to dampen Keller's spirits. Al will be able to take him for sure."

Ann saw Tom feint a move toward the entrance and deliver a hard kick to Al's chest, sending him reeling backward. The pipe fell out of his hands, clanking to the floor.

Recapturing his balance, Tom's assailant hurled himself toward Tom's gun. Tom kicked it out of his reach.

"I'll stay with her. You two help Al," the eldest one ordered. He wore wire-rimmed glasses and had an almost cherubic look. Yet Ann sensed he was the most lethal of all. "You stay very still while my friends tend to the cop," he said, holding the knife at her throat. "Then we're all going to have a little party."

Ann felt the tears washing down her cheeks. It was three against one; she had to do something to help Tom.

She saw the heaviest of the three dive at Tom, knocking him to the floor. Immediately, the other began to kick him.

"We have a message for you and the lady, Keller. Keep your nose out of the Jackson case. You think you can remember that?"

Al, bleeding from the nose, kicked Tom viciously in the stomach. "Feel good? You'll have plenty of time to think about it when you're both in the hospital."

Tom trapped the next kick with his hands and with a twist of his wrists, sent the man spiraling to the floor.

Anxious about the fight, the man holding Ann angled sideways, leaning toward the open door. As he did, the knife was shifted a few inches away from her face.

Reacting instantly, Ann struck the man's hand and jumped to one side. The man slashed at her, but she leaned away from the blade and kicked hard. Her heel smashed into his groin.

The man doubled over instantly, gasping and heaving. Virtually helpless with pain, he dropped the knife. Without hesitation, Ann scooped it up. Yanking the gag out of her mouth, she ran to help Tom.

One of the attackers, hearing her, turned to face the new threat. Tom, back on his feet, slipped under an assailant's punch and grabbed him by the shoulder. With a hard push, he threw the man headlong into the back legs of the one confronting Ann. Both men fell to the floor in a heap.

"My gun," Tom yelled.

Ann realized it was only a few feet behind her.

The two men scrambled to their feet, intercepting Tom before he could rush forward. The third one, still standing, came toward Ann menacingly. Unable to turn away, Ann forced him to keep his distance by threatening him with the knife.

As she struggled to keep him from getting past her, she saw the other two turn on Tom. They flanked him and when he knocked one of them backward, the other caught Tom with a punch, knocking him down again.

When the man in front of her lunged for her arm, Ann threw the knife in desperation. The throw was hard but wild, and although it missed her attacker, it managed to strike the man behind him in the shoulder. Tom's assailant cried out, reaching back blindly to extract the blade.

As her adversary turned around, Ann dove toward the gun. A second later she rose to her knees with it firmly in hand, then fired two rounds into the air. The man before her jumped away and sought cover.

"Get away from him," Ann yelled at the man still menacing Tom. "I'll shoot!" She fired another round and it went into the wall inches from where he stood.

The men scrambled toward the door, bumping into each other in their rush to escape. The one the knife had hit was still yelling. Tom jumped to his feet, but then grabbed his side with a groan.

Ann rushed toward him. "You need a doctor." Gun still in hand, she pointed to his side. "You're bleeding!"

He took the gun from her. "I'll bleed a lot more if that goes off," he muttered. "Come on. We'll use my car and see if we can catch them."

"*Catch* them? Are you crazy? I want to lose them!" She held on to his arm. "Besides, what would you do if you found them? There's still four of them and only one of you." She placed his arm over her shoulders. "Come on. Let's go find a doctor. You look like hell."

"No, I'm okay. I've learned to take a few punches without getting hurt. If you bend with the blows, nothing breaks." He took a deep breath, then moaned slightly. "You do bruise like crazy, though."

Suddenly they heard footsteps rushing toward them. Tom shoved Ann to one side, gun aimed at the door.

Bob Glenn appeared a moment later, then froze. "It's me, Tom."

"What are you doing here? And where's Denis Arteaga? He was supposed to meet me. Right after you gave me Ann's message, he got ahold of me on the radio. He'd heard what Ann was planning to do and also figured something wasn't right."

"Denis called to tell me he wasn't going to be here in time. He got stuck behind a traffic accident blocking a bridge. I got here as fast as I could." Bob holstered his gun as he approached Tom. "I tried to catch one of the guys who ran out of here, but he disappeared." Glenn stared at them both, then shook his head. "Tom, you look like hell."

Tom straightened, refusing any help. "Okay, you two. We've established that I don't look gorgeous, so drop it," he growled.

"You're a surly son of a gun," Glenn teased. "No wonder they wanted to beat your brains in."

Tom glared at him, but refused to comment. Suddenly they heard a muffled voice from somewhere nearby.

Tom turned toward a narrow door set in one wall. "Someone's in that closet," he said quietly. Gesturing for Ann to move out of their line of fire, he started forward.

Glenn stopped him. "You stay here. Cover me. I can move faster than you."

Glenn angled sideways to the door, then threw it open. A bound and gagged figure was huddled on the floor inside.

Recognizing the man, Tom undid the gag. "Well, Chuck, what are you doing here?"

"What's been going on?" he croaked. "I came by to check my building and lock up for the weekend, when some guys jumped me. Then it sounded like there was a war going on out here."

"It'll go down in our report, Chuck," Tom stated. "But if I ever find out that you had anything to do with this mess today..."

"Me? Look at this bump on my head!" He touched his neck gingerly, then showed Tom the blood. "I hate violence! It's bad for business."

"You answered the call officially, Bob. How about taking his statement and making out the report?" Glenn nodded his assent, waving Tom away.

Tom walked Ann to her car. "Now, I want to know why you came here without me."

She recounted the entire story. "But you can't complain. I *did* call you."

"You couldn't have waited?" he countered, then held up one hand. "Never mind. I've got to clean up and call Denis." He waited as she eased herself behind the wheel. "Bob will file this as his call, so hopefully the captain won't take too close a look at the report. I'd hate to have to explain why you and I were both here."

"Well, at least we have a lead now." Her brow furrowed. "Only it doesn't make sense. The kidnapper wants me to find the missing tape. Yet we're also being warned that if we look into Jackson's business, we'll be risking our lives. How are we supposed to do one without the other?"

"It looks like we're dealing with more than one group," Tom said softly. "And that means we're vulnerable no matter which way we turn."

ALTHOUGH TOM HAD RETURNED to the office claiming he was fine, Ann hadn't been able to stop worrying about him. Searching for Matt was becoming more dangerous for both of them. Somehow, she needed to find a way to tip the scales in her favor.

Slowly, an idea began to form in her mind. She could talk to the comic-book vendors in their area as a real-estate agent. If she piqued their curiosity by claiming an investor was interested in their properties, she might get a tour of their businesses.

And if she could get them talking, she might hear or see something useful. If the rest of the stolen art panels had been for sale, she felt certain they would have changed hands during the convention.

Ann dressed in her work blazer and a skirt. She covered the scratches the knife point had made with makeup, then put on the auburn wig and prop glasses Tom had loaned her and scrutinized her appearance until she was satisfied she wouldn't be recognized. Armed with the page from her phone book that listed the comic-book vendors in the area, she hurried to the car, ready to pursue her own leads.

Most of the stores that specialized in comic books were open on Saturday. There were only five, but as the hours ticked by, a pattern began to emerge. The owners were willing to talk to her, but she was learning absolutely nothing of value.

When she finally reached the last name on her list, a sense of hopelessness engulfed her. The idea just wasn't working. She walked inside the smallest of the retail shops she'd been to and glanced around. A young boy was sitting behind the counter reading the latest issue of *Powerhouse Mouse*.

"I'd like to see the owner or the manager, please."

A man peered out of the back office. "That's me, lady. I'm Mark Dobbs, owner and manager. What can I do for you?"

Ann went through her rehearsed speech and flashed the man her best professional smile. "I'd love to take a look at your shop."

He came out and stood behind the counter. "'Fraid there's not much to see. There's the front room and my office here. That's about it."

He was a large man, though not in stature. He barely reached five foot three, but he must have weighed close to one hundred and eighty pounds. In the breast pocket of his T-shirt were two chocolate candy bars.

"How about storage areas?" she encouraged. "You must have a wealth of that here to keep your inventory."

He shrugged. "A few closets, that's all. I don't keep that much merchandise on hand. Except for our special collection in the glass case, what I can't sell, I get rid of."

She walked around the shop, as if browsing. "I love some of these posters. They almost look like originals."

"Some of the pen-and-ink drawings *are* originals by the artists who created the characters. The majority of them, however, are lithographs. They're less expensive, easier for me to sell."

"You know what I think would be interesting to own? The original art work that actually makes up a page of a comic book."

"Art panels," he said. "That's what they're called." He began to unwrap one of the candy bars in his pocket. The heat inside the small store had taken its toll on it, however. Globs of chocolate stuck to the paper and to his fingers.

Ann tried not to turn away in disgust. "Are they expensive?"

"It depends on the artist and the subject matter. I've got one panel available right now. I could show it to you if you like," he offered.

She could barely contain her excitement. "Sure."

He pulled a moist towelette from a container on the front desk, wiped his hands, then waved them around. "I can't afford to have anything damage the merchandise," he explained. "You'll have to wipe your hands, too, and let them air dry if you want to touch the panel."

She followed his example, though she wasn't really interested in handling it at all. If it turned out to be a panel from *Manstalker*, she'd leave and call Tom and Denis immediately.

The man walked with her to the display case and unlocked it. "Here it is. This is from the horror comic book *Jack-O-Lantern*."

Her shoulders slumped as her hopes quickly faded into thin air.

He scowled. "Hey, so it's a brand-new comic book. You never know. This could become a collector's item, and then the price would shoot up in no time at all." Seeing he'd still not managed to interest her, he relocked the case and pulled the other candy bar from his pocket. "So what does this client of yours want to offer me for my shop?"

"I'm not sure. We'll work up an offer, then let you know."

She went directly to her car, then back home hoping that a new note had arrived. As she pulled into her driveway, she saw Joan turning away from her front door. Ann pulled the wig off quickly and left it on the seat.

As she straightened up, her friend smiled and waved. "Ann, I've been so worried about you! You haven't stopped by or called."

Ann stepped out of the car and walked up to Joan. After seeing there was no note on the steps, she asked Joan to come in with her into the den. "I'm tired, but I can't sleep. I'm restless, but no matter how much I pace, I can't get it out of my system."

"There's been no further news?"

Ann started to tell Joan about the notes, then stopped. "Nothing has changed," she answered. "The only thing I know for sure is that Matt's kidnapping is connected to that murdered man."

"Ann, be very careful who you place your trust in. You've got the CBI working on this and the cops. Those groups compete with each other as a matter of form. Don't let them play games with Matt's life. And don't let them con you. They're trained to get the responses they want from people. Remember that and stay on your guard." She stood up. "I better go back home. I've got a client coming by soon. But please, if there is *any* news, call me."

Ann nodded. "You know I will." She stood by the door. "I really wish the kidnapper would stop this war of nerves and contact me. The waiting is eating me up inside. I get so scared! I want to do something, anything, to get Matt back."

"You'll hear from him, Ann. Just hang on." Joan walked to the door. "Only remember, trust your instincts. The authorities are just doing a job and maybe thinking more in terms of promotions or making a name for themselves. Your only concern is Matt. That gives you an advantage over them."

"I won't forget," Ann replied. Walking back to the kitchen, she picked up her purse. "I'm going to go over to the police station right now and see if they've learned anything new. I can't just sit around here." Ann went outside with Joan.

"Good luck," Joan said as Ann got into her car.

Ann drove to the police station, her mind on everything Joan had said. Joan meant well, but her fear for Matt's life only resulted in compounding Ann's own. She couldn't handle that at the moment.

Ann pulled into the station and parked near the side door. She had just started down the corridor when she saw the vendor she'd visited earlier, Mark Dobbs, come storming out of Tom's office. A moment later, Tom appeared at the doorway.

Ann ducked back into an adjacent hallway, but she knew Dobbs would see her the moment he came by. Desperate, she glanced around. Near the small coffee machine next to the wall was a magazine. Making a quick grab for it, she leaned casually against the wall and held it in front of her face, as if reading intently. Relief swept over her as she heard footsteps pass by. Just as she was about to put the magazine down, she heard a second set of footsteps approach and stop right before her.

Without preamble, a pair of hands reached for the magazine, and turned it around in her hands. "Makes better reading right side up," Tom said. His gaze remained on her, never wavering. "Now would you kindly tell me what the hell you've been doing?"

Chapter Seventeen

Inside his office a moment later, Ann filled Tom in on her afternoon activities. "I thought I might be able to find out something you couldn't."

Tom leaned back in his chair, struggling to keep his temper. With the colorful cuts and bruises from the fight, he looked positively menacing. "What if they'd recognized you or your name?"

"I gave them a business card that belongs to one of the other Realtors, and I changed my appearance. I'm certain no one made the connection. Besides, I never even alluded to Matt, and I was purposely vague about everything else."

"Ann, unless you start checking with me first, we're going to end up getting in each other's way." He ran a hand through his hair. "For instance, it seems we both came up with the same idea this time. I asked Dobbs to come in, and made appointments with the other local comic-book dealers, as well. I figured it was time to turn up the heat. Only with you nosing around there first, the element of surprise may have been lost."

"You're right," she conceded. "Okay, from now on I'll make sure I check with you first."

"Now that we have that out of the way," Tom said as he walked around the desk and leaned back against it, "would you like me to update you on what I've learned?"

"You've got something?" She sat forward.

"It's not much, but it's more than we had before," he answered cautiously. "Jackson and Lenora apparently approached Dobbs at a convention three months ago. Jackson claimed to have several important collector's issues he wanted to sell. Of course, Dobbs denies involvement in anything illegal."

"Has anyone learned anything more about Lenora?"

Tom returned to his seat. "The CBI is still trying to establish her identity through those latent prints on the glass. So far, they haven't been able to find anything."

"How long can it take to feed the prints through a computer?"

"It's not that easy. The computer can pick out prints that fit the general pattern, but the actual match must be made by an expert." He ran a hand through his hair. "Denis and I also tried to get the informant who told us about Lenora to look through our mug files. But he refused, and legally we can't force him." Tom shrugged. "Dobbs might be able to help us. I'll ask him to volunteer when he's in a better mood."

Hearing the sound of heavy footsteps coming near, Ann turned around. The door to the office opened and Captain Lambert stepped into the room. "You and I are going to have a talk, Keller. In my office, now!" he bellowed, then strode back down the hall.

Ann stared wide-eyed at Tom. "Oh, boy! Do you suppose he knows you're still working on the case?" she whispered.

"I think that's a safe bet." Tom clenched his jaw, then looked at his watch. "But I'm on my own time now and my work is up-to-date. He has nothing to complain about." Tom stopped by the door. "Wait for me in the lobby, okay?"

Tom walked with her as far as the front desk, then continued down the hall. Before he could get to the captain's office, Lambert strode out to meet him. "You're taking your own sweet time, Keller. You wouldn't be trying to avoid me, would you?"

"I have no reason to do so," Tom answered calmly.

"Really?" the captain challenged. "I hear that you've continued to work on the Jackson case, ignoring my orders. What is it with you? Are you trying to see how far you can push me before I place you on suspension?"

"On what grounds? I spend my hours bringing you the highest arrest/conviction rate in the city, even when I'm assigned more cases than anyone else in the department. What I choose to do on my own time is my business." Tom kept his tone cool.

"Don't start with me, Keller. You've disobeyed orders and circumvented my authority too many times," the captain countered angrily. "And your attitude problem is the last straw. I'm going to get you suspended without pay."

Policemen in nearby offices had stopped what they were doing and turned to watch the confrontation.

Tom stood stock still, his gaze as intent as it was cold. "I'm not afraid of the review board. But if you're going to push me, you better be able to back it up with something."

The vein in Lambert's forehead bulged as his face turned a deep crimson. "You've been feeling sorry for yourself for years, ever since I pulled you off that missing-person's case," he growled. "Quit taking it out on everybody and get your act together. If you'd been able to swallow your pride and maintain a little respect for authority, you'd have made captain yourself by now."

Painful memories assailed Tom despite the ridiculous accusations they'd been couched in. "Your authority gets all the respect it deserves, sir," he replied cynically.

The captain spat out an oath. As Tom turned to walk away, Lambert grabbed his arm.

Tom shook himself free, his expression deadly. "Keep your hands off me." Tom started to walk away again, aware that the entire area had grown quiet. Even the handcuffed suspect before the arrest desk was staring down the hall.

"Keller, damn it!" Lambert lunged toward him.

Tom turned, disengaging the captain's hold with lightning speed.

Three other police officers appeared at almost the same time from different doorways. Grabbing Captain Lambert, they restrained him until he calmed down. "This isn't over, Keller, not by a long shot."

Tom walked to where Ann was standing. "Let's go."

Ann followed him outside. "Tom, there's got to be another way. I want my son back, but I don't want to destroy you in the process."

"I'm glad you're concerned," he said with a trace of a grin, "but Lambert can't touch me. I've closed two major cases this week already, and my record speaks for itself. He's got nothing against me and he knows it."

"He said you were bitter because he took you off a case once. What did he mean?"

Tom's face hardened as he led her across the parking lot. "There's a coffee shop not too far up the street. You want to drive over there with me?"

"Sure."

They arrived a few minutes later. Tom asked for one of the corner booths and sat facing the room. After their coffee was served, he leaned back and stared out the window for several long moments.

"Tom, you told me once that you had a personal stake in finding Matt. Is that tied to the case the captain mentioned?"

"It was a long time ago, Ann. I followed orders instead of listening to my own instincts and common sense, and the situation ended in a disaster. It's something I'm not very proud of. I try not to think about it, but I've never forgotten what happened."

"Maybe talking about it will help. It might get easier to bear once you share it with a friend who really cares about you."

He met her gaze. It was little wonder she was making a permanent spot for herself in his soul. He touched her hand lightly, then drew back. "It happened a month after I made detective, about ten years ago. I was placed on a case involving the disappearance of a teenager. Lambert, my supervisor at the time, kept insisting that the girl was just another runaway. Three days later he took me off the investigation even though everything I'd turned up contradicted his theory. The girl was an honor student with no reason to run away." Tom clenched his fist. "But I followed orders. I dropped the case and went on to something else. A month later, the girl's body was found in a shallow grave near her home. Apparently, she'd been held by two men, then finally killed. Had I stayed on the case, I might have been able to prevent her murder."

Ann felt her blood freeze. A kidnapping that had resulted in the death of the victim played on her worst fears. "Tom, you had no way of knowing," she said weakly.

He took her hand and held it inside his. "I followed orders back then and didn't listen to my instincts, Ann. I won't make the same mistake again. I'm a damn good cop. I'll bring your boy back to you. I know how much you two need each other." He paused. "And maybe I need both of you, too."

His words held the promise of a future, and she clung to their soothing comfort. "I trust you, Tom. No matter how tough this gets, I know I can count on you."

His gaze softened, but for a moment the words didn't come. "I won't let you down."

"I believe you," she answered softly. Ann lapsed into a thoughtful silence. "I wish Captain Lambert wasn't so against you helping me out."

"I've come up with a theory about that. Lambert's determined to become public safety commissioner. He's made no secret about his plans to apply for the job when the current commissioner retires next month. To do that, he knows he'll need the support of the town's leading citizens." Tom narrowed his eyes pensively. "Many of these people have been victimized by the burglary ring, but almost all of them were insured. Let's say that the captain discovered an insurance scam going on. It could be quite tempting to some to report things stolen that actually weren't. The captain could end up with some very grateful friends if he purposely looked the other way." Tom shrugged again. "But it's all speculation."

"What we need is a lead we can pursue right now." Ann pursed her lips. "I have an idea that might just work."

Seeing Tom lean forward with interest, she continued. "Remember Jerry, our contact at the convention? You said his brother was a cop."

Tom nodded. "Sure. Jerry Kyle."

"If Jackson and Lenora frequented conventions, then it's possible Jerry might have also met them. Why don't we ask him to come look at mug files? He might recognize Lenora."

"That's a great idea. You might make a cop yet."

"No thanks, I'll stick to real estate," Ann observed wryly. "Life's unpredictable enough as it is."

"So you do believe in stacking the odds in your favor and playing it safe," he commented.

She shook her head slowly. "No, not really. You could cheat yourself of the best life has to offer that way. I've learned that since there are no guarantees, you have to reach for happiness whenever and wherever you find it."

He considered her words as he walked out to the parking lot with her. "I'll drop you off at your car," he said at length. "Then after I'm sure the captain's gone, I'll ask Jerry Kyle to come by." Tom weighed his options carefully. "If he agrees, it'll also probably be a good idea for you to pick him up. You can bring him in through the side door and we'll avoid the main desk that way."

As Tom pulled to a stop near her car, she turned and glanced at him. "Let me know where to go to get Kyle and when I should pick him up. I'll be waiting for your call."

Fifteen minutes later, before she'd even arrived home, her mobile telephone rang. Tom gave her the directions to Jerry Kyle's place and she drove directly to the house. Tom had said Jerry remembered seeing a woman with Jackson at the conventions. At long last, they were going to get a break.

It took another twenty minutes before they were together at Tom's office. Tom extended his hand. "Jerry, thanks for coming. I know the circumstances must seem a little unusual to you, but believe me it's for a good cause."

"My brother speaks highly of you, Tom," Jerry said as he shook Tom's hand. "I'm sure your reasons are good ones, whatever they are."

Tom placed several thick volumes in front of Jerry. "Exactly how did you meet Sean Jackson?"

"He came over to my booth at one of the conventions and introduced himself. He was trying to get the names of some serious collectors in our area. I started to tell him, when my partner kicked me under the table. Because of that, I kept my mouth shut. After he left, my partner, Mike, told me Jackson was a lowlife."

"These are the women we have in our mug files. There're more books there." Tom gestured to one corner of his office.

"I didn't realize you'd have so many," Jerry said hesitantly.

"Did you have to go someplace?" Tom asked.

"No, it's just that after a while, I'm afraid the faces will all run together."

Ann felt an oppressive heaviness settle over her. She wasn't sure how she'd be able to handle another disappointment. "Maybe if you take breaks..."

"I'll try," he said, giving her a reassuring smile. "I know how the press hounded you, and I don't blame you for trying to find a lead."

Ann smiled but said nothing. Her problems back then seemed trivial in comparison to what she was facing now. At least the press hadn't found out Matt was missing. Without Matt at her side, she felt empty inside and lost.

The minutes ticked by with agonizing slowness. She watched Kyle's face, hoping for a sign that he'd recognized one of the women. After a while, she averted her gaze. She couldn't stand seeing him turn page after page in a fruitless search.

"I think I should get us all some coffee," Tom said as Jerry started on his third book.

"I'll go with you," Ann said. As they walked down the empty corridor, she tried to hide her growing discouragement.

They walked to the coffee machine. "How do you like yours?" Tom asked, fishing some change out of his pocket.

"Black with—" She stopped speaking as a familiar voice boomed down the hall. Alarmed, she glanced up at Tom. "Is that who I think it is?" she asked in a harsh whisper.

Tom moved cautiously to the far end of the hall, then stopped and strode back quickly. "I just heard him say he came back for some papers. If he finds you here, there's going to be all hell to pay."

He took her arm and quickly led her back to his office. "Kyle, there's a problem. Would you mind if we cut this session short? We could pick it up at your convenience later on."

"That's probably a good idea anyway," Kyle answered. "I've looked at so many faces, I can't picture Jackson's girlfriend anymore."

"Then let's go." Tom was escorting them toward the side door when he heard the captain coming down to their wing of the building. "Duck into that lunchroom on your right."

The smell of a pipe burning cheap tobacco penetrated the air around them as Captain Lambert strode by. Holding his hand over his nose, Jerry moved noiselessly to the door and peered out.

Perplexed, Tom moved aside and watched him. A second later, Jerry ducked back inside and gave Tom a satisfied look.

Tom didn't stop to ask. As soon as the captain was out of sight, he led them out to the parking lot then asked, "By the way, what were you trying to tell me back there?"

Jerry grinned. "It looks like I'm going to be some help to you, after all." He glanced from one to the other. "That awful pipe smoke triggered my memory. I remembered a certain man approaching Jackson while he was still standing near our booth. He reeked with that same tobacco smell and I was afraid that our comics would absorb it." He spoke eagerly and quickly. "When I decided to poke my head out, I did it mostly out of curiosity. But you know what? It was the same man!"

"The captain knew Sean Jackson?" Ann's surprise was complete.

Chapter Eighteen

Tom glanced around the parking lot, making sure no one else was nearby. Things were breaking at last. The direction the case was taking, however, made his muscles tighten with apprehension. "Could you hear what was said?" Tom asked quickly.

"No, but they talked for a long time and then finally walked off together." Jerry Kyle paused, then his expression suddenly brightened. "Wait a minute. I just remembered something else. Right before they moved off, Jackson's girlfriend gave me a piece of paper with an address and a telephone number on it. She told me to call them if I heard of any major collectors who'd be interested in trading original art from golden-age comics."

"Do you still have that note?" Tom asked quickly.

"I don't know," Jerry answered, "but I can look as soon as Ann drops me off."

Tom's gaze darted around the parking lot. "You two better get going. We don't want anyone who might recognize either of you coming out now."

Ann gave Tom a quick glance, certain they'd uncovered the most important lead so far. "I'll be in touch with you."

"Do you have Denis's number for after hours?"

"Yes. Should I try to reach you there?"

Tom nodded. "As soon as you can. And by the way, if Jerry still has that note, try not to handle it. Stick it in a plastic bag or an envelope."

Ann drove quickly to Jerry's home. His two-bedroom duplex was small but meticulously furnished. Jerry walked to a large rolltop desk in the corner and opened one of the bottom drawers. Files were organized with a neatness that rivaled Ann's own. "If I kept it, it's in here. I have a miscellaneous file that's filled with information I don't want to throw out but don't have a place for."

Ann smiled. "I've got one of those, too."

"Here it is." He extracted a piece of paper from the manila folder. "I've got to warn you, though, I have no idea what this address and telephone number correspond to. I never tried calling." Jerry walked to the kitchen and placed the paper inside a sandwich bag. "And I doubt fingerprints are going to do much good now. I handled it a couple of times."

"It's worth a try. But even if it doesn't pan out, it won't matter. We think we have the woman's prints already. At least this is a sample of her handwriting, and that's new. Thanks, Jerry. Someday I'll tell you exactly what's going on here."

"I hope so. I'm really curious."

Ann hurried out to her car and dialed Arteaga's number. Identifying herself, she stated, "Tom was on his way over to talk to you. Is he there yet?"

As she completed the question, she heard someone pick up a second receiver. "Did he have it?"

"He sure did, Tom, and I've got it in my hand now."

Denis interrupted. "Can you bring it to us here?" He gave her the name of the hotel they were in.

"I'll be there in ten or fifteen minutes."

By the time she arrived, both men were waiting outside for her.

"Everything go okay?" Seeing her nod, Denis urged them back inside the hotel. "Come on. I've got the computer doing a search."

As they entered the agent's room, Ann asked, "What are you checking?"

Tom closed the door behind them. "I asked Denis to run Captain Lambert through his computer."

Ann was filled with questions. "How does he fit into this? I still haven't quite figured that out."

"Neither have we," Denis answered. "Here's the information now." He read it as Tom glanced over his shoulder. "There's nothing unusual here, old buddy. Lambert's been spending lots of money recently, but that's not illegal."

"Denis, there's something about this that really stinks, but I can't put my finger on it."

Ann handed Tom the paper enclosed in a plastic sandwich bag. "Here's the note. How long will it take to do a handwriting analysis on it?"

"That really won't help us much until we have something else to compare it to," Tom warned. He studied the address and telephone number. "This, I think, is Jackson's apartment."

Denis took it from him, then checked some notes he retrieved from his briefcase. "It's Jackson's all right."

There was a knock at his door, and Agent Murphy came in. "You still working, boss? I got your message."

He listened as Denis filled him in, then reached for the note. "I took a course in handwriting comparisons a few years ago. Maybe I can help."

"What are you going to compare it to?" Denis countered.

Murphy smiled. "I did the preliminary investigative work on everything that happened to Mrs. Dixon prior to her son's kidnapping. Her employer gave me a photograph of the spray-painted message that was left inside a house she was showing. He'd taken it for insurance purposes."

Murphy placed the photograph and the note, still in the plastic, underneath a lamp. With a small magnifying glass attached to his key ring, he studied first one, then the other. "This could have been written by the same person. Notice they're both printed, not in cursive writing. Of course, it's hard to make a comparison because the writing media are different, but there are similarities. Look at the way the *L* is shaped. There's a loop of sorts at the bottom. A handwriting expert should be able to confirm if it's a match or not."

Ann turned to Denis. "But what would it tell us if it did match?"

He rubbed his chin pensively. "First of all, the sample of Lenora's writing gives us hard evidence that links her with Jackson. It's also part of a chain that could lead us to her identity."

"And if she also turns out to be the person who left that message on the wall," Tom added, "that places her in town at a critical time and connects her to you. That message could cost her and help us. If we can prove she wrote it, then find her, we might be able to trade for information that could lead us to Matt."

"I see," Ann said. All they'd really managed to get was another reason to hope. There was still nothing solid to hang on to. Another night would pass without her son. Determined not to appear hysterical in front of the men, she began to walk to the door. Her throat was so tight, she prayed her voice wouldn't betray her. "Good night, fellows. It's time I went home."

Tom glanced at Denis as he followed her out. "I'll be back in a minute."

Tom and Ann walked in silence as they left the hotel and crossed the parking lot. "I can't stand to see you this way, Ann," he said, stopping by the side of her car. "Come to my apartment tonight and stay with me." Seeing her start to protest, he interrupted her. "I'll sleep on the couch. You can take my bedroom."

She smiled slowly. "I'd get even less sleep then," she teased halfheartedly.

"Then I'll stay at your place," he said with an air of finality. "I'll take your couch."

She shook her head. "I'm depending on you too much already, it scares me."

"Why are you afraid? You can trust me with anything, don't you know that by now?"

"Tom, my feelings for you confuse me. My life is in shambles right now. I'm afraid of creating an even bigger mess for all of us."

"Don't shut me out, please. You see, I'm the one who needs you." He pressed his palm to her cheek. "When I was a kid I often wondered how my father and mother ever got along. Dad was always quiet and never very demonstrative. Mom was outgoing and very affectionate. Mom would say that Dad needed her, that she brought him out of himself. With her, he could laugh and let go enough to love." Tom caressed Ann's face lightly. "You've done the same for me, Annie. You make my life special. I can't give you security and all the other things you should have, but I can offer you my friendship. Please don't take that away from us."

His words touched her deeply. "I couldn't get through this without you, and you know it. But you're six feet of temptation, and I need time to myself," she teased gently. "I'm going home. Call me tomorrow?"

"Just as soon as I get back in town," he answered. "Denis doesn't know it yet—" he grinned "—but I'm going with him to Denver."

She felt the enticing power of Tom's gaze as it came to rest on her throat and her mouth. If they kissed, they wouldn't be able to part tonight, and the time wasn't right for them. She opened her car door and ducked quickly inside. "I'll talk to you tomorrow, then. Take care."

"Call me here when you get home, so I'll know you got there okay."

She smiled. "Yes, sir, Lieutenant."

He laughed. "Did that sound like an order?"

She nodded.

"Well, that's because it was. Call me, please."

Ann continued to smile as she pulled out of the parking lot. She didn't have to look back to know he'd be standing there, still watching. Like a guardian angel, he'd protect her with his life if he could. A warm feeling spread over her. Some people went through a lifetime never finding love. Was she going to be lucky enough to find it twice?

WHEN ANN WOKE UP it was still dark. She turned her head toward the curtained window. It was only three in the morning. Not even a glimmer of sunlight had lightened the horizon. Unable to sleep, she lay in bed, staring into the darkness. Overwhelming feelings of guilt assailed her. Was her son spending tonight in a soft, clean, comfortable bed? Had he eaten dinner? She lay on her side and held her pillow against her.

Tom was trying his best, but more had to be done. But she wasn't sure what she could do to speed things along. Slowly an idea formed in her mind. She weighed the pros and cons, trying to anticipate potential disasters. The last thing she needed was another run-in with the men who'd captured her before.

As the hours of darkness ticked by, she worked out the details. At eight in the morning, she finally tossed the covers aside.

With her contacts in real estate she could find out a great deal more about Captain Lambert. Tom and Denis had checked his bank account and work record, but credit checks also turned up interesting things about people. Undoubtedly, they'd follow up on that later, but her way was faster and less likely than theirs to get back to Lambert.

She checked the newspaper, hoping against hope that some word would be there from Matt's captors. Nothing was.

Ann closed her eyes and used all her will power not to give in to despair. Her son was still alive. He had to be. Surely some instinct, some connection between mother and child, would have warned her if he was not. The kidnapper was trying to rattle her, that was all. Or maybe he was making sure she had time to find the right tape before contacting her again.

If only she could find it! Then she'd have the bargaining power she needed to get her son back. Squaring her shoulders, Ann mentally scolded herself for getting ahead of herself. That was one way to guarantee she'd fall apart and become totally useless to her son! First things first. Today she'd find out about Lambert.

She chose her contact carefully. A quick phone call confirmed her faith. Maggie Carstairs would see her right away. Over the years, they'd closed many real-estate deals together. Maggie was used to prequalifying prospective buyers, so this would be simplicity itself for her. All she'd have to do is access a few credit-bureau files. And with no one else around at the mortgage company office on Sunday, the task would generate little attention.

Ann arrived shortly before nine. The mortgage company's doors were locked and no one else was in sight. She sat on the steps and waited.

Maggie walked up less than three minutes later, holding a steaming cup of coffee in her hand. Seeing Ann, she smiled broadly. "I'm glad you called this morning; I've been thinking about you! I tried to call you at your office, but the receptionist said you took a leave of absence."

"It's been rough lately," Ann answered obliquely.

"I bet. I read the papers. Hey, do you want to share this cup of coffee? I think there's another mug in my office."

"Let me take a rain check on that." Seeing Maggie nod, Ann continued. "Like I told you on the phone, I need your help."

Pulling out a large ring of keys, Maggie opened the door. Once inside, she locked the door behind them and led Ann to her office. Maggie sat and regarded Ann thoughtfully. "This must be very important. You never ask anyone for anything."

Ann nodded and sat across from Maggie. "It is."

"In that case, tell me what you want and I'll do my best to help you out."

"I need you to prequalify someone for me and include an extensive credit check."

"A client of yours?" Maggie's brow furrowed.

"No, and that's where the favor comes in. I need to know all about this man, Maggie, without having him know what I'm doing. He's rather important in the community, too."

"Okay," Maggie said after a moment. "If I'd come to you asking for a favor, you'd have helped me, so let's get the details. Who am I running a check on?"

"Captain Howard Lambert of the police department."

Maggie grimaced. "You want to sneak something past a cop? Great idea, old friend," she added cynically. "How soon do you need this?"

"I was hoping you could do this right away. The computer files can be accessed anytime, I believe?"

"Twenty-four hours a day, seven days a week—Realtor hours." Maggie laughed. "Okay, I'll do it, but you'll owe me dinner at the best place in town."

"You've got it."

Ann left Maggie's office thirty minutes later with more information than she'd ever dreamed of getting. But she wouldn't be able to act on anything she'd found until she spoke to Tom. This lead put everything right in his backyard.

She was a few blocks from home when her mobile telephone rang. Hearing Tom's voice made her pulse quicken. "I've got so much to tell you! How soon can we get together?"

He groaned. "Please don't tell me that I should have been worrying about you this morning," he muttered, then added, "then again, why should Sunday be any different?" She heard him exhale. "Have you been out investigating on your own again?"

"I'd rather talk to you about this in person."

"Okay, you're right. I can meet you at your place in about an hour. Watch your back until I get there."

"And then what?" she baited, in high spirits. She could almost see his smile.

"Then I'll watch it for you."

Laughing softly, she hung up the receiver. Her thoughts remained on Tom as she drove home. As she pulled into her driveway, she saw one of Matt's old toy cars gleaming in the sun. It lay against the side of the porch where it had been mislaid long ago. Her chest tightened painfully. Confusion and remorse left her with a sick feeling at the pit of her stomach. Tom was becoming an ever-present part of her thoughts. But was she letting her interest in him interfere with her goal of finding Matt? Was she failing her little boy when he needed her the most?

The possibility cut through her heart like a blade. With new determination, she made an effort to push Tom out of her thoughts.

As the minutes ticked by, she learned that some things were easier said than done.

TOM SAT ACROSS FROM HER on the sofa. Ann seemed more distant now, though he couldn't figure out exactly what was wrong. "Okay. Tell me exactly what you did while I was in Denver, then I'll tell you what we found out."

"I went to see a friend of mine. Her computer is linked to the credit bureau and she was able to run quite an extensive search on Captain Lambert."

Tom sat up abruptly. "You ran a check on the captain? And on a Sunday?" He smiled slowly and admiringly. "Weren't you worried about getting into trouble?"

She smiled back. "Who's to know? Besides, I know a cop who'd fix things for me."

He laughed loudly. "Are you kidding? It's more likely we'd both end up in jail." Her courage and determination never ceased to amaze him. Would she be able to apply that courage to her relationship with him? And would the love he could give her be enough to offset the uncertainties of life with a cop? He brushed aside the thought and tried to concentrate on business. "Okay, go on. Tell me what you found out."

"The mortgage company had a report already on file, so it didn't take very long at all. It seems that the captain purchased a home recently. The company Maggie works for has the best lending rates currently available, so many local homes are being financed through them. The captain's was one of them."

"Buying a new home is scarcely illegal. Even if he made a huge down payment, he could have saved the money."

"It was an expensive home, but not outrageous. What caught my attention was that Lambert's been moonlighting as a security consultant for Safeguards Unlimited. It seems strange, don't you think? Here he was meeting with a known burglar at a comic convention, and he works for a security company?''

"Safeguards Unlimited," Tom repeated. "That name sounds familiar." He stood up. "Let me make a quick call." He picked up her phone and called Bob Glenn. "Could you pull the file on Sean Jackson that's on my desk? Then check and see if you can find any mention of a security company called Safeguards Unlimited." He waited for several long moments. "Thanks. And, Bob, for the time being, forget we ever had this talk. Believe me, this is one case you don't want anything to do with."

He placed the receiver back in its cradle. "We've got a big problem. I'd say a little over three-quarters of the burglary victims used that same security agency."

"So the captain's involved?"

"It sure looks like it. Did you know Lambert's new address?"

She handed it to him. "It's in that new area of country homes about three miles from here."

"The captain's at home today, so I'm going to go over there and talk to him myself." Tom's lips formed a thin, white line. "I want to hear what he's got to say about this."

"Now *you're* the one who's acting on impulse," she warned sternly. "You can't just show up at the captain's house and expect him to confess. He's tough. Remember what happened the last time you two talked?"

Tom scowled. "If Lambert's gone bad, our only hope of proving it is by forcing him to make a mistake. I've got to do something to rattle him."

"Then let me drive over there." Seeing him about to protest, Ann placed a hand gently over his lips. "I can go and demand the police department do more to get my son back. Then you can show up saying that you learned I was coming to see him and came to get me. While you're leading me out, you can mention to the captain that you've heard burglary's got a new lead and that those unsolved thefts should be wrapped up soon. You don't know much about it, but you understand it has something to do with a local security company."

"That should shake him up," Tom conceded. "Okay, we'll play it your way and see what happens."

"Give me five minutes after I go inside his house, then come after me." She walked out to her car, then flashed him a thumbs-up sign.

Tom followed her at a discreet distance, his gaze never leaving her car. Abruptly, the loud squeal of tires invaded the serenity of the quiet neighborhood street. Glancing ahead, he saw a black van turn the corner and head toward them at high speed. A few car lengths in front of him, Ann swerved as the vehicle skidded wide and nearly collided with her.

Tom trained his eyes on the van, looking for distinguishing features. As it flashed past him, he saw a mud-obscured license plate on an otherwise spotless vehicle. This was the same van he'd seen at Jackson's place, he was certain of it. But what was it doing here? He put out a call, asking that the driver be located and detained.

Seeing Ann pull up to the curb farther down the street, Tom followed and parked behind her. There was a small gathering of people standing by a driveway gate, next to a mailbox.

Ann left her car and went in for a closer look. Tom followed and quickly closed the few feet between them.

Verifying the house number at a glance, Ann turned and looked at him. "That's the driveway to Lambert's house."

It was the quiet that alerted him. People in groups usually talked in animated tones. Flashing his badge, he stepped quickly past two people who'd left a small gap in the ring. The sight before him confirmed his worst suspicions. "Ann, use my radio to call for an ambulance."

Tom knelt beside the man lying on the driveway. Mail was scattered around him. Blood flowed from a wound in the man's abdomen, trickling down to turn the gravel beneath him crimson. "Help's on the way, Captain. Hang on," Tom said.

Chapter Nineteen

Ann returned from calling the ambulance and approached the captain, who lay motionless. Tom was crouched by his side, trying to stem the flow of blood with his folded handkerchief.

"I'll stay with him while you radio for a backup unit, if you'd like," she volunteered.

Tom nodded. "Hold your hand over the compress and apply only slight pressure. There's a bullet lodged in there somewhere."

Ann rested on her knees next to the captain as people continued to gather around them.

Tom returned moments later and saw Lambert's wife, Caroline, hurry toward them. She sat down oblivious to everyone else, and began talking softly to her unconscious husband.

As Ann tried to make Lambert comfortable, she saw that his keys had dropped out of his pocket. Taking them from the ground, Ann handed the keys to Tom, who stood beside her.

When the paramedics arrived, Ann and Tom stepped away from the injured man. Seeing that Caroline hadn't moved, Tom went to her side and gently helped her up. "These fell from the captain's pocket," he said, distracting her temporarily with the keys.

She accepted them, scarcely looking at them. Her eyes were wide, and her complexion pale. "Will he be okay?" she asked the paramedic who was checking her husband's vital signs.

The man nodded. "We're going to take him to the hospital now, ma'am. The police will want to speak with you first, then you can come to the hospital and see him."

Ann went to Mrs. Lambert's side. Facing the loss of someone dear was a soul-wrenching torment she'd come to know intimately. Wordlessly, Ann placed her hand over Caroline's shoulder and helped her walk back to the house.

"I've never felt so useless," Caroline said, her voice breaking.

Ann nodded. "Believe me, I know exactly how that feels."

Caroline's eyes mirrored her anguish as they focused on Ann. "No, you can't possibly. It's like your heart's being torn out a little bit at a time. If there is a hell, then that must be what it's like."

"But I do know," Ann answered quietly. "My son was kidnapped last week." She took a deep breath.

Caroline's gaze filled with compassion. "You're Mrs. Dixon, aren't you? Maybe you do understand."

Ann nodded. "Lieutenant Keller and I helped your husband, Mrs. Lambert. Will you help us now?" She was asking a great deal of Caroline Lambert. What made it worse was that she couldn't warn Caroline how damaging it might be to her husband's future.

"What could I possibly do for you?"

"Your husband's been working on some burglaries that might be connected to my son's kidnapping," Ann explained. "It's possible he might have had some information that could help me find my son." She would not add to Caroline's burdens, but the questions had to be asked.

"Howard's been trying hard to get a lead on that burglary ring," Caroline admitted. "It's made him look bad in front of our friends. My husband's been moonlighting as a security consultant, and he set up security systems for some of these people."

"Do you know if he actually turned up any leads?"

"Everything's been quite unofficial, I know." Caroline smiled an empty, sad smile that touched Ann deeply. "Howard has been going out on many errands late at night or on weekends. At first it didn't bother me, but then I began to get worried. You hear about men who fall for younger women, and Howard's at that stage in his life where he's dissatisfied with the gains he's made. I'm ashamed to admit this now, but one night I decided to follow him." She stared at a photo of her husband on the coffee table. "But it was all right. He was just meeting a man in the parking lot of the Hog's Breath Saloon."

Caroline picked up her purse and slipped it over her arm. "Afterward, I felt so guilty about not trusting him that I told him what I'd done. At first he was angry, then I guess his male ego took over. I could swear he was pleased that I was jealous."

Ann smiled. "Do you remember anything about the man he met? It might help."

Caroline made a face. "He looked cheap, though he wasn't bad-looking. His hair was either light brown or blond, it was hard to tell from the floodlight in the parking lot. He had on an open-collared sport shirt and dressy slacks."

Ann heard Tom come inside. "Ma'am, there's a detective here who needs to talk to you," he said. "Afterward, I'm sure he'll be glad to take you to the hospital."

Bob Glenn walked in, introduced himself to Mrs. Lambert, then looked at Tom. "Did you see the shooting?"

"No, but I saw a man in a black van with a mud-obscured license plate speeding away down the street. I put in a call to traffic to have him stopped for questioning. That was right before I saw the captain."

Mrs. Lambert nodded. "Yes, the black van. It pulled up when we were walking out to get the Sunday paper. Howard told me to go back inside, it was one of his contacts. Then I heard the shots. I ran to the driveway, but the only person I saw was Howard lying on the ground. I rushed back to call the ambulance. Then, by the time I came out, all the neighbors had showed up. And you two—" she gestured toward Tom and Ann "—were taking care of him."

"Tom, do you still have a photo of Sean Jackson with you?" Ann asked, playing a hunch. Seeing him nod and start to take it from his wallet, she asked "Was that the man you saw your husband meeting that night?"

"That's him." Caroline gave Ann a hesitant smile. "I hope I've helped you. As soon as Howard's better, I'll ask him more about it, if you want."

"Thanks." Ann averted her gaze. She didn't have the heart to tell Caroline that her husband was mixed up in some very nasty business. "Couldn't the police talk to her at the hospital?" Ann suggested to Tom. "That way she could be with her husband."

Tom glanced at Glenn. "It's your case."

Bob considered it, then nodded. "Let's go, ma'am. I'll drive you there myself."

Caroline glanced at the keys in her hand for the first time. "Where did I get these?"

Tom reminded her gently. "Why? Don't you recognize them?"

She stared at the two keys. "One of these might be to his car, but I have no idea what this other one goes to." She held up the smallest one. "Are you sure they're Howard's?"

"If you'll let me borrow them for a little while, I'll find out," Tom answered.

She handed them to him without question, then hurried outside with Detective Glenn.

Ann slowly walked out of the house with Tom. "Now we're out of leads again," she commented in a soft voice. The acute and constant apprehension was becoming impossible to bear. It tore at her, gnawing away at her confidence and ability to hope. "I'm going out to my car so I can call Joan. There might be a phone message or a new note. The kidnapper *has* to contact me today, it's been so long!"

"Ann, remember that to him, it's a game. He'll use time as a weapon to manipulate you. Disappointment and frustration can destroy you quicker than the pressure of waiting."

"I can't let go of my hope, Tom. At the moment that's all I have." She sat behind the driver's seat and called Joan. A moment later she hung up the receiver. "She'll give me a call in a few minutes."

Unable to remain still, she began to pace beside the car. Her hands were trembling. Not wanting Tom to see that, she jammed them deep into her pockets.

Lost in thought, Tom stared at the keys in his hand. Silence stretched between them.

Ann finally stopped pacing, his silence capturing her attention. She watched him for a few long moments then, unable to take the suspense, she interrupted him. "What are you thinking about?"

He glanced up. "We've been searching for a lead, and now I think we have one."

"The keys?" She looked at them again, but then shook her head, bewildered. "Caroline doesn't even know what they're keys to."

"Unless I miss my guess—" he held up the smallest key "—this fits a storage locker someplace. There's a three-digit number stamped on it. We should be able to track it down from that."

"Maybe it's from the Denver airport."

"Could be, or maybe from the bus depot here. Let's check that out. If I wanted to store something of value away from my home and still have it accessible, that's the place I'd pick."

"You think we'll find proof the captain's involved in the burglaries?"

"I'd like to think that, but I'm not sure. All I know is that he didn't want anyone at home stumbling onto whatever he has in the locker this key fits. Also, he didn't want the key to be out of his sight."

When the telephone rang, Ann started and grabbed the receiver. She began to tremble. "Joan found another note under my back door," Ann told Tom. "Open it, Joan, and then read it to me slowly, so I can tell Tom exactly what it says." Ann waited a few seconds, then began to repeat what she heard. "'Quit stalling. Your son is still alive, but not for long unless you find that cassette. You have twenty-four hours before I start sending him to you piece by piece.' " Ann's voice trembled but she continued to repeat the words Joan read. " 'Let me know when you have the cassette, by placing a big sign on the telephone pole at the intersection of Pine and Quartz. The flyer should offer a reward for a cat named Artemis. Be ready. Artemis.' " Her voice finally broke. Handing Tom the telephone, Ann turned away from him.

A layer of perspiration coated her body, and for a few moments she thought she might pass out.

"Ann, Joan said there was also a snapshot of Matt holding today's paper. I'll have Denis's people go over that photo. Maybe there's a clue in it somewhere."

She turned around, desperation giving way to determination. "Let's get going. We'll track down that locker first."

He nodded. "Maybe the contents will give us a clue about what's supposed to be on that tape. If we could find that out, we may have something to force the kidnapper to negotiate."

They arrived at the bus station twenty-five minutes later. Dashing up and down the rows, they finally located locker 133.

Tom reached for the keys and tried the lock. Nothing moved. He jiggled the key and tried again. This time it slipped into place. "This is it."

Ann scarcely breathed as Tom turned the key and opened the door. "It's an old athletic bag."

Tom tilted it toward him and undid the zipper. Twenty-dollar bills bound in stacks of fifty filled it to capacity. He inspected the interior carefully. "There's something else down here." He pulled a large manila folder from the bottom and flipped it open. "Now we have evidence." He held it open for her to see. "It's one of the stolen art panels."

Taking everything with him, Tom hurried with Ann back to the car. "The captain's involvement places a different slant on everything. I've got to see if I can get the chief to put me back on the Sean Jackson investigation. I need to have the freedom to act officially now."

"Do you think the captain will be able to tell us something?"

Tom considered it for a moment. "Not for a while, probably. But Caroline Lambert may know something, even if she's not aware of what's been going on." He considered the matter for a moment. "Our fastest lead may come from the storage bag the art panel is in. It's high clarity and of very good quality. We may be able to use the label to track down the fence who's handling the stolen merchandise."

"Do you think you'll be able to find anything else in there that will point us in a new direction?"

"There's a good possibility. This wasn't something we were ever expected to find. The captain wasn't worried about clues, just about hiding his stash."

Minutes later Tom and Ann rushed to the station. "Go to my office and wait for me there. I'm going to talk to the chief."

Ann felt her pulse racing. In Tom she'd found her staunchest friend and ally. But he'd also brought her another, infinitely more precious gift. Hope. Tom had taught her to reach out to another person again. She'd never realized that by making Matt the center of her world and excluding everyone else, she'd been trying to protect them both from another loss.

Tom's support, however, had seen her through those times when her courage had faltered and optimism had grown dim. A bond had been forged between them. A part of her would always be his.

Ann walked to Tom's office. With his help, her son would soon be home. She felt like a child at Christmas.

A second later, Tom rushed in. "I'm back on the case officially," he blurted out. "I'm also on the trail of a very important lead. I asked a policewoman to call one of the comic-book dealers who's open on Sunday. It turns out that particular brand of storage pack is carried by only one of the vendors here in town. Remember Dobbs?" Seeing her nod, he continued. "That's when I decided to play a hunch. I tracked his vehicle through DMV and discovered Dobbs owns a black van. I'm going to pay him a visit now. His store is closed today, but I've got his home address. I'll let you know what I find."

"I'm going with you," she said staunchly. "My son's life is on the line and we're reaching the final stretch. If Dobbs had the stolen panels, he must have been Jackson's fence. It's also possible that Jackson double-crossed Dobbs and kept some merchandise from him. Maybe the tape the kidnapper wants indicates where the missing art panels are. For all we know, *Dobbs* could be the kidnapper."

Tom groaned. "All right, come on. At least then I won't have to worry about where you are. But you'll stay in the car once we get there."

"Maybe. Now let's go," Ann replied, following him out to his car.

As they got underway, Tom switched his radio frequency to the one being used by the CBI. Contacting Denis, he quickly filled him in, then added, "Meet me there. I think you're the one who should be my backup on this."

"I understand. Let's do it."

Tom turned to Ann, who was almost on the edge of her seat. "I'm not sure who I can trust in the department besides Glenn, and he's at the hospital with the captain. Until I'm certain that the captain's activities didn't involve anyone else in the force, I'm going to play it safe."

"Good. Can't you drive any faster?" She glanced at her wrist watch.

Tom placed the flashing red light he kept stowed in his car on top of the roof, and increased their speed. "Satisfied?"

"For now."

She was quite a lady. Throughout her ordeal, Ann had managed to keep her fear under control. She'd shoved it aside and found the courage to do things she'd never done before. "You're a pushy little thing, aren't you?" he teased, trying to help her cope with the tension.

"Some people need a little prodding," she countered.

He chuckled. "I rest my case."

As they neared Dobbs's neighborhood, they both grew quiet. Tom reached out and removed the flashing red light from the top of his car. "I don't want to announce our presence until Denis is here and we're actually ready to make our move.'' Tom picked up the radio's mike and ascertained Denis's location, then turned and glanced at Ann. ''He'll be here in five minutes.''

Tom drove down the dead-end street, his eyes glued on the house numbers. ''It's in here someplace.''

''Up ahead,'' Ann said, spotting the house number. ''Dobbs's house is the blue one on the left.'' She saw him study it, then glance around the nearly empty street. ''Since we're here, let's go talk to Dobbs,'' she suggested. ''Denis isn't that far behind us.''

''No, Ann, we'll do this my way,'' his tone made it clear that an argument wouldn't do any good. ''If Dobbs shot Lambert, he's dangerous, and we have no idea who else might be there.'' He pulled over to the curb, two houses down from Dobbs's. ''I'm going to approach on foot and try to get an idea of what we're up against. If I can get close, using the shrubbery as cover, I will. So don't worry if I duck out of sight for a few minutes.'' He started to get out of the car, then stopped. ''I don't expect any trouble, but stay alert.''

''I intend to, though it would be hard for anyone to sneak up on this car. You've parked it right in the open.''

''That's the idea.'' He checked his pistol, then placed it back in its holster. ''Now sit tight and wait for me.''

She watched him approach the yard, then stop and walk around to the side where a thick juniper hedge shielded him from view. There was an equally thick hedge obscuring the front of the house, near what she supposed was the living room window. She could see shadowed figures moving on the other side of the sheer curtains.

Why had Tom opted to go to the back of the house? The cul-de-sac was deserted. He could have had an ideal spot to eavesdrop right beneath the living room window. Perhaps the preferred method was to approach a suspect's house from the rear, but an opportunity like this one couldn't be missed. Time was critical now, and they had to take a few risks.

Ann glanced around, verifying that no one had come up. Then she left the car. She'd be silent and careful. Her son's life was at stake, but over-cautiousness now could end up placing Matt in even greater danger.

Noiselessly, she ducked behind the juniper barrier, oblivious to the sharp needles pricking her skin. She could hear a woman's voice inside and a man's, but she couldn't quite make out what they were saying. She crawled a little farther, then leaned against the wall, directly beneath the window.

"You shouldn't have come here," the man snapped. "I've got problems of my own."

"Take me with you. I wouldn't be in your way."

Suddenly a hand clamped hard over Ann's mouth. She couldn't breathe past the obstruction. She reached up to try and pry it away when she heard Tom's voice at her ear say, "Quiet."

He pulled her away from the window. They'd reached the driveway when Tom heard the garage door opening. When the black van rocketed out of the garage, he stepped in front of Ann, grasped her hard by the waist and pulled them both clear of the speeding vehicle's path.

Ann landed on her side on the grass, Tom's arm still wrapped around her. Stunned, she gasped for air, then moved away.

"Are you okay?" he asked.

She nodded. "I managed to catch a glimpse of them and I know it was a man and a woman, but they're getting away!"

"They must have heard us." Quickly he helped Ann to her feet. "Don't worry, they can't outrun the radio. I'm going to have every cop in town looking for them."

Ann matched Tom's pace as he ran back to the car. Suddenly the loud squeal of brakes ripped through the air. An instant later, they heard the dull scrunch of metal striking metal.

Tom didn't stop by his car. Instead he kept going until he reached the corner. Farther down, where the neighborhood street met the city's traffic, the van lay on its side. Its wheels were touching the smashed side of a pickup he remembered seeing parked there earlier. A third car, a tan sedan, was halfway up the sidewalk, its front grill twisted around a metal sign post and mailbox.

"That's Denis's car." Tom grabbed Ann's hand and ran back to his own vehicle. He gunned the accelerator as he picked up the microphone to call for help. "Denis had better not be hurt," he mumbled. Less than fifteen seconds later, he pulled up beside Denis's wrecked car.

Ann stared at the van. "There's someone getting out. It's a red-headed woman. She's running away!"

Tom muttered an oath. "I'm going after her. Stay here and check Denis. He hasn't moved."

"I'm okay," Denis said, emerging from the car. Obviously still dazed, he held a handkerchief over his forehead. "Just a cut." He drew his weapon and watched the cab of the van for the other occupant.

Tom sprinted after the tall, red-headed woman, but before he could get fifty feet, he heard Denis yell out Ann's name. Turning, he saw her running toward the van. "Ann, no!"

She went to the rear doors and tried to pull them open. "My son could be trapped inside!" She looked at Tom, then Denis. "Help me!"

Chapter Twenty

Tom drew his weapon and ran to get Ann away from the wreck. Denis, still shaky, continued to cover the front of the van.

Ann tugged at the rear doors, but they wouldn't budge. "Matt!"

Tom arrived and holstered his gun. "Ann, let me give it a try. Move to one side." Tom glanced back and saw that Denis had moved into position behind him, gun at the ready. "Here we go."

He pulled at the door, using the weight of his body as leverage, but nothing happened. "The frame's twisted. I'm going to have to go through the front." Unholstering his weapon once again, he went to the open passenger's door.

With ease, he hoisted himself onto the overturned van and peered inside. "Dobbs is unconscious. I think he hit his head against the steering wheel. I'm going in to search the back."

The moments ticked by with agonizing slowness. It seemed as if an eternity had passed before Tom called out once more. "Matt's not here, Ann, but I've found another of the stolen art panels. There are also dozens of microcassettes here." As he crawled out of the van, the wail of sirens could be heard coming up the main street.

"Tom, could one of those tapes be the one we've been looking for? And how are we going to find out which? The kidnapper said if I played it, he'd know."

"I don't think it's any of these, Ann. If the tape the kidnapper wanted was one of many, I think he would have told you how to identify it."

The weight of shattered hopes fell around her shoulders and numbness seeped over her. With cold detachment, she watched Tom climb out of the van.

"Ann, I'm sorry. But it's probably a good thing that we didn't find Matt in there. He would have been hurt for sure. The back is filled with suitcases and all sorts of things." He saw an emergency medical team and ambulance pull up and paramedics began to attend to Dobbs and Denis. Other police units were not far behind.

Denis stepped toward the van. "That man's wanted for questioning in the shooting of Captain Lambert and for receiving stolen merchandise," he told the rescue team pulling Dobbs from the van.

"And for attempted homicide," Tom snapped. "That sleaze tried to run us down."

Recognizing Tom, one of the officers approached.

Tom briefed him quickly and asked that a patrol car be sent to look for the woman who'd escaped. "Special Agent Arteaga and I will need those tapes as soon as possible," he said. "We'll also want everything in there tagged as evidence."

"We'll have the crime unit come out and I'll make sure the tapes are released to you right away. Will you be at the station?"

"I'm staying right here. The crime-scene unit can tag those first, then I'll turn them over to Special Agent Arteaga. Those tapes could be linked to a case they've been working on."

Denis came up, a bandage above his left eye. "I'll sign the necessary papers and take the tapes into our custody." As the patrol officer moved away, Denis stood beside Tom. "About how many were in there?"

"Dozens," he answered, shaking his head. Tom glanced at Ann and saw that her face was void of expression. "Denis, can you watch over everything here? I'd like to talk to Ann for a few minutes."

Denis glanced at Ann, then nodded. "I don't suppose sending her home would do any good," he suggested tentatively.

"You suppose right," he muttered back.

Tom took Ann by the arm and led her away from the scene. Standing in the shade of some large pines, he grasped her gently by the shoulders. "Ann, look at me."

She met his eyes but for the first time, felt nothing. Something vital had shut off inside her.

"You're giving up, Ann. You can't do that."

She shook her head. "I'm not giving up. But I don't want to hope anymore. I build up expectations then when something goes wrong, it practically destroys me inside."

"You can't separate yourself from your emotions. Don't even try. Believe me, Annie, I avoided life that way for years. It's tempting to withdraw and find a spot where nothing can hurt you. Building walls around yourself can keep unpleasant things out, but it also locks you in."

She took one step closer to him. "Then help me now, Tom."

"Annie." Her name was no more than a husky whisper as he pulled her against him. His arms wrapped tightly around her, molding her against him.

She pressed herself into his warmth. "I've asked so much from you, yet you've never held back. What I feel for you—"

"Is gratitude." He released her slowly then turned to watch the men gathering evidence from the van.

"Yes, that, too." She followed him out onto the sidewalk. "But that's not the only thing. You've opened my world and my—"

"Lieutenant." A uniformed patrolman ran toward them.

Tom swore softly. "Hold that thought. I have a feeling I'm going to want to hear the rest." With one last look at her, he went to meet the police officer.

Ann walked back to the van. The ache for her son had returned. But with it had come the desire to fight for what was rightfully hers.

Fear, with its cold, deadly hand, had undermined her for the last time. Since Warren's death, it had haunted her with such subtlety that she hadn't even recognized it. It had tempted her never to surrender her heart to anyone outside her carefully arranged life. And now it had tried to rob her of hope at a time when she needed it most.

"We've got the tapes," Tom said. "Let's go."

She rushed to his car. Denis was already waiting in the unmarked vehicle. "Where are we going?" Ann asked.

"The station," Tom replied. "We need to listen to all these tapes. Maybe then we'll be able to figure out more about the one the kidnapper wants."

TWO HOURS LATER, when Denis walked into Tom's office, Bob Glenn followed half a step behind.

The taut expressions on their faces convinced Ann that nothing they'd heard would help in locating Matt. Unfortunately, neither her luck nor Tom's had been any better.

Bob pulled up a chair and straddled it. "Dobbs had quite a select clientele for his fencing business. I recognized a councilman and the head of one of our town's oldest families."

"All these individuals make ideal blackmail victims," Denis added. "They all have a great deal to lose if their activities became public. With Dobbs re-recording the tapes to alter his own voice as he did, he could use them freely against his clients."

"But what's the link between these tapes and the one the kidnapper wants?" Ann asked.

Tom glanced at Denis then at Bob. "Did you guys make a list of the people Dobbs recorded on the tapes you had? None of the ones we heard speaking are connected to Ann in any way."

Bob Glenn flipped open a small notebook he kept in his pocket, then handed it to Ann. Ann read over the list, then handed it back, shaking her head. "I know most of these people by reputation. But I've never met any of them."

Denis leaned forward. "Then the tape the kidnapper wants probably isn't here. It's my guess, though, that the one he's looking for is similar in content. The kidnapper must believe that it's one-of-a-kind, though, and that's what puzzles me. From what we've learned about Artemis, he's not stupid. If Dobbs was blackmailing him, Artemis should have figured that he wasn't the only victim. Yet he's never addressed the possibility of there being more than one tape.''

''What if the kidnapper knows Dobbs doesn't have this particular tape? Could the red-headed woman we saw running away have stolen the tape from Dobbs?'' Ann suggested.

''It's possible, but why would the kidnapper think *you* have it?'' Bob countered.

''Okay.'' Ann leaned forward in the chair, her thoughts racing. ''Let's say this woman stole the tape from Dobbs and went to meet Jackson in the wooded area by the ditch on the night he was killed. Dobbs, realizing this particular tape was missing, followed her there. The woman passed the tape to Jackson, but then spotted Dobbs and ran away. Jackson and Dobbs got into a fight, and Dobbs ended up killing Jackson. Dobbs then moved the body to my car, but before he got a chance to look for the tape, Matt came up.''

Denis shook his head. ''Then where did he get the new trash bag, and why did he put it over Jackson's head? We've all concluded it was to avoid leaving traces of blood. Why should the murderer care about getting *your* car messed up? Your theory has too many holes in it, Ann.''

Her shoulders slumped and she returned to her chair. ''Okay, then you guys think of something.''

''The bag would have kept blood off the murderer's clothes and have prevented him from leaving a trail of blood we could follow back to the murder site,'' Tom said.

''But that still doesn't tell us the identity of the murderer.'' Denis added, ''Could the killer be one of the people Jackson burglarized—and Artemis too?''

''That leaves us a lot of people to investigate,'' Ann concluded.

The telephone rang, interrupting their discussion. Tom picked it up and after a brief exchange, placed it back on the hook. "Dobbs is conscious. I think we should go talk to him."

"If we don't learn anything new," Ann challenged, "will the police turn over one of the tapes to me? I can at least try to exchange it for Matt."

"You want us to pick a tape at random? You're going to be giving Artemis license to blackmail someone else." Glenn shook his head. "There's no way we can do that."

"You'd leave me without anything to exchange?" Her voice rose an octave. "You're not serious!"

"Ann, calm down," Tom soothed. "Bob's right. We can't give you one of the tapes, they're evidence. But we can do something else. Since we know what's on those tapes, we can make one of our own. In fact, you might consider overseeing that job while we talk to Dobbs. Go to our lab, there are some real electronics experts there. Then, if we don't turn up anything new, you'll have a very accurate facsimile to exchange for."

"Tom, those weren't just random voices on those tapes. It was obvious who some of them were."

"We'll find an impersonator and then alter the sound so it's barely audible. Remember, all we're trying to do is use the tape as backup, in case something goes wrong. Our real goal is to catch someone picking it up."

"I'll only permit something like that as a last resort," Ann said. "The best we could hope for is that it'll whet the kidnapper's appetite. He might give me more time if he thinks I'm already on the right track. But if he even suspected that I'd tricked him purposely..." She couldn't finish the sentence.

"Then I'll have to get Dobbs to talk, that's all," Tom stated flatly. Gesturing with his head, he signaled the others that it was time to leave.

As Denis and Bob walked out of the office, Tom tarried behind a moment longer. His eyes met Ann's. "I'll call you here and let you know what we find out from Dobbs. And, Ann, I *will* get answers. On the streets, I've acquired a reputation for being a very tough cop." He paused, choosing his words carefully. "It's not unjustified."

She stood and touched his face in a light caress. "You're not tough at all, Tom. I'm surprised that more people haven't seen through that act of yours."

He covered her hand with his own for one brief instant, then moved away. "Whatever good you see in me, you bring out," he murmured. "Now I've got to go. To do the things that have to be done, I can't afford to be the same man I am with you."

THEY ARRIVED AT THE HOSPITAL a short while later. Dobbs was conscious and not critically injured, and he refused to talk to any of them about the tapes.

"If you cooperate with us, Dobbs, we can make things go easier for you," Denis insisted.

"I have nothing to say to you. In fact, I'm not really sure what tapes you're talking about."

"Give me a break," Tom spat out. "You're in this quite deep. I chased an intruder out of Jackson's apartment and he took off in a van *exactly* like yours. I also saw your van speeding away from Captain Lambert's right after he was shot. The evidence against you is growing. We could end up putting you away for a very long time."

"Nice try, smart boy, but the only case you have is against my van."

"We listened to the tapes, Dobbs. We can track down the people you were blackmailing easily enough. Once they realize you're tied to a murder rap, they'll all rush to testify against you, if only to save their own skins."

Dobbs shifted, then sat up higher against the pillows. "You can't tie me to Lambert. You have nothing."

"Not Lambert," Tom countered. "Sean Jackson. We believe you killed him."

"You're out of your mind. I had nothing to do with his death. When was he killed?"

"Around five in the morning on the twenty-third of the month." Tom gave him a stony glare. "Let me guess, you're going to tell me you were in bed with your girlfriend, right?"

Dobbs grinned. "What's the matter? Can't *you* get any company at night?"

Tom took three steps toward him, but Denis quickly blocked him. "Cut the crap. Do you have an alibi or not?"

"You bet, check it out. I was on a red-eye flight coming back from Albuquerque."

"That doesn't get you off the hook, you know," Tom countered evenly. "Captain Lambert's alive and ready to make a statement telling us who shot him and why. Prison's a rotten place for a cop, so he's ready to deal."

Tom signaled Denis, and they strode to the door. "When you're rotting in prison, just remember, we offered you a chance to cooperate. It was your choice not to take it."

Tom and Denis came to a stop at the other end of the corridor near the lounge.

"What do you think?" Tom asked. "Will he talk once he gets a chance to stew for a bit?"

"I'm certain of it." Denis nodded with a wry smile. "You didn't see his face as you turned to walk out of the room. He looked like he'd been hit by a sledgehammer."

Detective Glenn approached them a moment later. "Lambert's doctor says two of us can go in to question him now, but we're not to stay in there for more than five minutes."

"It's police business, so I'll sit this one out," Denis said. "If anything comes out that relates to the kidnapping, you can fill me in."

"No, what I have in mind would carry more weight if you came in with me, Denis." Tom glanced at Glenn. "I need all the bargaining chips I can get."

"Hey, it's fine with me," Glenn replied. "I've had my fill of hospitals already. Rooms crammed with heart monitoring machines, and IV drips make my skin crawl."

Tom laughed. "You're a real tiger, Glenn."

"Hey, I'm honest. If I'm given a choice, why should I do something that makes me uncomfortable?"

Tom chuckled. "Okay, Bob, you can check out Dobbs's alibi. He was very smug about it, so I think it's probably true." Tom gave Glenn the details.

As Glenn walked off, Tom glanced at Denis. "I'm going to try a bluff. Let's see if we can play Dobbs and Lambert off against each other."

As they went into Lambert's hospital room, the captain opened his eyes. "I hear I should be thanking you," Lambert said in a hoarse voice.

Tom shook his head. "Not just me. Mrs. Dixon, too."

Lambert closed his eyes and said nothing.

"Captain, we have the contents of your bus-depot locker. That connects you to the fence, Dobbs. We know he's a blackmailer, and we know he's the one who shot you. He is associated with the kidnapping of Mrs. Dixon's son, as well, and she has received a note warning her that her son will be killed in less than twenty-four hours unless she gives the kidnapper what he's asked for." Seeing that the captain's eyes remained closed, Tom searched for a sign that he was being understood.

"I can't help you with anything concerning the kidnapping." The captain's voice was weak but his tone was adamant. "I don't know anything about that."

"Captain, if you're withholding information from us now, it could go very badly for you. If Matt Dixon dies, your connection to Dobbs could make you an accessory to kidnapping and murder."

Lambert opened his eyes. "I want to make a deal, Keller. Have the district attorney come in and I'll make a statement. Also, get my attorney, Phil Gardner."

"I need to know everything you can tell me as soon as possible."

"Then get them here. As soon as they arrive, I'll start talking."

An hour later, the group met in Lambert's room over the protests of the captain's doctor. A police stenographer sitting in one corner prepared to take down everything Lambert said.

Tom was eager to get started. Bob had checked out Dobbs's alibi and it had held up. Dobbs couldn't have killed Jackson. That meant that the captain's answers would be crucial to them now.

The captain sat up slightly. "So I'll get immunity from prosecution in exchange for my testimony?"

The district attorney, a middle-aged man with a protruding belly, sat next to the hospital bed. "That's the agreement."

"You think I'm getting off easy, don't you?" Lambert's eyes strayed over Tom and Denis. "Don't you realize that I've forfeited everything?"

Tom shrugged noncommittally. "It's not up to me to judge you," he answered.

"Why couldn't you have kept your nose out of it, then? I tried to warn you off with those hoods I hired to work you and the Dixon woman over. I knew I couldn't buy you off. You're one of those people who never seem to be tempted by power or money. I've never understood that. Well, Keller, I'm just not that holy myself," Lambert spat out, then he glanced at the stenographer. "You ready?"

Seeing the stenographer nod, he began. "I gave Jackson the information on the security systems we'd installed so his ring could circumvent them. Then when he got killed, Dobbs, who'd known I was Jackson's inside man, contacted me and I agreed to work with him. But I gather you already knew this." He glanced at Tom who nodded, then continued. "If Dobbs wanted to be the head of the burglary ring, I had no qualms about that. Since Dobbs was also a fence, getting rid of the merchandise would be even easier. That meant that I got my cut on a regular basis."

"Why did you do it?"

He lapsed into an uncomfortable silence for several seconds. "My wife and I were heavily in debt and I could see no way out. Even having a second job wasn't helping much. I realized that my financial situation could keep me from becoming commissioner, so I took steps to rectify it. I heard on the streets that Jackson owed some major loan sharks and that he was getting beat up on a regular basis. I decided to approach him with a plan I knew would help both of us."

"How did you get him to trust you?"

"I gave him the information and took part in the first burglary. Once he had something on me, he felt safe."

"You agreed to work with Dobbs once Jackson was dead. According to you, everyone was happy. So why did Dobbs try to kill you?"

"Once my finances were back on course, Dobbs became a millstone around my neck. I was worried that if Dobbs got arrested, he'd pull me down with him. That's when I came up with a plan and broke into his home. I found a large stash of tapes on his desk, and that made me curious. When I started listening to them, I realized that he'd been blackmailing some very prominent people." Lambert exhaled softly. "I took the tapes and set them in a box at the back of a closet. Then, using some plastic explosives and detonators I'd taken from the evidence room, I wired a bomb to the refrigerator door."

"How come Dobbs is still alive?" the district attorney asked.

"He was kind enough to explain it to me right before he shot me," Lambert replied sarcastically. "He wanted me to know why he was going to kill me. You see, besides the security system I'd sold him, he'd installed a motion detector. That activated a hidden video camera and tape recorder. When he came home and checked the sensor, he knew someone had broken in without setting off the alarm. He taped me going into the kitchen, and then heard me messing with the refrigerator. It wasn't hard for him to find the trip wire after that."

"You said you moved the tapes into the closet. Was there a reason for that?" the D.A. asked.

"I planned to be on the scene immediately after word of the explosion reached the station. Once I found Dobbs's blackmail evidence in my official search, I'd be a shoe-in for the job of commissioner when he steps down next month. The public would have loved me for bringing down some of the town's fat cats. The honest people who'd been victimized by the thefts would have been able to track down their stolen property. And there would have been no one left alive who could connect me to the thefts."

"That still doesn't explain who killed Jackson or who has the Dixon boy," Tom challenged. "The deal was you weren't going to hold anything back."

"Now look, Dobbs was really upset when he found out that Jackson had stolen seven panels but sold him only four. You know now that Jackson gave me one of them as payment for what turned out to be our richest take. Another turned up in Jackson's apartment. That means there's still one missing. My guess is that Dobbs was chasing Jackson and caught up with him on the Dixon property. He killed him and then stuffed him in Ann Dixon's car to place the heat on her. When he didn't find the missing panel on Jackson, he concluded it had been hidden at the Dixon place somewhere. Ann Dixon ignored his notes, so he took the kid hoping he could either force her to find it for him or give it back, if she already had it."

Tom gestured to Denis and a moment later they met out in the hall. "What do you think? Is he telling all he knows?"

"I think so. His theory is logical from his point of view. Only it doesn't tally with the evidence we have. First of all, Artemis wants a tape, not a panel. Also, Dobbs had only three panels with him, not four. That leaves two out of seven missing. There're still some players in this we haven't found."

Tom muttered a curse. "We know that Dobbs didn't kill Jackson, and I don't believe he has Matt, either. There was no trace of the boy at his house or in his van. Also, I think he would have mentioned a hostage by now, if only as leverage to get us to ease up on him. He knows he's in for a lengthy jail term."

Hearing the sound of someone running toward them, Tom turned quickly around. "Ann! What are you doing here?" He strode toward her and met her halfway.

"I've got the phony tape ready. The lab guys dubbed Dobbs's voice in with one of theirs, only they made it sound like the microphone wasn't working right. Unless you've found out where Matt is, I'm going to put the sign up on that intersection. I'm almost out of time."

Tom briefed her on what they'd learned and watched her try to control the pain of another disappointment. "Ann," he said quietly, then reached for her hand.

Ann stared at the floor for a moment, then threw her shoulders back and looked at Tom. "That settles it. I'm going to post the sign. In the meantime, you'd better start making plans. Once the drop is made, someone is going to have to follow the kidnapper." She hesitated for a moment. "And please," she managed through the lump in her throat, "choose well. If we fail and the kidnapper loses whoever's tailing him, I may never see Matt again."

Chapter Twenty-One

For a moment neither man spoke. Ann's pain reached out to them, devastating the facade of cool professionalism they tried to maintain. Tom cleared his throat. "Ann, wait a few more hours before you put that sign up. You've got time left, so let's try to use it."

"I keep thinking about something Lambert said," Denis commented thoughtfully. "The kidnapper seems very sure that you have this tape. Is it possible that you haven't searched everywhere? Maybe Jackson didn't die immediately. If so, he might have found a way to dig it into the soil or maybe toss it away from himself."

"I suppose it's possible, but honestly, I've searched both the inside and outside of my house and so have the police and the kidnapper."

"So what's one more try?" Denis insisted. "You don't have anything to lose at this stage."

She nodded. "You're right. Let's go right now."

They took separate cars. Tom followed Ann in his vehicle as she weaved through traffic and hurried home. "I wish she'd slow down," he muttered.

"You know, I never thought I'd see the day, but around this lady, you're one hell of a nice guy," Denis needled Tom playfully.

"Yeah, but around you I don't have to be, so watch your step."

"Let me know when I should start shaking in my boots," Denis said teasingly.

Several minutes later Tom pulled into Ann's driveway and parked behind her car. "Now let's see if we can find that damn tape."

They scoured the driveway and garage area with methodical precision. Twenty minutes later, with nothing to show for their efforts, they met by Tom's car.

Ann took a deep breath that sounded ragged, as if she were struggling to hold back a sob. "I'm going to go put that sign up."

"Will you try one more thing?" Denis asked.

"What do you have in mind?" Ann asked wearily.

"Let's go back inside the house. I want you to *relive* everything that happened the morning you found Jackson's body. After repeating the story to the police several times, you tend to remember the last telling, not what really happened. The best way to avoid that is to actually recreate everything you did that day."

She nodded. "All right." Ann unlocked the front door and led them inside. "I don't think I'll ever forget anything about that morning. I have tried to block out certain things though, like the way Jackson's face looked. But even that comes back to me in my nightmares."

"Don't shut your mind off to any part of it now," Denis insisted. "Try to remember the way you felt and everything you saw."

"You're asking a hell of a lot," Tom snapped.

Ann placed a hand on his arm. "This is for Matt's sake, and there's nothing I wouldn't do for him." *Or you,* she added silently, and wondered what he'd think of that if he knew.

Tom's gut wrenched painfully. She looked so vulnerable and fragile. If only he'd been able to bring her son back to her!

He watched her as she went through the scenes in her mind in response to Denis's prodding. He felt her pain and wanted to soothe it, but there was nothing he could do.

His thoughts drifted ahead to the time Matt would return home, and a new fear stabbed at him. Ann didn't want to share Matt; she'd already told him that. Even if she could accept the uncertainty of his job, would she open the circle of her family to include him? A cold emptiness seeped through him as he faced the possibility of losing her.

Ann's words brought him back to the present. "Matt came rushing inside," he heard her explain. "He was so scared! He had Commando clutched tightly against him, and one of his toys."

"Which one?" Denis insisted. "I want you to remember everything. Think back and see him as you did that day."

She closed her eyes tightly and concentrated. "I can see his face as clearly as if he were standing in front of me. I know he had his guinea pig, but I can't remember which of his toys he had with him." She opened her eyes and met his gaze. "But, Denis, surely that's not important."

"Was it something small?" Denis insisted.

"I guess so, or I would have been able to get a clearer look at it." Realization flooded over her features. "Are you thinking that he picked up something he found near the body?" Her voice dropped to a hush. "Like the tape?"

"What did Matt do that morning, Ann?" Tom asked, alert to the implications.

"He went to his room. No, I took him to his room." She shook her head. "I remember coming back after seeing the body, then I think I took Matt to his room." She placed her hands on both sides of her head, as if trying to stop a raging headache. "Give me a minute. My thoughts are all jumbled right now."

"We're running out of time," Denis warned, "but there's one method that might help you remember everything quickly. It can be very reliable, too, if you're willing to try."

"You're thinking of hypnosis?" Tom asked. Seeing Denis nod, he turned to Ann. "The police department has a psychiatrist on call who's done this type of thing before. What do you say?"

"Call him right now."

Tom made the necessary arrangements within fifteen minutes. "He'll be ready at his Medical Center office by the time we get there."

Ann picked up her purse. "Let's go."

"We'll take my car," Tom said. "The emergency lights will cut down on travel time."

They reached the Regional Medical Center in less than ten minutes, even though the trip should have taken twice that long. Tom led the way through the clinic wing of the facility to the doctor's office. Seeing the nurse glance up, he flashed his badge.

"Dr. Myers is waiting for you. Just go on through," she said.

The doctor, a tall, thin man with glasses, studied them as they came into his office. He listened to Tom and then gazed at Ann. She looked as if she were about to explode from the tension. "You're distraught. I'm not sure you'll be able to relax enough to go under," he cautioned gently. "But we can try."

"Doctor, I'll go under. Now let's get going."

He smiled. "You see? That's precisely what I meant. You can't rush it, you have to let your subconscious mind take over." He glanced at the men. "I don't think you two should stay."

"They have to," she snapped desperately. "Look, Doctor, we don't have time to fill you in on everything. Just do your best. I'm as willing a subject as you'll ever have."

He looked at her with new respect. "Okay." He walked over to a switch and dimmed the lights. "First, I want you to sit comfortably in front of me and close your eyes. Now take a deep breath and as you let it out, feel a sense of re laxation coming over you."

It took twenty-five minutes before Ann's body drooped slightly in her chair and her breathing became even. It seemed longer.

The doctor glanced back at the men sitting quietly in the dark. "I've used a technique to increase the depth of trance. But it took her a long time to relax. I didn't think this was going to work."

"She's a strong woman," Tom answered softly. "She can accomplish whatever she sets her mind to." For the first time in days Ann looked peaceful and serene. Tom's muscles tensed, a sense of failure sneaking through him. What good were all his skills as a cop if he couldn't use them to help the people who mattered most to him?

Denis moved forward. "Doc, you've been briefed on what we need to do. See if you can help her remember what her little boy was holding when he came back into the house. Help her to retrace everything her son did that morning, if necessary, to find out."

When Dr. Myers posed the question, Ann's face took on a look of intense concentration. "It's hard to see it. I know the top corner is square. But the rest is covered by his hand. I can't get a good look." Her voice rose slightly.

"It's okay, Ann. Relax now, you're safe here and nothing can harm you."

The tension seemed to flow out of her again. The doctor stood and took Denis and Tom aside. "It could be a tape. Do you want me to go on? She's really going through a struggle to remain calm. I don't know how much longer she'll stay under."

"No," Tom said.

"Yes," Denis answered at exactly the same time. He gave Tom a surprised look. "What do you think she'd want?"

Tom gritted his teeth, then nodded. "Go ahead."

The doctor sat back down across from Ann. Questioning her step by step, he helped her visualize and recount the details of that day. "You've seen the body, but now you're safely inside the house. Tell me what you're doing and where Matt is."

She glanced at her hands and grimaced, as if something was there. "I've got to get this blood off and calm down. I don't want to frighten Matt." She held her hands out in front of her as if washing them. Suddenly she jerked upright. "Matt's not in his room!"

She tried to stand up, but the doctor gently guided her back into a sitting position. "Where is he?"

She smiled with relief. "Playing over the furnace grating. He's fishing."

"That's it!" Tom whispered to Denis, who nodded solemnly. "That's the only place we haven't looked. If it was a tape, then that's where it is. You can bring her out of the trance now, Doctor."

The doctor talked to Ann quietly for a few moments, then snapped his fingers sharply.

Ann lifted her head slowly and opened her eyes. "What . . ."

Tom took her hand and helped her up, and Denis turned up the lights. "Are you okay?"

"Fine. Everything's so vivid in my mind now. I'd be willing to bet that we're going to find the tape we want down there."

"Who could have known?" Denis countered.

"Can we go now?" Ann strode to the door and turned anxiously to the three men.

Tom came forward and opened the door for her. "I'll take you back and we'll search the furnace."

"I can't believe this is finally going to be over," she said, relief easing the tension that had been etched on her face.

Denis and Tom exchanged a quick glance. Tom placed his hand over her shoulder. "Finding the tape is only half the battle, Ann. We still have to get your son back."

"The kidnapper doesn't want Matt, he wants the tape. Once he has that, why wouldn't he give me back my son?" Ann thanked the doctor, then walked with Tom and Denis to the car.

"The actual exchange could get tricky," Tom warned. His heart ached as he tried to find a way to make things easier for her.

Denis waited until they were underway. "Tom's trying to prepare you, Ann. We don't know the identity of the kidnapper. If we had a lead on who he was, then we could predict his actions. As it is, we'll have to take his word for things, and that's not something we like to do."

Tom glanced over at her, but remained silent. If he failed to bring Matt back, he wouldn't be able to look Ann in the eyes again.

Hearing his call sign on the radio, Tom picked up the mike and identified himself. After a brief exchange he hung the mike back on its hook. "So Dobbs is ready to deal."

"Do you think he knows anything about the kidnapper?" Ann asked quickly.

"I don't know," he answered honestly, "but I'm going to find out. I'll drop you off at your house first, Ann. You can start looking for the tape while Denis and I go to the hospital. As soon as we're done with Dobbs, we'll come back and help you search."

"The grate might be difficult to pull up, but if I need help, I'll call Joan. She'll be glad to help." Ann narrowed her eyes, her mind racing. "Make your conversation with Dobbs a fast one," she warned the men. "My twenty-four-hour deadline is up tomorrow morning, and I don't want to cut it too close. Remember that we don't know exactly when the note arrived."

"We'll be back here in less than two hours." It was easier to stop a tornado than it was to dissuade Ann once she made up her mind. Still Tom knew he had to try. "Annie, this once, try to wait for me?" He parked in her driveway and turned to look at her.

Instead of answering, Ann leaned over and gave him a quick, gentle kiss.

Before he could say anything, she got out of the car. Tom watched as she strode to the house in the light of early evening. "Damn," he muttered.

Denis laughed loudly. "Oh, buddy, have you got it bad! I must say, though, she's quite a woman. She'll keep your life interesting. That is, if she doesn't drive you crazy in the process."

Tom smiled and backed the car quickly out of the driveway. "She's already driven me nuts, you dumb jerk, so quit laughing at me. You don't bait a crazy person."

As they drove back to the hospital, silence descended between them. Tom finally spoke. "Denis, if Ann has to make the drop, I'm going to be the one tailing her."

"I figured that, so I've already included you in my plan."

ANN LIFTED THE GRATING OUT, then pointed a flashlight down into the dark interior. The gray ductwork gleamed under the beam of the light. She shifted the light from side to side, straining to reach all the places where a small cassette could have gotten wedged. After a few minutes she sat up and rubbed her back. Dirt covered her hands and the front of her blouse.

Had they been wrong? No, it was too soon to give up. She went to the bedroom and changed into a pair of faded jeans and an old blue sweater. If Matt had dropped a cassette down there, it might have gone clear through. The only way to find it was to go into the crawl space under the house and look in the furnace itself.

The thought of going beneath the house made her cringe. Undoubtedly all sorts of bizarre insect life lurked down there. Grumbling, she took the flashlight and walked outside to the garage. She'd need a hammer and screwdriver to get the plywood cover off the crawl space.

Tools in hand, she crouched by the wall. The board cover was harder to remove than she'd anticipated and working in the fading dusk required her to keep one hand on the flashlight.

"What on earth are you doing?"

Ann jumped. The voice had come from directly behind her in the dark. "Joan, I never heard you come up!" She took a deep breath, then turned to tackle the problem with the board. "I've got to take a look in that crawl space."

"Why do you want to go down there? Are you having problems with your plumbing?"

Ann looked at her directly. "Joan, I haven't been completely honest with you. After reading that last note the kidnapper left for me, you must know that there's been a special ransom demanded of me. It seems Matt picked up a cassette he saw near the body. I didn't know it until today when I was hypnotized for recall. Matt probably dropped it down the furnace grating in the hallway and that's why I never found it. I've already looked from inside the house. I'm hoping that by searching the furnace from the bottom up, I'll be able to spot it."

"Have you decided to keep this from the police? I don't see Keller here."

"No, I can't afford to do that. I've got to get my son back, Joan. I'm going to get the tape the kidnapper wants, then Tom and Denis can help me make sure he upholds his side of the bargain."

Having finally removed the plywood, Ann aimed the beam of the flashlight into the crawl space. "Nothing except my son could ever persuade me to go in there," she muttered. She started forward, the flashlight gripped in her right hand.

"You're going to need both your hands to get through there and search, and that flashlight's too bulky. Let me use the big flashlight to light the way from here. Then, you can use a smaller penlight to check around the inside of the furnace."

"I don't have a penlight, so this'll have to do," Ann stated flatly.

"I have one at home and it'll take me less than five minutes to go get it for you. I've also got a big battery-powered lantern that should light up the entire crawl space. Wait for me and I'll be right back."

"Okay." Ann watched Joan dash through the back gate. There was no time left for mistakes now. She had to find that cassette tonight, and if Joan's lantern could help, then it was worth a few minutes delay.

Joan returned shortly holding a big red lantern and a penlight. "Believe me, this is going to work much better."

Ann took the penlight wordlessly and Joan turned on the lantern. Now she'd be able to see all the spiders and crawly creatures between here and the cassette with incredible clarity, Ann thought. "Thanks. Now it's time for me to get going." Taking a deep breath to bolster her courage, she crawled through the narrow opening into the dark space beneath her house.

TOM STARED AT DOBBS, his face an expressionless mask. "I can promise you only one thing. Your cooperation will make it easier for you in the courts. But if I find out that you've held back anything, particularly regarding the kidnapping, I'll make sure you spend the rest of your days in jail," he growled.

"I don't know anything about that missing kid, but I can help you catch Jackson's murderer." He paused, shifting in the hospital bed. "I might be able to fill you in on details about the robberies, too."

"Start talking," Denis prodded. "And make it good, Dobbs. We're not in a patient mood."

"The red-haired woman in the van with me was Sean Jackson's girlfriend, Lenora Wells. She came to me last night, scared to death, wearing that ridiculous wig. She wanted to get out of town fast. Everything was closing in on her."

"And you agreed to take her with you? Why?"

"We were both in trouble. I had to get out of town fast, too, and she felt that the cops were on her tail. Apparently she had threatened Mrs. Dixon. She'd made an appointment with her, then spray-painted a message on the wall of the house where they were supposed to meet. Later, when the Dixon woman almost caught up with her at a restaurant, she figured that Ann Dixon was connected to the police. Lenora's really afraid of going to jail."

Dobbs looked at the men. "Lenora's a good-looking woman and she offered to pay her own way. She had one of the art panels that Jackson had swiped. She knew I wanted it. She offered it to me in exchange for helping her."

"Where could we find her now?"

"I have no idea."

"This is all interesting, but how's that going to help us catch Jackson's killer?" Tom countered pointedly. "Are you saying that you believe Lenora Wells killed him?"

Dobbs shook his head. "No, though Lenora was convinced that you'd think it was her because of the message she'd spray-painted on that wall."

"So if it wasn't her, who was it?" Tom prodded.

"On the afternoon of the day Jackson died, I met with a client who'd already bought one of the art panels from me. This woman's father had been the original artist for *Manstalker*, but the publishing company had kept all of his drawings. She claimed her father had been used, then fired without just cause. Her old man later committed suicide, right in front of her and her mother. It must have really freaked her out because from what I could tell, she idolized her father."

"Okay, so you sold stolen merchandise to her, but what's that got to do with the murder?"

"As you know, I tape-recorded all my business transactions, then later I altered my voice so the tape couldn't be used against me. The day this client was at my office, I got called away from my desk for a few minutes. I stepped out to talk to someone, and when I returned the client was gone. So was the tape. She must have found the machine and panicked." He sat up and leaned against the pillows. "That's when my real troubles started. I had to get that tape back. My voice was on it, too. She could have used it to blackmail me."

"So you went to her house and stole it back?" Denis asked.

"It wasn't that easy. The name she'd given me was phony, but I still managed to track her down through her telephone number. I asked a friend of mine at the telephone company to get me her real name and address. Then I called Jackson. I had an important sale to finalize that night in Albuquerque, so I hired him to either get the tape back for me or destroy it."

"Are you saying that he got killed during a burglary?"

"When I read about Sean's death the next day, I assumed that the lady had caught him in the act and killed him. I kept quiet since she still had the tape. There was no way I could say anything against her without incriminating myself.''

''What's her name and address?''

''I met her as Nell Collins, and that's the name that sticks in my head. I've got her real one jotted down in a piece of paper in my wallet. Can you reach it for me? It's in the top drawer.''

Tom handed the wallet to Dobbs, and he extracted a small note from inside. ''Her name is Joan Richardson.''

Tom swore with surprising eloquence. Without waiting to hear the address, he shot out the door.

Chapter Twenty-Two

"Do you want me to shift the beam, or is the light helping where I'm aiming it?" Joan asked.

"It's fine right where it is, thanks," Ann answered. "It's really dusty and cramped down here, and without that light, I'd never be able to see well enough to search."

"Have you spotted the cassette?"

"Not yet. The furnace is at least another five feet away, and it's rough to maneuver around some of these floor joists. Something's down here, too," she added in a tremulous voice. "I can hear it moving from time to time." She suppressed a shiver.

"Try not to think about it, Ann, just keep crawling toward the furnace."

It wasn't easy. Her knees were being chafed on the hard, dry ground and, since she hadn't thought of wearing gloves, her hands felt raw. "Okay, I'm here. Now move the beam to the right. I'm going to get beside the furnace, open it and shine the penlight up in there."

Minutes ticked by as she maneuvered the tiny beam where it was needed. "There's something caught between the burner and the base, if I can just reach it . . ." She groaned, trying to force her hand into the small opening. Ann pushed her face against the cold cast iron and strained upward, guessing at the spot. "I've got it right at my fingertips. I think it might be the cassette." She pulled her hand out slowly, her skin scraping against the sheet-metal sides.

Seeing the small red-and-white plastic microcassette in her palm, she let out a whoop. "Finally! I've got it!"

"Good, now get out of there," Joan urged, her voice sounding distant.

Ann had just turned around when the light suddenly wavered and she heard a muffled voice. Then darkness engulfed her. "Joan, what happened to the light? I can't see anything."

Getting no response, Ann moved the tiny penlight from side to side, trying to spot the opening into the crawl space. All she could see was the underside of the house and two concrete pillars. Everything else faded to black. With no light filtering in from the outside, there was nothing to orient her. "Joan, damn it, where are you?"

Once again, no one answered. Fear began to creep through her. It wasn't like Joan to leave her stranded; something must have happened. Had Artemis decided to come after the tape himself? She forced down the panic that was making her shake and tried to retrace her route. Keeping the penlight on, she followed the marks she'd made on the ground on her way in. If Artemis was out there, this would be just as good a time as any to negotiate for her son.

Something scampered along the base of the foundation ahead of her, then dropped down onto the ground. Ann froze and listened. Her stomach lurched as she tried to pinpoint the sound. Was it coming toward her or going away? She forced herself to start moving again. It was time for reason, not blind fear. What was waiting outside could prove infinitely more dangerous than any animal she could encounter in here.

Something hanging down tickled against her face and she swatted it away furiously. *Calm down. It's just a spider web.* She forced her thoughts to clear. Something moved again to her right, but this time Ann didn't stop. As she pressed on, she tried to breathe through her mouth to avoid the stench that surrounded her. It was like the smell of dead animals and rotting leaves, only worse. The dark, she discovered, was filled with sounds and smells, all magnified and never ending.

Suddenly the bright beam of a flashlight only a few feet away blinded her completely. "Ann?"

"Tom, is that you?" She shaded her eyes, trying to see his face.

"Yeah, it's me. Are you okay, honey? Can you get out?"

She almost started laughing with relief. "Just shine that light to show the way and shoot anything that slithers toward me."

She heard him laugh nervously. "Come on, just a few more feet."

He held out his hand and pulled her through the opening onto the soft, moist grass of her lawn. Gently, he brushed the soot and dirt from her face. "Are you sure you're okay?"

"I need a bath, no doubt, but I've got it." She held out the microcassette triumphantly in the palm of her hand. "But something must have happened to Joan. She was helping me, then she disappeared."

That's when Ann saw that Tom was shaking. His face was deathly pale, even in the warm glow of the flashlight. The realization that it was fear she saw etched on his face stunned her. "I'm really fine," she said, uncomprehendingly. She placed her hand against his cheek, her own heart hammering in her chest.

He pulled her against him so tightly she could barely breathe. "I've been through hell thinking that I practically handed you over to your worst enemy."

"What on earth are you talking about?" She pulled away slightly and glanced up at him.

He told her the highlights of Dobbs's confession. "He's convinced that Joan was the one who killed Jackson. Dobbs made a lot of sense, too, once he told us the story."

"Then she's got Matt." Ann glanced around, fear alive in her voice. "She couldn't have gone far, she was just here."

He nodded. "I saw her out here when I came up, but I couldn't see you. I thought she might have hurt you. Then, when I yelled to her, she took off like a shot. I think she realized from my tone that I was on to her."

"I told her that you'd been talking to Dobbs." Ann clutched her throat. "Dear heaven, she's got my son, she knows I've got the tape and she's killed one person already." Ann grabbed the flashlight from Tom's hand and sprinted forward.

"No, Ann, wait! Backup's on the way. You can't—" Suddenly he realized that he was talking to himself. Ann was already running up the trail leading to Joan's house. Cursing, he rushed after her.

She was on the other side of the little footbridge when he finally caught up to her. Grabbing her roughly by the arm, he spun her around. "Will you stop and think? You can't rush in there! You'll get yourself *and* Matt killed."

"No, you're wrong. That's exactly what she's *not* expecting. Surprise is on my side and I'm going to use it." Without a second's hesitation, she kicked Tom hard in the shin.

The pain caused him to release his grip slightly, and that was all she needed. She broke free and ran again for Joan's house. It was dark now, inside and out. Joan had turned out all the lights. Ann went to the back door Joan normally kept open. But this time, when she twisted the knob, it was locked.

Ann picked up a large rock from the ground. She'd smash the glass, then reach inside and undo the lock.

"Wait." Tom was a few feet behind her. "I'll kick it—" Before he could complete the sentence, the glass was shattered. Ann tapped the remaining shards off the door frame. As they landed with a tinkling sound on the floor, Tom reached her side. "Damn it, why do you find it so hard to do as I ask?"

"Because sometimes my plans are better," she answered flatly. As she started to reach through the broken pane, he grasped her arm, stopping her. "Just what do you think you're doing?" she challenged in an angry whisper.

He didn't answer, but instead reached inside and undid the lock himself. "Stay here. I'm armed and I'm trained to handle this kind of situation."

She gave him a four-step lead before following him inside. Ann stopped by the kitchen wall and tried to turn on the light switch.

Hearing the sound, Tom spun around, pistol aimed and ready. "What are you trying to do?" he demanded in a muted voice. "I almost shot you!"

"The power's been turned off," she warned. "Maybe Joan's not here anymore and she wants us to waste our time looking for her in the dark. She could have made a run for it, and left Matt hidden somewhere." She tried to rush past Tom, pointing her flashlight around the living room frantically.

Tom grabbed her around the waist and pulled her against him. "Be quiet and stand still!" he demanded in a soft voice. "If she's here and hiding, you're going to give our position away." He released her waist but gathered her hand tightly in his. She held the flashlight, pointing it a few feet ahead of them. "Look at this collection," he muttered. "There's everything in here, from license plates to dolls." He quickly added, "Does she collect guns, too?"

"Not that I know of." Ann studied the room. As she searched for some clue to Matt's presence, a quick step and a moving shadow broke the stillness. "Look out!" she yelled.

Tom whirled in a crouch, pistol extended. Before he could bring his weapon to bear, he caught a glimpse of Joan in the beam of his flashlight. She was swinging something toward him so fast her hands were a blur. Instinctively, he ducked to one side, but he was unable to avoid the blow completely. Pain erupted from the side of his skull and his shoulder. Yellow-green lights appeared behind his eyes briefly, then gave way to blackness.

In the bright yellow cone of her own flashlight, Ann saw Tom fall. His pistol slid across the floor, disappearing into the blackness edging the room. Joan stood before her, grotesquely distorted to an unnatural height by the single beam of light. She held a blood-streaked baseball bat high in the air, ready for her next victim.

Blinding Joan with the beam of her penlight, Ann dove out of the way. Joan's errant swing missed by inches. Taking advantage of Joan's off-balance position, Ann hurled herself against the other woman, knocking her away from Tom.

Joan fell backward onto the floor. With a screech of rage, she pushed Ann away and rolled over to Tom's pistol.

A heartbeat later Ann stared at Tom's gun, pointed at her. Tom's flashlight, which had fallen on top of the sofa, illuminated the room slightly with its beam. "Joan, please, where's my son?" Ann's heart pounded in her throat. "You can take the tape and run as far away as you like. I won't stop you."

A ripple of something akin to pity crossed Joan's features. "I never meant to harm anyone. I've spent my life collecting things to trade for the original *Manstalker* panels my father created. I bought one from Dobbs, but when I had enough money to buy another, that scum tried to double-cross me. He'd been taping our conversation. I stole the tape from him because I figured he'd found a way to use it against me. Only when Jackson stole the cassette from me and I couldn't find it, I knew I was in trouble. If someone else found it and recognized either Dobbs's or my voice, I'd be up for murder. Dobbs would have been happy to turn state's witness and get me convicted, in exchange for his own freedom."

"But why did you involve me and Matt in this? It has nothing to do with us!" She remembered Tom saying that he'd called for backup and prayed that it would get here in time.

"It was never my intent to involve you. Jackson broke in at about five in the morning. He woke me up when he opened the desk drawer in the den. You know, the one that squeaks? I grabbed this bat. It's the one Grand Slam McClanahan used to hit his last home run. Jackson turned right into the bat and the blow killed him right away. It never occurred to me that he'd already found and taken the tape."

"But why didn't you call the police and report a burglar?"

"When I saw his face, I recognized him immediately. He was with Dobbs when I bought the first art panel. I was afraid if I called the cops, someone would figure out the connection between us and Dobbs. I'd go to jail for sure. I'd done nothing wrong except try to get back what should have been mine all along. But I had to get rid of Jackson. I placed a bag over his head so I wouldn't leave a trail of blood, and dragged his body to my car. Only the damn thing wouldn't start. Then I remembered yours was in the driveway. I knew you kept a set of spare keys in the tire well so I carried him down there. It wasn't easy, believe me. I was almost set to drive away when I heard Matt. I had no choice then except to take off. Once I was out of sight, I brushed away my footprints on the path and came home."

"So when did you realize Jackson had already stolen the tape?" Ann glanced over at Tom, hoping he'd revive quickly.

"As soon as I got home, I went to where it was hidden, intending to find a safer place for it—I'd kept it in a vase in the living room. Only when I reached inside, I discovered the tape was gone. I knew right away what had happened. As soon as I could, I retraced my steps to your driveway. When I didn't find the tape and the police didn't come to arrest me, I figured you had it. Only I was certain you weren't aware of what it was. I knew I'd have to force your hand somehow."

"Joan, what did you do with Matt? I can't believe that you'd hurt him."

Tom stirred, fighting his way back to consciousness. "It would be easier for him if he stayed asleep," Joan added sadly. She stepped back, pointing the gun halfway between Ann and Tom. Tom rose to his knees, his eyes half open.

"Ann, your son's safe. I'll take Matt with me and I'll raise him as my own, I swear." Her face lost its human quality and became a mask once more. "Neither you nor Tom will suffer, if you don't spoil my aim. Goodbye, Ann," Joan said, gripping the pistol with two hands and shifting the barrel so it pointed squarely at Ann's chest.

Ann held her breath, expecting pain and then darkness. There was nowhere to run. Then, without warning, the house lights switched on, blinding them all in the sudden glare. Simultaneously, two monstrous blasts sliced through the room. Joan was knocked sideways by an invisible fist and thrown roughly down. Tiny fragments of glass showered through the air.

Tom pulled Ann to the floor. Breaking their fall with his shoulder, he rolled over, covering her with his body. "Stay down!"

Joan lay halfway across the room in an unnatural sprawl, an ever-widening crimson stain flowering on her lavender blouse.

"Oh, no! She can't be dead!" Ann tried to squirm free, but Tom held her firmly. "What did she do with Matt?"

Tom stared out the picture window that now had two quarter-sized holes at chest level. Between the holes, the plate glass displayed a spider's web of interlaced cracks. In the glow of the room lights he could see Denis Arteaga standing on the lawn just outside, his pistol still pointed at the spot where Joan lay.

"Are you two okay in there?" Denis shouted, never taking his eyes off the fallen woman.

"We're fine, Denis!" Tom shouted. Just then, a policeman leaped through the doorway, his shotgun ready. He looked at Tom, then relaxed slightly. "Anyone else here we should know about, Lieutenant Keller?"

Tom shook his head. "I think she was alone. Better check out the rest of the house, though, just in case."

Ann grabbed his sleeve, forcing Tom to turn and look at her. "Matt! What about Matt?" Without waiting, she ran to Joan's side. She placed her fingers at the pulse point on Joan's neck. "What are we going to do? She's dead!"

Tom went to her side. "Honey, there's nothing we can do about it now. Matt's probably not here anyway, or we would have seen or heard something. But I'm sure there'll be a clue here somewhere that will tell us where he is. Let the officers look for it." He urged her away gently.

Denis came toward them. Giving Ann a look filled with compassion, he turned toward Tom. "Why don't you take Ann back to her house? I'll stay here and oversee things. We'll turn this place upside down, if we have to."

"I'm not going anywhere." Ann pulled free of Tom, then glared at Denis. "Matt's here," she assured them as calmly as she could. "This is where Joan would have kept him. She would have wanted him close by."

"If he's here, we'll find him," Tom answered. "But let us do the looking." Her fears sliced through him. He wouldn't be able to stand the look of betrayal on her face if anything had happened to Matt. He'd done his best and she'd trusted him, but right now he had no way of knowing if his efforts had been enough. "I'll have an officer walk you home and stay with you while we search."

"I'm not leaving."

Tom looked at her silently for a moment then with a nod, he turned and began to look for Matt. They went from room to room but found no trace of the little boy. Tom glanced at Ann and felt his gut knot painfully.

As they repeated the search, two officers checking the attic and crawl space, Denis came up to her. "I thought you might be interested. We caught up with Lenora at the bus station. She switched hair colors again and was trying to buy a ticket out of town. Apparently she'd picked the night Jackson was murdered to move out on him. She found out that Jackson had been seeing other women behind her back. Then the morning after she left his apartment, she learned he'd been murdered."

Ann watched the uniformed men going over each of the rooms, searching for anything that might provide a clue to her son's whereabouts. "Has anyone figured out why Sean Jackson came to my house the afternoon before he was killed?"

"We believe he was casing the neighborhood. Your house and Joan's look very similar in layout, so he decided to try for a closer look."

After an hour of fruitless searching, the men gathered in the front room. Sensing that they were about to give up, Ann walked to the den and continued to look around.

Tom went to her side. "We've already been through everything in this room and the others repeatedly. The crime-scene unit will be arriving shortly. I'm sure they'll be able to find clues we haven't even thought about."

"I'm still not leaving," she replied staunchly. "He's here, I can feel it."

"Then why hasn't he called out to you or signaled us?" Tom countered, hating himself for having to force her to face reality.

Ann's eyes glittered with a sharp intensity. "That's the answer," she said, then smiled. "Maybe he doesn't know we're here. Matt!" she yelled at the top of her lungs.

As the other officers ran into the room, Ann turned toward them. "You've all got to be as quiet as possible. Please. Not one sound."

Tom remembered how Joan had sneaked up on them earlier, appearing out of thin air. Maybe there was a hiding place! He raised his hand, palm outward.

Silence fell over them. Tom held her hand in his, giving it a gentle squeeze.

"Matt! Honey, if you can hear me, call out or make some sound!" She yelled at the top of her lungs until her voice broke from the strain.

Finally several of the policemen began shaking their heads, exchanging worried glances.

Tom held her hand in his all the tighter. They needed to hang on to each other now more than ever.

Finally Denis placed his hand on her shoulder. "Come on, Ann. We gave it our best—"

She put her hand to his mouth. "Listen!"

A faint thump was coming from somewhere deep within the house.

"Do you hear it?"

Denis nodded, then glanced at Tom. "Where the hell is it coming from?"

Tom felt a tingling that went all the way from his neck to his soles. That sound meant his future. "It's coming from within the walls." He splayed his hands against the wood paneling and pushed, but nothing happened. "There's a space behind the walls, and there's got to be some way to get back there."

The men began tapping the walls, searching for a hollow sound that would indicate a room on the other side.

Ann's spirits soared. She gave Tom a bright smile. "He's here," she whispered.

Tom felt a surge of possessiveness more powerful than any he'd ever known. His family...his woman...his son? He mulled the thought over in awe. It seemed right, more right than anything else in the world.

Ann stood in one corner and pushed. "I think I felt something give way here, but I'm not sure."

Tom was at her side instantly. He felt the panel move slightly, yet his path remained blocked. Denis came up behind him. "Maybe we're pushing it the wrong way."

"What wrong way? It doesn't slide," Tom countered.

"But maybe there's a catch that makes it swing open," Denis explained, running his fingers along the wall.

"Good point. It wouldn't have to be right here," Tom ventured. "The bookcase on the other side..."

Ann needed no further inducement. Reaching it first, she started to toss all the books onto the center of the floor. Behind one of the largest volumes was a square panel set flush with the wall. Ann pushed it in. A second later, the bookcase swung out, revealing a small room. A battery-powered lantern bathed the interior in a muted glow.

Amidst paintings, children's toys and boxes of comic books was a small cot. Matt sat on it, kicking his heels against the floor. As soon as they removed his gag and the rope around his waist that had kept him from reaching the door, he smiled and ran to Ann.

A loud cheer erupted as Ann pulled him into her arms. Tears of relief ran down her face. "He's okay, he's really okay," she sang out.

A rock-hard lump formed in Tom's throat as Ann's eyes met his. Smiling, she held out her hand to him.

Tom wrapped his arms around Matt and Ann. He was rewarded when the little boy's arm wound easily and naturally around his neck. Oblivious to the others, he caressed Ann's cheek with the side of his hand. "I love you both, Ann," he whispered.

"We love you, too." She touched his face lightly, then leaned over and kissed him as if they were the only ones in the room.

Tom felt Matt snuggled against him, and he curved his arm tightly around the little boy. Out of the corner of his eyes, he saw the others leaving, granting them the privacy they needed.

Ann pulled away slightly and smiled. "Being a parent takes a lot of patience," she whispered, "but I think it's something even a hard-nosed cop could learn to do."

Tom brushed a kiss on Matt's forehead. "What do you say we go home, partner?"

"All of us?" Matt gave Tom a look filled with questions and hope.

"Is that what you want?" Tom asked him.

He nodded eagerly. "I've already told Mommy, but she never listens."

"Don't I know!" Tom answered. Then, seeing the look on Ann's face, he began to laugh.

She walked back home with them, noting how tightly Matt and Tom held on to each other. At one time she'd thought that it would be difficult sharing Matt. But now she knew differently. With the right man, it was the most natural thing in the world.

Nicole had a second chance...
to live.

One moment Nicole was standing in the deli's doorway, smiling at the handsome oceanographer. The next, she reached out to stop the gunman who'd jumped out of the rain-shrouded Manhattan day.

But when Nicole awoke, it was early morning August 30, a full week earlier. Had she been dreaming? Doubt grew stronger as the day unfolded—a day she remembered before it had even begun. Then she again met the oceanograher—David Germaine—and her world shifted on its axis.

David was her desire, her destiny, her only hope of averting disaster. Could this memorable stranger help her reverse fate? Meantime, dark forces gathered....

Don't miss this exciting Harlequin Intrigue coming this July wherever Harlequins are sold.... Watch for #142 *Déjà Vu* by Laura Pender!

HI-142-1

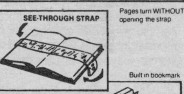

COMING SOON

In September, two worlds will collide in four very special romance titles. Somewhere between first meeting and happy ending, Dreamscape Romance will sweep you to the very edge of reality where everyday reason cannot conquer unlimited imagination—or the power of love. The timeless mysteries of reincarnation, telepathy, psychic visions and earthbound spirits intensify the modern lives and passion of ordinary men and women with an extraordinary alluring force.

Available in September!

EARTHBOUND—Rebecca Flanders
THIS TIME FOREVER—Margaret Chittenden
MOONSPELL—Regan Forest
PRINCE OF DREAMS—Carly Bishop